Screaming Yellow

by
Rachel Green

Kind regards,
[signature]

Screaming Yellow

© 2010 Rachel Green. All rights reserved.

ISBN: 978-1-291-21603-5

First published in eBook by Lyrical Press
eBook edition ISBN: 9781616501945

DISCLAIMER

This is a work of fiction. Names, characters, places and incidents are either the product of the author's imagination, or are used fictitiously. Any resemblance to actual persons, living or dead, business establishments, events, or locales is entirely coincidental.

All rights reserved. No part of this publication may be reproduced in any form or by any means without the prior permission of the author.

Screaming Yellow

by

Rachel Green

Dedication

For the holder of my own tattooed sigil, DK

Acknowledgements

Thank you to DK and Luisa for living with a writer, Nerine and the staff of Lyrical Press for all the help, and to the players in the UK Leather and BDSM scene for letting me watch and play.

Prologue

The rope went taut, followed by a frantic drumming of leather against the old oak banisters, a kicking and jerking of legs until one shoe, a sensible brown slip-on with a decorative buckle, slipped from a stockinged foot to drop twenty feet to the carpet below.

Above, the legs shuddered and were still. A line of urine ran down, soaked up by the coarse nylon but copious enough to drip onto the Persian runner on the ground floor. Fingers that once held a flute in the Wiltshire Women's Symphony Orchestra before arthritis took its toll fell limp and lifeless, the wedding band that hadn't budged in forty years slipping off and following the shoe, though it hit the floor on its edge, bouncing and rolling silently away.

Grace Peters would look better in her coffin. Hanging from a rope around an open beam in the loft was not how she'd have wanted to be remembered. Her tongue protruded from yellow teeth and her eyes were red from burst blood vessels. Hanging was an uncommon means of suicide for women, but was still in the top five.

She swayed slightly in the breeze from the open kitchen window. Grace had been a recluse for the three years since her husband's death and there were few visitors to the three-story house on Wightwick Drive. At least in winter decomposition was slowed: there would be little change in her appearance before she was discovered.

Downstairs Mitsy, Grace's tabby cat, sniffed at the fallen drops and looked up, just the tip of its tail twitching.

Chapter 1

Susan Pargeter winced as a fourteen-gauge needle sank into her skin then again when it poked out an inch farther along. It was a shallow wound--she could see the ridge of metal under the flesh, the last in a long line of parallel needles down the top of both breasts from her collarbones to her areolae.

"Keep still."

Robert's voice was commanding, a tone expecting absolute compliance. His fingers slipped another sterile needle through, perfectly parallel with the rest. "There." He dropped the plastic cap into a yellow sharps bin. "A pretty ladder for an angel to climb."

He ran his finger down each set of ridges in turn, causing Susan's heart to flutter. Her pelvis flooded with warmth.

The overhead lights went out as Robert set up his digital camera. Her blissful expression would not appear in any photograph, just the needles taken from the perspective of a surreal landscape. She would have the honour of appearing, albeit anonymously, in his latest collection of fetish photography.

Lights flashed as he took several photographs from different camera positions, changing the direction of the floods when he felt a new angle warranted it. His voice softened as he stroked her cheek. "Do you need water?"

When she shook her head, he straightened an arm, cleaning it with an alcohol wipe. He inserted a sterile hypodermic, finding the vein with the assuredness of many years of practice and drew out a few fluid ounces of blood.

"The ancients thought this was the life essence." He removed the syringe and pressed a wad of cotton wool onto the spot, securing it with a plaster and tucking it out of sight of the camera lens. "Many still do. God forbade His creation to drink of it lest they become as demons." He set his cameras on automatic shutter and poured the blood over her breasts, the splashing accompanied by the twelve frames per second shutter clicks.

As both cameras beeped to indicate full memory cards, Robert threw a towel over Susan's stomach to catch the drips. "All done. I'm proud of you. You took it without a murmur. Not even a single call of 'yellow.'"

She smiled, watching him withdraw each needle and drop it into the sharps bin. "It might have spoiled your design if I'd asked you to stop. Besides, it was very relaxing."

"Good." Robert smiled and leaned forward to brush her lips with his own. "Come to my room later."

"I will. Thank you, sir." Susan stood and held out her arms as Robert drew a silk dressing gown over her naked body. The marks where the needles had been were a series of raised scarlet ridges that would be gone by morning. Beads of blood from the deeper needles were already scabbing over.

She raised his hand to her lips and kissed it. "Thank you."

Robert smiled. "Away with you." He gave her bottom a gentle pat. "I have work to do. I've got to download all those pretty pictures I've just taken and work on them."

Susan nodded and turned, skimming up a five-pack of the sterile needles and slipping them into the deep pocket of her robe.

The door closed softly behind her.

Chapter 2

The front door slammed hard enough to rattle the leaded glass in its eighteenth-century fanlight. Jennifer winced, remembering the time it fell out and they'd had to find two hundred pounds to have it repaired before the bishop visited. Simon had been forced to ask the people at the manor for help and they'd been crowing about it ever since.

She logged her status to "global away" and pushed her executive chair from the computer. She stood and padded to the study door, her bare feet sinking into the antique Persian carpet. "Simon? Is that you?"

Her brother stood in the hallway shrugging off his overcoat and dripping water all over the runner. His face was an angry red as he pulled his arm out of the sleeve, heedless of the cotton turned inside out in the process. "Who else would it be?" he asked, a little too harshly for Jennifer's liking. "I live here, don't I?"

Jennifer drew herself to her full five feet, eight inches and flicked her long hair out of the way. "I'll thank you not to take that tone with me, Simon Brande. I may only be your sister but I think I deserve a little more respect than that. More than the carpet, at any rate. Look! You're dripping everywhere!" She tutted and swept forward to take the coat from him. "Here, let me. How many times have I asked you to take your coat and shoes off in the porch?"

She opened the cloakroom door and pulled out a coat hanger, pursing her lips as she thrust an arm into the wet sleeve to pull it out again. She hung the coat in the downstairs cloakroom where the tiled floor was easily mopped. "Honestly, anyone would think I was a harridan when really I'm just concerned for your well-being."

Simon's shoulders sagged and his face relaxed. "Of course you are, Jennifer. I'm sorry." He stepped toward her and offered a peck on the cheek. "I've had a rotten day."

"Oh?" Jennifer looked down. "So have your shoes by the look of it. What have you been walking in?"

Simon looked down and grimaced. "I parked too close to the rose bed. I must have stepped in the mud."

"Oh, Simon! You've probably crushed the aubrietia I planted yesterday. I wish you'd be just a little more careful. Take your shoes off before you tread it through the house."

"Sorry." Simon used the toe of one shoe to lever his foot halfway out of the other, then swapped feet, leaving him in just his socks.

Jennifer took two sheets out of the property section of the newspaper and laid them next to the front door, Simon's shoes on top. She passed him his slippers. "What happened to give you such a horrid day?"

"I don't know if I should say." Simon worried his feet into the slippers, picked up his battered old briefcase and carried it into the living room. "I don't want you spreading it all over the bloody internet as soon as my back's turned." He poured himself a scotch and drank it in one swallow.

"I don't know why you'd say that." Jennifer took a seat on the sofa and patted the cushion next to her. "I never say anything you don't want me to."

"Ha!" Simon poured himself a second drink and sat. "Like that time I found Mrs. Westman and the verger going at it like hammer and tongs in the belfry? 'I won't tell a soul' you said, but the following Sunday there was a lynch mob outside the church doors."

"I'm sure that was nothing to do with me." Jennifer picked up a Homes and Garden and began flicking through it. "I didn't tell anyone other than Marge."

"Yes, exactly. Marge at the grocer's. I'm surprised the bishop didn't turn up to re-sanctify the church." He sighed and leaned back against the horsehair stuffing. "Well, it's not as if you wouldn't find out soon anyway. Grace Peters is dead. I've just had to identify her body."

"Oh, that was you, was it?" Jennifer turned away to reach for a glass.

"What do you mean, 'that was me?'" Simon stared at her. "Do you mean to say you already knew about it?"

"Of course." Jennifer smiled and poured herself a gin. "Margaret told me. She works on the emergency ward at the hospital and dispatched the ambulance."

Simon threw his hands in the air. "I should have guessed you'd already have all the gossip. You and your webcam cronies. I bet if I wanted to know Sergeant Davies's cock size you'd be able to tell me."

"Don't be so crude." Jennifer smacked his arm lightly as she sat. "What did she die of?"

Simon rubbed his eyes, the third finger of each hand digging into the corners to wipe away the grit. "Suicide. They found her hanging from a beam, the rope through the trap door to the loft. The poor soul. I shall say a prayer for her."

"Nonsense." Jennifer put the glass down on the coffee table, careful to use a coaster to avoid leaving a ring. "She took a long drop because couldn't take the guilt any more."

Simon sat forward in his seat, frowning. "What guilt? What are you on about?"

"Henry, her husband. Everybody knows she killed him for the insurance."

Simon shook his head, unable to stop a bark of laughter. "Don't be ridiculous, Jennifer. Everybody knows that was an accident. The inquest cleared her of any complicity as I've told you before. I'd know if it was anything else, wouldn't I?" He stood, leaving his glass on the wooden surface.

Jennifer moved it onto a coaster, her face pinched in irritation, then turned away to stare at the painting of Jesus baring his heart on the wall. "She wouldn't have confessed a murder to you, would she? How many times has that happened? I bet that even when you had the parish of St. John's Wood you never got a 'Bless me Father, I've strangled my husband and made it look like an accident.'"

Simon scowled. "Of course not, and Henry's death was an accident as well you know. Besides, if she was such a cold-blooded killer, she'd hardly be likely to commit suicide, would she?" He pulled off his white collar and unbuttoned his shirt.

"Just because she didn't confess doesn't mean that she wasn't racked with guilt." Jennifer was unfazed by the double negatives. "What about all those sleeping pills she took? She couldn't sleep for the guilt eating her up inside."

"She didn't take sleeping tablets." Simon shook his head. "Really, Jennifer. Where do you get all these ideas?"

"Was there a suicide note?"

"Why would there be?" Simon stood. "She was obviously very depressed."

"What makes you so sure there wasn't?" Jennifer held out a hand and Simon pulled her to her feet. "Have you seen the crime scene?"

"Of course not. I haven't been to her house, only the hospital. The police called me there to identify her."

"Why you?" Jennifer led the way into the kitchen and took the oven gloves off the hook. "Who found her?"

"The police. Susan Pargeter dropped in to see her and when she didn't get a reply she called the police. My name was in her wallet on the 'in case of accident' card. The Lord knows why."

Jennifer smiled. "She liked you. You were the only person in fifty miles who didn't think she'd murdered her husband."

"That's because she didn't. It's a moot point, anyway. Whatever she did or didn't do in her life is between her and God now. That smells good."

He nodded toward the lasagne Jennifer was pulling out of the oven. "I'm famished."

"It's a bit overdone," she said. "It's gone crispy on the top. I had the oven set to 'flames of Hell' for the first forty minutes."

"Now who's being disrespectful?" Simon smiled. "Shall I put the plates out?"

"Please." Jennifer carried the dish to the small table. "Have we got any of that pinot blanc left? It'd go well with this."

Simon put the plates on the work surface and checked the wine rack. "We have, yes." He took the bottle out and ferreted in the cutlery drawer. "Where's the corkscrew?"

Jennifer blushed. "It's probably next to the computer. I'll go and get it." She trotted back to the study, pulling off the oven gloves.

"Straight back, mind." Simon rattled the cutlery. "No chatting to your friends. I don't want this conversation spread all over Laverstone."

"As if I would," Jennifer called, stealing a glance at her contacts list. Margaret was still online as well as Catherine from The Larches. She couldn't wait for dinner to be over so she could log back on. She returned to the kitchen and gave the corkscrew to Simon. "Shall I be Mother Superior?"

"That got old the first time you said it." Simon opened the wine, holding the bottle between his knees for leverage. "I wish you'd give it a rest."

"Why should I when it needles you so?" Jennifer laughed and patted his arm. "How will the bishop react to a suicide in your parish?"

"He'll give me one of his hard stares and a lecture on the saving of souls." Simon broke into a grin. "I just hope she left something to the Church in her will, else he'll probably demote me to St. Jude's."

"That's Anglican, though."

Simon laughed. "My point exactly." He carried the plates and cutlery through while Jennifer took a loaf of garlic bread out of the oven and sliced it up. She arranged it in a bowl and went through to find Simon already dishing up two generous portions of lasagne. He raised his eyebrows when he saw the bowl. "Don't let me have too much of that," he said. "My parishioners would never forgive me."

"Nonsense." Jennifer put three of the twelve slices on his plate. "Garlic is good for you."

"Not when it's swimming in butter it's not." Simon held out his hand and Jennifer took it while he said grace. As soon as she repeated his "Amen" Simon bit into one of the pieces and chewed, a line of grease speckling his upper lip.

"What did she look like then?"

"Who?"

"Grace Peters."

Simon gestured with the piece of bread. "You know what she looked like. Sixties, grey hair in a bun, all her own teeth."

"No, silly." Jennifer picked up her knife and fork. "What did she look like when you saw her? Was her neck broken? Bulging eyes from the blood pressure? What?"

Simon picked at the lasagne with his fork. "She looked…pale," he said at last. "Look, do we have to talk about this? How was your day?"

"Fine. Same as always." Jennifer knew her brother well enough to know when not to push a subject. "The bookshop in Dark Passage was having a sale. I bought you a nineteenth-century bible for your collection."

"Thank you." Simon smiled, though she suspected it was more for the change of subject than the gift. "I hope it's not like the last one you got there."

"With all the 'Gods' replaced with 'G-dash-d?'" Jennifer laughed. "It was an American bible. They've decided naming God is disrespectful."

"A Jewish tradition, I think you'll find." Simon pointed at her with his fork. "If God hadn't wanted us to say His name He wouldn't have given us vowels."

Jennifer laughed and the rest of the course was eaten to small talk. She finished long before her brother, who had a second portion, and waited patiently for him to finish his plate. She cleared up and brought out the second course. "Pudding?"

"Lovely." He opened his arms to allow easier access to the table. She put a dish in front of him and a can of pressurized cream on the table then returned to the kitchen for her own.

Simon squirted cream over the top of his pudding and picked up his spoon. It was a simple affair of apricot yoghurt poured over sliced banana. "I'm sorry." He pushed the dish away and rose. "I'll put the kettle on."

Jennifer looked up. "Don't you want that?"

"No, thanks. After identifying corpses, this looks like chunks of dead flesh over empty eyes." Simon clenched his lips as if she'd try to force him to eat it. "I'm not in a pudding mood." He rubbed his forehead and cheek with one hand, brushing away the lock of hair that fell into his eyes. "Do you want coffee?"

Jennifer was torn between wanting to talk more about the suicide and wanting to get back onto the computer. She looked at her brother's face. He looked tired. It was worth the sacrifice of another hour offline to encourage him to go to bed early, for then she'd have all night online if she wanted.

"Yes, please," she said. "Make it a sweet one, though."

"Coming right up." Simon picked up his pudding dish and carried it into the kitchen.

Jennifer watched through the serving hatch as he switched the kettle on and emptied the yoghurt and banana into the bin. He stood there while the kettle boiled.

Jennifer finished her pudding and followed him into the kitchen. "Then send it to them."

Simon laughed. "How did you know I was thinking about Mum?"

"You always do." Jennifer dumped her dish into the sink and turned on the taps. "You always hesitate when you throw food away." She mimicked their mother's stentorian tone: "Don't you waste that good food. There are children in Africa who'd be glad of it." She smiled, reverting to her own voice. "No wonder you entered the priesthood."

"What else could I do?" Simon smiled and added his empty bowl to the swirling water. "It was either that or start work at the factory. At least I got a grant for my education."

"I didn't need one." Jennifer took the coffee mugs down from their hooks. "I had that scholarship to Middlesex. Not as prestigious as Queen's, perhaps, but I did all right for myself."

"You certainly did, dear." Simon squeezed her hand. "I know you're an excellent writer but I do think your imagination gets a bit carried away sometimes."

"It's my job." Jennifer spooned coffee into the cups and passed them to him to add the hot water. "I have to think the unthinkable or nobody would read my books."

Simon laughed. "Just stick to your pen name is all I ask. The bishop would have a fit if he connected me with the author of She Died for Passion." He filled the cups and passed them back.

"I didn't know he'd read it." Jennifer smiled and added cream to the coffee, followed by a sprinkle of cocoa powder. "Do you want sugar in yours?"

Simon laughed. "No thanks, I'm sweet enough. Hey! I said I'd make the coffee."

"I know, but you make it too strong." Jennifer sprinkled brown sugar over the cream, allowing it to dissolve. "All the parishioners think you're sweet enough to eat."

"Who am I to dissuade them?" Simon smiled, the lines of fatigue easing from his features to leave him looking the part of the dashing young priest once more. "At least it keeps the church full."

"Beauty equals bums on pews," agreed Jennifer. "Even some of the men come just to ogle you."

"All sinners saved as part of the service." Simon winked at her.

"And a few damned for impure thoughts to keep the books even." Jennifer carried the coffees into the living room. "Leave the washing up. I'll do it later."

"Thanks." Simon followed her in. "I might have an early night, I think."

"No work to do? That makes a change." Jennifer sat in the armchair while Simon kicked off his slippers and lay on the sofa, propping himself into a seated position using the arm. His left sock had a hole in it.

"I wish you'd throw those out," Jennifer said with distaste. "What if someone saw you with holes in your socks?"

"They'd think me a darling for devoting my life to poverty and the church. They might even put an extra pound in the collection box." Simon waved his foot at her. "If they offend you that much you're welcome to darn them."

"Not a chance." Jennifer shuddered. "Nobody darns socks any more."

"Why not?" Simon sipped his coffee. "Mum used to darn socks."

"That's because we couldn't afford new ones. Now that Tesco sells three pairs for a fiver there's no need to mend them any more."

"That's a shame." Simon took a sip of his coffee. "I think the world wouldn't be in such a crisis if we did a bit more making do and mending."

"You won't save the world by darning socks."

"It's not just socks, though, is it? Plastic milk bottles. Whoever thought of plastic milk bottles should be excommunicated. What was wrong with the milkman's glass bottles, eh? That was pure recycling at its finest."

"And ten pence on the pop bottles," said Jennifer. "I made my make-up money collecting pop bottles."

Simon laughed. "Yes, sometimes you collected them from the back of the pub. You were a tearaway in those days."

"So were you, before you decided the priesthood was a cushy number."

"I was called to it," said Simon. "I renounced my worldly passions."

"Only after Eleanor Page dumped you." Jennifer smiled and changed the subject. Simon would never go to bed if she wound him up. "What was that I heard about Old Tom digging up a grave today? Apparently he got the plots mixed up and tried to bury Mrs. Daniels over the top of Mr. Peabody." Jennifer looked over at her brother. His eyes were closed, his hands still clasped around the coffee mug balanced on his leg. She stood and relieved him of it, setting it on the coaster he'd used for his glass.

She dimmed the lights on the way out of the room and sat in front of her computer again, logging on to her messenger program. She put her coffee to one side and poured herself a generous glass of wine while her chat program connected, the string of names changing to green or red to show their online status.

"Guess what?" she typed to her friend Catherine. "Grace Peters has taken a long drop off a short rope."

Chapter 3

Susan writhed under Sir Robert's gloved hand, the hot wax spilling onto her back and hardening. All the colours of the rainbow, or at least in the online catalogue of the candle merchant, had been dripped, poured and ladled onto her back, bottom and thighs, running like the rivers of Eden across her smooth skin.

He used the head of one candle to round off the tip of a two-inch diameter church candle and pushed it inside her.

"Oh God, yes," she said. "Please, Master, more."

He smiled, one hand manipulating the candle inside her while the other held a hot red taper candle over her spine, adding another layer of colour to the canvas spread across her willing flesh. He left off fucking her, twisting her hands up off the bench and behind her back and switching to white tapers, fixing the red one vertically into the soft wax already pooled in the small of her back. The white candles, lit in a bundle of three from the red, spilled a torrent of wax over her fingers and wrists. Susan shrieked, twisting around the thick rod of wax filling her on the inside.

"Please, Master, please."

If he could have seen her eyes he would have smiled even more. He knew they would be opened wide, desperate for release.

"Not yet," he commanded, fumbling open the fastenings of his pants. He stopped the rain of wax in order to free his erection, rubbing it in the hot pools covering her body to share the pain and pleasure she was yielding to. He rubbed against her, feeling the pressure build. "Now!"

"Thank you, Master," she cried, going into convulsions. The candle clattered to the floor as her vaginal muscles contracted, her juices spilling over the wax in a torrent of white foam.

Robert came, his semen spilling over her and mixing into the wax.

Chapter 4

"Watch the cat!" Meinwen yelled as her best friend barely avoided the tabby.

Dafydd Thomas almost dropped the box on the way to the truck, his dreadlocks swinging wildly as he recovered from almost treading on the cat. "Meinwen Bronwyn Jones! What have you got here?" He steadied the box with a knee as he sought a better purchase. "I think I've put my back out with this one."

"Stop your yammering, Dave." The box's owner trotted out of the house carrying an aspidistra as tall as her and a transistor radio by means of hooking one finger through the carry strap. "That's my computer and all the discs I need to get it running again after its journey in there. You drop that box and I'll make you sorry I was ever born."

"I already am." Dafydd put the box onto the back of the truck and slid it forward. "I must have been bonkers to offer to help you move." He stood at the back of the truck surveying the boxes, his hands on the small of his back and grunting. "Where did you keep all these bits of… collectables?"

"I heard that unspoken thought, Dafydd Thomas." She tucked the plant under one arm and tucked the radio into the computer box. "And don't call me by my full name. Only my mam called me that and I was tired of it before I was six. I was surprised by the amount of stuff I was keeping in my wardrobe and under the bed as well. I just haven't had time to go through it all and decide on what to chuck."

"I wish you had. It would have made this job easier. Less weight means less fuel too, you know."

"Sorry. I had to close the shop in a hurry. Half of these boxes are stock from Reincarnations and worth too much to ditch. Look, can you take Mildred off me?"

"Yeah, well. Sorry about the shop an' all." Dafydd took the plant out of her hands and wedged it into the truck, using Meinwen's duvet to protect it from damage. "Even sorrier you're going to Leighton."

"Laverstone," Meinwen corrected. "I told you. There's nothing left for me in Dovey now the shop's closed. I've been itching to leave ever since Mam died and that was five years ago."

"Why Laverstone though? Why not Aberystwyth or Cardiff, even? There's plenty of tourist trade in Cardiff ever since they started filming Torchwood and Doctor Who there."

"I'm not going into the Dr. Who market." Meinwen sat on the

tailgate. "It's too competitive. Besides, there are other areas of interest in Laverstone."

"Such as?" Dafydd sat next to her and began rolling a cigarette. "My gran says there's nowhere quite like home."

"And thank any god listening for that." Meinwen glanced up at the second floor window she'd spent the last five years looking out of. "If I never see this place again it'll be too soon." She went to the passenger seat of the truck and pulled out a slim volume called Folklore of Laverstone. She waved it at Dafydd who stared at it while he lit his cigarette.

"You wrote a book, did you?" He nodded toward the author's name.

"No. Another M Jones did. I can't claim to be the only one." She sat again and opened the book at the introduction. "I'd have had to be in my sixties to have written this. It was published in nineteen sixty-four."

"Laverstone is a quiet backwater surrounded by the fields of Wiltshire and the arteries of London avoided, by accident or design, by the twentieth century. The fever to build roads and motorways never seemed anxious to include this historic market town.

"The hamlet of Laverstone was founded in fifteen forty-eight as a travelling inn for coaches on their journey between the metropolis and Oxford, and provided the basic needs of food, shelter and stabling. Within a year it had grown a smithy and several rude houses that took advantage of the river Laver and the pastureland surrounding it for several acres on each side.

"A village grew around the hamlet. Landowners carved up slices of the countryside and settled. The village became recognized as a town when the first of the three churches, that of Our Lady of Pity, was erected in eighteen sixteen. The inn grew into a manor, which flourished up to the late nineteenth century then fell upon hard times. The current owner, Frederick Waterman, became a reclusive poet after tragedy struck the family in the late nineteen fifties.

"The town, like Avebury, is surrounded by a ring of standing stones, reputedly either fifteen or seventeen of them, depending upon the proclivities of the counter. There are several legends warning of straying too near the stones at certain times of the year, the vernal and autumnal equinoxes, for example. It is reputed that Laverstone is where William Shakespeare found the inspiration for A Midsummer Night's Dream.

"See?" Meinwen punched him on the shoulder. "The whole town is magical. I'd be daft not to go there."

"There're other towns not so far away." Dafydd pulled on his cigarette. "Tintagel. Boscastle. Glastonbury. They're places steeped in magic. You could open a shop there."

"And be one among dozens?" Meinwen snorted. "I looked Laverstone up. There isn't a single witchcraft shop in the whole town."

"Aye. They probably burn them down." Dafydd dropped his cigarette and ground it out with his foot. Without a filter, it would vanish into the soil within a day or two. He looked at her through his dreads. "Look, I don't want you to go, okay?"

She nodded, flicking through the pages of the tour guide as if there was a script inside. "I know," she said eventually, "but I have to go. I'm so sick of this town I could cry."

"Why there, though? You might as well be moving to the moon. Or France."

"It's as good a place as any." Meinwen closed the book and looked directly at him. "I'll be honest with you, Dave. I met a bloke and he lives in Laverstone. Okay?"

"What sort of bloke? A boyfriend sort of bloke?" Dafydd frowned and stood, putting his hands on Meinwen's shoulders. "I thought you and me had something special?"

"We did." Meinwen winced as he let go and turned away. She caught his arm, pulling him around. "We do, I mean. We're buddies, though. We're not partners."

Dafydd took her hand. "We could be."

Meinwen almost laughed but stopped herself, shaking her head. "What about Madge? You've been seeing her on and off for nearly ten years."

"Only because you were too proud." Dafydd looked down. "I love you, Manny. Always have, always will."

"I know." Meinwen reached forward and opened her arms, relieved Dafydd returned the hug. "That's why we'll always be best mates. One for all, remember?"

"Yeah." He smiled. "You haven't said that since Billy left when we were kids. All for one and one for all."

"Like Dumas's heroes." Meinwen smiled, her eyes glittering with tears.

"Nah, like on the telly." Dafydd ran the knuckle of his index finger below her eye, caught the unshed tear and licked it off his finger. "Just you and me now."

"One for all and two for one?"

"Yeah." He pulled her in for another hug. "You're my bestest buddy."

Meinwen laughed and went inside for her bedding. "Two more boxes in the kitchen and we're done. Then we can get off."

"I thought you said we were just friends?" Dafydd grinned and ducked her mock punch, coming back out a minute later with both boxes and a mug perched on top of them. "Shall I take this back again? You only ever used it when I came 'round."

Meinwen stared at it for a moment. "No. I was going to give it you back, but can I keep it instead?"

Dafydd nodded and grinned. "Sure," he said. "It'll be something for you to remember me by."

While he finished packing the truck, Meinwen dropped her house keys inside the envelope and licked the flap to seal it. It wasn't much to show for five years of living in a one-bed flat on Gwelfor Road but it had overlooked the estuary and for that she was grateful. She turned to the south-west, taking in every last detail of Cardigan Bay to store for the weeks and months of being landlocked in Laverstone.

"You ready?" Dafydd stood with the keys to the truck in his hand. "We'd best get a move on or the sun'll come out and we'll never get away from the crowds wanting a Mr. Whippy."

Meinwen smiled, shoving the envelope through the letterbox before climbing into Dafydd's ice-cream truck. She'd timed her moving date to his day off so he could drive her. "Yes. Let's go before I change my mind."

"Is that a possibility? I could drop my keys down this drain."

She laughed. "No, I'm going and I won't be back."

"Not even for my Mr. Whippy?"

"Maybe for that." She climbed into the passenger side. "I never could resist your strawberry syrup."

"Now you're talking." Dafydd laughed and climbed in, turning the engine over to warm it up. Meinwen winced at the sudden peal of Greensleeves through the loudspeaker.

Dafydd lunged to switch it off. "Sorry."

"Thank you." Meinwen shook her head, grimacing. "Honestly, I don't know why ice-cream trucks play that tune at all. It's so sad."

"Is it?" Dafydd pulled off and headed downhill. "It's just an old English madrigal, isn't it? All about true love and delightful company."

"Unrequited love and a king pining away for want of a woman," said Meinwen. "You might as well be playing Madonna's Sex through your loudspeakers."

Dafydd laughed. "I'd probably sell more ice cream, too." He slipped in a CD of nineties chart hits and they drove through the rest of Aberdovey in companionable silence. Meinwen was wrapped in thoughts of the town she'd grown up in and how Dafydd would fare without his best friend.

"There's your old shop," he said as they passed the vacant building. "They've not started renovating it yet."

"Never," said Meinwen, "am I calling a shop 'Reincarnations' again. It's just asking for the lease to be cancelled."

"Well, it is coming back to life," said Dafydd, trying to hide a smile, "just as a bookies. It could be worse."

"In what way?" Meinwen turned her attention from the beach front properties to the driver. "What could be worse than a bookies?"

"A butcher's?" He allowed a grin to break through. "Or a Methodist church."

Meinwen punched him on the arm. "Oh, very funny, I don't think. Watch out for that bolt of lightning!"

"Where?"

"It must have been my imagination," she said. "Because at least I have one. I didn't go into a dead-end job like you."

"Ice-cream trucking isn't a dead-end job," he said. "Well, except when you park up in dead ends."

"It's not a life's ambition, though, is it? Didn't you want to be a rock star?"

"I'm still working on it."

"How far have you got?"

"Three Blind Mice on the recorder. I'm a bit stuck on getting the G-sharp, see."

Meinwen laughed. "What about the winter? I've seen you with all sorts of jobs in the winter. Didn't one of them grab you?"

"I quite like the burger truck," said Dafydd. "Not that there's much call for burgers in the middle of winter. You freeze your tits off just getting your money out, sometimes, let alone driving to Aberystwyth or Machynlleth, and then I'm digging trucks out of snowdrifts, see." He glanced across at her. "What about you, then? How did you meet this fancy man of yours? What does he look like?"

"Robert, his name is." Meinwen rolled the R across her tongue. "He's charming and charismatic and sensible and mature and he has this tiny dimple in the corner of his mouth when he smiles." She demonstrated with her finger on her face. "He's lovely. I fell in love with him the moment I saw him."

"Oh, aye?" Dafydd paused for a moment, concentrating on the road. "Mature, you said. Just how mature? Big brother sort of mature or my old man and a coffin mature?"

"Well, he's a little bit older," said Meinwen, on the defensive. "You have to be a bit older to achieve true wisdom and harmony with the world."

"'Struth, he's old enough to be your granddad, isn't he?"

"No." Meinwen looked out of the window at the mountains dotted with sheep. "He's in his early fifties, which is no age, these days."

"If he's told you early fifties he's pushing sixty." Dafydd frowned. "How old does he think you are?"

"I might have been a bit conservative with my age."

Dafydd snorted. "Go on."

"I said I was twenty-five. All right? Are you happy now?"

"There's no way you still look twenty-five, love. What did he say when you told him?"

"He didn't say anything. Just how much he was looking forward to us being together."

"Where was this? In the shop?"

"Sort of, yes." Meinwen reached in her bag for the flask of tea then put it back again. "Look, can we stop in Machynlleth? I need to find a bathroom."

"Aye, we can." Dafydd glanced across again. "What did you mean 'sort of' in the shop?"

"I was in the shop." Meinwen looked away. "And he was at home."

"Eh?"

"I said he was at home. We were chatting on the internet, all right?"

"On a computer?" Dafydd frowned. "Have you not met him in real life, like?"

"Not exactly, no."

"How do you mean, not exactly?"

"I mean I haven't, okay?"

"You mean you're packing up and moving three hundred miles for a man you've never even met? What are you like?"

Meinwen folded her arms and returned to looking out of the window. There were scattered houses now they were on the approach to Machynlleth. "I'm not moving just for Robert," she said after a while. "I had to get out of Dovey. It's stifling there. When they wouldn't renew the lease on the shop I thought 'Well that's it then. There's nothing else stopping me.'"

"But what will you live on, *cariad*?"

"I've got my savings, and what's left from when the council bought

Mam's house and Robert's found me a little cottage to live in that isn't too much rent."

"You're not moving straight in with him then?" Dafydd pulled to the left to let a car overtake safely. "That's a bit of a relief to be honest. Sensible of him, like. If you'd moved in and then found you didn't get on together you'd be stuck."

"Oh, he wanted me to move in all right," said Meinwen. "It's his wife that didn't."

Chapter 5

Robert Markhew leaned back in his chair and watched the girl in front of him with lidded eyes. She stood stock-still, her gaze lowered and fixed upon the paperclip he twirled from finger to finger. As the minutes ticked by she began to fidget, first rubbing her fingers together, then scratching her arm and jigging her leg. Finally, her eyes strayed to the window.

"What am I to do with you?" he said at last, his soft voice crashing against her eardrums after the silence of his study.

She mumbled something and his hands stopped moving, the glint of reflection from the twisted steel pausing in its endless rotation.

"What?" he asked. "Speak up girl."

She brought her eyes up to meet his for just a moment. "I said 'anything you like, sir.'" The ghost of a smile flickered across her mouth.

"Anything I like?" Robert smiled and dropped the paperclip into a shallow tray on his desk where it became lost among its brothers. "Ah. The opportunities you offer with such a simple statement." He paused, one finger pressing his pursed lips as he considered the merits of this action or that. He stood and walked around his desk until he was standing behind her. She tensed, as if expecting a slap at the very least but still jumped when he spoke.

"I think I'll have you stand in the naughty corner for the rest of the day." His voice was sibilant in her ear and he had to fight to prevent the warble betraying the smile.

"What?" She looked up, defiant, her head turning to the side to catch a glimpse of his expression. "I'm twenty-seven years old. I'm not a child."

"Are you not?" He grasped her shoulders lightly and turned her to face the mirror. In the dim light her slim figure looked years younger compared to his. His white beard served to accentuate their differences in age. He reached to open the door with one hand. "Then leave."

She hesitated. "I've work to do."

"You have your choices." Robert returned to his seat and took a pair of bunny ears and a camera from the top drawer. He reached forward and tucked the ears into her hands. "Put these on while you decide."

Chapter 6

Simon stepped out of the rectory to walk to the Church of Our Lady of Pity, the centre and lifeblood of his parish, with his head bowed and one gloved hand thrust deep in his pocket against the April wind. The other clutched his briefcase as if the wind might pluck it from his grasp. As he opened the gate to the road, his attention was caught by the incongruity of an ice-cream truck, faded stickers advertising the delights of summers past, parked in the driveway of The Herbage next door.

A middle-aged woman with red hair in a braid that reached almost to her waist was carrying boxes into the house, accompanied by a young dark man with dreadlocks. He paused and frowned before setting off again.

He crossed the road, heading to the church tucked into a side road that also served both the Royal Park and St. Pity's Primary School. The children in the playground were playing hopscotch and bulldog, and he watched them for a moment, a gentle smile tugging at the corners of his mouth, before walking on to the church.

He stopped in the nave to genuflect and touch the base of the marble statue of Mary Magdalene, the namesake of the building. The stone around her feet was worn from countless touches as people begged for her intervention in their prayers.

Jean Markhew was in the apse, tending to the candles. She waited for him to finish his silent prayers before she approached, her feet silent in soft shoes.

"Father." She nodded and half-bowed.

"Jean. How are you?" Simon smiled and took her hand in both of his. He nodded toward the display in the transept. "You've done us proud again with the flowers."

"They're just daffodils from the garden." She smiled and looked down to conceal her blush. "I thought Our Heavenly Father would like them as much as I do."

"I'm sure he does." Simon patted her arm. "How is Robert?" Jean was the widow of Robert Markhew's brother Anthony, and lived at The Larches with him, her daughter Mary and his stepson, Richard. Like the manor, they were one of the few houses in the parish that were sufficiently well-off to employ staff, since Robert was a highly successful writer and internationally acclaimed photographer.

"Like a bear with a sore head," she said, her face dark. "Like a little boy who's dropped his sweeties."

"Why?" Simon squeezed her hand. "Though now you have me

imagining the famous Robert Markhew in short pants."

Jean forced a smile. "He's racked with guilt over Grace Peters. They had a fight, you know, and now that she's dead he's inconsolable. They never made up their differences."

"Oh?" This was news to Simon. "What did they fight about?"

"He didn't tell me. I expect it was all the pills she took."

"What pills? I knew Grace quite well. I never saw her voluntarily take pills for anything." An image of Grace choking on little white torpedoes sprang into his mind. He shook his head to rid himself of it.

"Sleeping pills. She took them for nightmares. Didn't you know? I thought everybody knew."

"I'm sure it's just a rumour, Jean. Pay it no heed." Simon handed her another votive candle. "I'm amazed at the speed with which gossip spreads through the town, but gossip is all it is. Certainly it's nothing to set your stock by. How are things at the house?"

"All right, I suppose." Jean's mouth twisted into a grimace. "At least they would be if Richard left for good."

"Oh?" Simon dropped his voice to a whisper. "There's no trouble, I hope?"

"Nothing new, no. He has his mind set on money from Robert and treats me like I'm his servant sent to fetch and carry. He's an angry young man. Robert can't see what a money-grubbing little sod he's dealing with. Only the other day I caught him poking his nose in Robert's private room." She lit the candle, placing it in the rack before crossing herself.

"I'm sure it was perfectly innocent. Richard's a good lad." Simon tried to be reassuring. "I didn't even know Robert had a private room."

"Maybe it was and maybe it wasn't. All I'm saying is that he shouldn't be poking around where he's not wanted. Robert's got no time for me but as much as you like for the servants. I'm sure he shares his bed with them too. That's what I was lighting the candle for."

"I'm sure you must be mistaken." Simon clasped her hand. "There must be a reasonable explanation."

"Not one he'd confess to you or anybody else." Jean pursed her lips. "They'll be damned, the both of them."

Simon laughed. "I shouldn't think so. There's always time to repent."

* * * *

The church was filled with shadows when Simon turned the lights off at four o'clock. It was usually enough to send people scurrying to the refuge of the open doors at the end of the nave. The only light inside the church now came from the flickering votive candles as they burned away the prayers said over them.

Simon's footsteps rang against the wood floor and echoed from walls of eighteenth-century granite as he walked past the pews, checking for lingering parishioners and lost possessions. He paused at the third row from the back at the sight of a silent figure on her knees, a rosary in her hands as she prayed.

"I'm sorry, I'm closing the church for the night." His voice was soft enough to prevent her from being startled.

She looked up, her face translucent in the dim light from the stained glass windows. "I'm sorry, Father. I'll go."

Simon held out a hand to help her to her feet. "It's Susan, isn't it? Susan Pargeter?"

"That's right, Father." Susan took his hand and edged out of the pew. "I was praying for Mrs. Peters. Is it true she killed herself?"

Simon shook his head. "There's no doubt about it. I feel responsible. I used to see her regularly but I had no idea whatsoever she was so depressed or likely to do such a thing."

"Nor I, Father. I saw her every day to take her a hot meal and she never once said she was tired of her life. I don't like to think of her going to Hell. She was a good woman."

Simon nodded, holding out his hand to help the woman out of the pew. "I'm sure that at worst she'll spend a little time in purgatory, Susan." He led the way to the doors. "What sins she had are between her and God now."

"Then I'll pray for Our Lady to intercede on her behalf." Susan paused at the door. "Father? Is it true that she took sleeping tablets?"

"That's just a rumour, Susan." Simon held the door open for her and repeated what he'd said to Jean. "Gossip for old women and nothing to take any heed of."

"But there's no trace from sleeping pills, is there? How would anyone know if that's what she took?"

"She didn't, Susan." Simon took out his set of keys in an effort to chivvy her out. "Besides, if she'd taken any pills at all it will be picked up in the autopsy. Your body can't digest pills after you're dead."

Susan frowned, lingering on the threshold. "But what if the sleeping pills were just a cover for something stronger? What if she'd taken heroin or worse after the sleeping pills? How would anyone be able to tell that?"

"She didn't take any pills, Susan, and she didn't take any heroin, none at all." Simon ushered her out and locked the great oak doors behind them. "If she'd eaten or injected anything it would come up on the blood test."

Susan stared at him for a moment, until Simon felt like looking away. "That's good to know, Father, Thank you."

Susan turned and hurried down the path toward the park, her coat tails flapping.

At the door, Simon turned to look back into the shadowed nave. A second image of Grace intruded, this time of her red and bloated face, looking up at him as she hung from the banisters. He rubbed his eyes and left, locking the church doors before his rounds.

* * * *

It was evening before Simon had finished visiting parishioners and was walking back through the cemetery on the way home. At least it was beginning to get lighter at night now, only a month ago it was already dark by six o'clock. When he passed the gate to The Herbage again the truck had gone and his remaining steps to the rectory door seemed a little lighter. He stepped out of the wind into the inviting warmth of the house and was surprised to find Jennifer was not on the computer but in the living room. She called out to him as he closed the door.

"Simon?" Her voice trilled with suppressed excitement. "We have a visitor."

He shrugged off his coat and went in, setting his briefcase on the floor next to the armchair. The large gentleman sitting on the sofa next to his sister was none other than Robert Markhew himself, a trail of biscuit crumbs leading from his goatee to the treasure of a half-empty plate on the coffee table. He made to rise as Simon entered, pulling himself up with the aid of his stick, but Simon waved him down again.

"No need to get up. We don't stand on ceremony here." He turned to Jennifer and bent to plant a kiss on her cheek. "Is there any tea left in that pot?"

"It'll have gone cold now." She stretched upward for the chaste peck. "I can easily make up a fresh one for you, though."

Simon waved a hand. "Don't worry about it." He lowered himself into the easy chair and threw a leg jauntily over the arm. "Good to see you, Robert. To what do we owe the pleasure?"

"I came to invite you to dinner one evening." Robert held his chin with one hand, his thumb stroking the grey hairs of his beard and dislodging crumbs over his sports jacket. "All this business with Grace dying has got me thinking about the afterlife."

"Heaven, you mean?" Simon smiled. "I shall be delighted, of course. What day are we talking about?"

"Would tomorrow suit you?" Robert asked. "I don't know when Grace's funeral is yet, but it shouldn't be this soon, and I know you're busy on Sundays, of course."

"Tomorrow will be fine." Simon pulled out his pocket diary and wrote in the appointment. "Shall we say seven o'clock?"

"Capital." Robert heaved himself upright and turned to Jennifer. "You're invited too, my dear, naturally."

"Thank you, Robert." Jennifer smiled up at him. "Will Richard be present?"

"Ah." Robert hesitated. "I'm afraid not. He's in London at present."

"Is he?" Simon stood to show his guest out. "I thought I saw him in the cemetery a day or two ago. He and Jean were leaving flowers on her late husband's grave and chatting. They seemed to be quite close."

"You must be mistaken." Robert made his way to the front door. "He's been there all week, looking for work in the museums."

Simon shook his head. "My apologies." He opened the door. "It must have been a trick of the light. We'll see you tomorrow then. Seven o'clock sharp."

Chapter 7

Nicole yelped as the hemp rope bit into her thigh. "I'm sorry, Sir." She spoke through the two strands running vertically across her lips. "I don't think I'll be able to take this for long."

"As you wish." Robert relaxed the cord, allowing her to lower her foot to the floor again. "Good girl for telling me before I went any further with this form of binding." He felt her hands. "Are your fingers all right? They feel a little chilly."

"Fine, Sir, thank you." Nicole shifted her weight to the other foot.

"How about this?" Robert used a length of silk rope wrapped several times around her thigh as padding against the bite of the hemp.

Nicole danced on one foot as her leg was hoisted in the air again. "Much…better, Sir."

Robert laughed. "Relax. You're not going to fall. Most of your weight is supported by the karada I've worked around your torso. Lean back."

"I can't."

"Trust me." Robert forcibly bent her supporting leg until her weight was suspended by the network of hemp and jute attached to the hook in the ceiling. He plucked at each of the ropes, refining and adjusting the web until each one supported her equally.

"Ooh," she said. "I don't think I can take this for very long, Sir. The ones around my waist are too tight."

"Relax." Robert stroked her hair. "How long can you manage, do you think? Ten minutes? Five? Do you need to call yellow immediately or do I have time to tie off the other leg and take a few shots?"

"Five, perhaps." Nicole grunted as a lark's hitch was tossed over her free ankle and attached to the hook. Her angle tilted nearer to the horizontal as Robert tightened the ropes supporting her foot, wrapping several loops around her to keep her leg straight. "You're fully suspended now." He brushed his lips across her shoulder. "I want you to count to two hundred and it will all be over."

"Yes, Sir." Nicole began. "One, two, three…"

"I meant in your head."

Nicole stifled a giggle. "Sorry."

Robert set up his lights with an efficiency born of practice. Hemp glowed under the bright lamps, every fibre visible against the dark cloth he'd attached to the picture rail. "Lovely," he said, his camera flashes firing as she spun in a lazy circle. "This may well become the cover of the book. Turn your palms upward and lose the grimace."

"I'll try." Nicole's face dropped into a more relaxed expression.

"Excellent." Robert's cameras clicked through their maximum shutter speed. He was glad he'd switched to digital cameras when the quality became comparable to film. Scenes like this would have cost a fortune to develop otherwise, never mind the expression of the lady in the chemist when he went in for his prints.

"Two hundred, Sir. Yellow." Nicole's voice cut through his thoughts.

"Coming." Robert stepped forward and kissed her nearest shoulder. "Not literally, mind." He untied knots with a quiet efficiency and within moments he'd released her legs and allowed her to support her own weight. His rope-work was designed to be easy to take off and Nicole was completely free, but for the chest harness, in under a minute.

He smiled and kissed her properly. "Well done." He stepped back and took several more shots of the rope marls left on her skin. "Now coil the ropes while I download these photographs."

Chapter 8

Breakfast at the rectory was a civilized affair. Jennifer made toast while Simon set the table and put out bowls and their three boxes of cereal. They both took tea and although he professed to prefer Earl Grey, Simon drank the brand Jennifer bought at the local supermarket. They sat together, each lost in their own thoughts until their bowls had been pushed to one side.

"Was it just me, or was it a bit strange that Robert thought Richard was in London?" Simon asked, spreading a generous amount of Seville marmalade on his toast.

Jennifer nodded. "I thought it was, too. Everybody knows he's been staying at the White Art in town."

"Everybody meaning your webcam cronies." He took a sip of the tea, holding the cup around the rim instead of by the handle. Jennifer thought the method uncouth. "Have they said why he's staying there and not with his stepfather?"

"No." Jennifer leaned forward, the tips of her hair brushing across the strawberry jam on her toast. "Haven't you found out from your sources?"

"No. Not that I'd be able to reveal anything I learned in the confessional."

"Heaven forbid." Jennifer smiled. "I know people gossip to you though. Outside of your little rosewood box, I mean."

"Not that I'd listen to such idle chatter." Simon took a bite of his toast, a little of the marmalade slipping off and adhering to his chin. He wiped it off with a napkin. "Perhaps he just wants to be out of the way of Robert's harem."

"Don't be ridiculous." Jennifer took a sip of her tea. "All the women who visit The Larches have good reason to do so. I can't imagine Jean having truck with a harem." She giggled at the thought of the balding Robert Markhew as an Arabian sultan.

Simon waved the butter knife at her. "Scoff if you must," he said with a grin. "I'm sure Robert is a very attractive man when clad only in his boxers. If I weren't a priest I'd be tempted, and not least by the biscuit crumbs in his beard."

Jennifer snorted tea from her nose.

"You can spray what you like," Simon continued, "but he probably has a huge bed for six in that private room of his."

"Private room?" Jennifer wiped her face with her napkin. "What private room?"

"The one that Jean isn't allowed in." Simon smirked at the expression on his sister's face. He picked up his cup again. "Didn't you know about it?"

"You know I didn't." Jennifer poured more tea and did her best to remain composed against his insufferable smugness. "I shall do soon, though."

"I wouldn't doubt it." Simon held out his cup for a refill. "What about our new neighbours then? Do you know anything about them?"

"Not much," Jennifer admitted. "The ice-truck is registered to a company in Machynlleth, so they must be Welsh. Her name is Meinwen Jones and she used to run a shop in Aberdovey but it closed down a month ago according to Melanie at the post office. I don't know anything about him other than he's called Dafydd Thomas."

"I saw them yesterday when they were moving in." Simon chose honey for his second slice of toast. "Not to speak to though. She looks to be a bit of a hippie, all floaty skirts and patchouli oil."

"That's odd." Jennifer finished her toast and pushed the plate away. "What does she want to come here for? Nothing ever happens here."

* * * *

Meinwen smiled at the customers. "I haven't really opened yet." She nodded to the boxes of merchandise stacked two or three high, all waiting to go on display. "Is there anything in particular you're looking for?"

The girl in the t-shirt pushed her friend forward. Her purple hair looked nice, but clashed with the zebra-striped vest top, the bondage pants and the Doc Marten boots. Her stripy purple socks went well enough though, and were a match to Meinwen's own.

"Do you do love potions?" She bit her bottom lip, looking at everything but Meinwen. "Or a spell I can do myself?"

"Certainly." Meinwen reached under the counter and took out a small blue bottle. "Here you go, Mary. You need to add a hair of the two people you want to fall in love and bury it at the root of an oak tree overnight. That'll be a tenner."

"Wow." Mary grinned, holding the tiny bottle up to the light. "You must be a good psychic to have guessed my name." She dug into her pocket and pulled out the money. "How long will it take?"

"No more than a week or so." Meinwen tucked the money under a statue of Buddha and rubbed his belly for luck. "Wear a little of it whenever you expect to see the object of your desire."

Mary sniffed at the contents. "Cool," she said. "It smells like musk."

Meinwen watched them walk down the street before returning to her unpacking. Her reputation as a witch would grow exponentially, at least among the town's teenage population. She was glad she hadn't mentioned she knew Mary's Uncle Robert, who had not only sent her Mary's picture but described her to a T.

* * * *

Later, Meinwen was working in her new garden when the vicar appeared next door. She didn't stop digging, but caught a glimpse of him every time she lifted a spadeful of the damp, chalky soil. Had she been looking for a man to share her life with, she could have done worse than this young chap. He looked to be forty or so, with an easy smile and ash-blond hair that fell across his eyes. He was, as far as she could tell, quite physically fit. Probably from pushing the ratty old car she'd spotted in the driveway. She paused, leaning on her spade as he approached the low wall dividing the two properties.

"Good morning." He flashed her a smile, displaying a set of teeth unavailable on the National Health. "Or afternoon, I should say."

"Hello there." Meinwen stood, smiling over the waist-high stone. "I hope I'm not disturbing you. I didn't realize I was moving in next to a vicar."

"Simon Brande." He offered his hand. "Although I'm not a vicar but a priest. Not just any old riff-raff here."

"Ah, Catholic. Transubstantiation and all that." Meinwen smiled and shook his hand. "Meinwen Jones. I was brought up Methodist, though it's years since I went to Sunday Service."

"I promise not to hold that against you." Simon grinned. "I saw you moving boxes yesterday. How are you settling in?"

"Well enough, thanks. I don't have much, see. That's why I rented this place. It's fully furnished, though the bed leaves a lot to be desired. I may have to invest in a new mattress."

Simon laughed. "I'm sure I wouldn't know. What about your young man?"

"My young man?"

"The burly fellow with the dark skin who was helping you move in yesterday." His voice trailed upward into a question.

"Oh, you mean Dafydd. He's away back to Dovey now. He's not my young man though, just a friend with a truck. I slipped him the fuel money and he helped me move."

"I see. Well, welcome to Laverstone. What brings you to our corner of the world then? You're a long way from…lava bread and *bara brith*."

Meinwen leaned in closer. "It's the energies. Do you know there are three ley lines that converge on this town? I reckon I'm only a mile or so from where they meet here."

"Ley lines?" Simon pulled back with a nervous laugh. "I'm afraid I don't believe in them."

"Of course not. I'm sorry." Meinwen touched his arm. "You wouldn't, would you, being a priest. I expect you're not allowed to. It doesn't matter though, because they're here whether you believe in them or not. I bet you have good energies in your little church though. Full pews every week, people grateful for the good harvests, that sort of thing?"

"I suppose." Simon frowned and twisted a little to block the sun from his eyes. "That's down to God looking after us though, not some blessed ley line."

"As I said, believe what you will." Meinwen grinned, warming to him despite their contradictory beliefs. "We're all on the same side in the end, aren't we? Holding back the darkness, I mean."

"If you say so." Simon looked back at the house and Meinwen followed his gaze to see a woman watching them from a window.

"Who's that?" Meinwen waved and the figure vanished. "I thought priests weren't allowed to marry?"

"We're not. That was my sister, Jennifer."

"Ah. Not living in sin after all then."

"Indeed not." Simon turned back to her. "Good will always triumph against evil, though I suspect the town will soon be rife with speculation now I've been seen talking to you."

"Only if you give it a bit of a nudge." Meinwen picked up her spade again "Well, I must get back to it. I've only the long weekend before I open the shop and I've already lost the morning stocking shelves."

"A shop as well?"

"Oh yes. I've rented one near the market." She turned some soil. "Thirty-four, Knifegate, if you want to drop in some time for a chinwag. I promise I won't talk about ley lines and if you ask nicely I'll bake some Welsh cakes."

"That sounds delightful. I look forward to it." Simon leaned farther over the wall "What are you doing exactly?" He looked into the hole. "Putting some potatoes in?"

"Bless you no, Father." Meinwen chuckled. "I'm building a witch's circle."

"Goodness!" Simon took a step backward. "I'm not sure you're allowed to do that."

"Why?" Meinwen smiled. "It's not like I'll be sacrificing goats on the Sabbath. It'll do no harm to anybody. Think of it as a patio, if you like. You've got one of those yourself."

"It's hardly the same thing, is it? You'll be conversing with heathen gods on yours."

"You're the first priest I've met who's admitted to their existence." She shovelled another load into a wheelbarrow. "You're the most progressive I've ever met, I think, or should that be recessive?"

Simon laughed. "Progressive, I think." He brushed the hair out of his eyes in what looked to Meinwen to be an affected habit. "Anything else would be admitting that yours were here first, and that would be blasphemous."

"Which of course they were." Meinwen grinned and leaned on the wall. "Isn't it against your doctrine to believe in the existence of other gods?"

"Perhaps." Simon looked up at the sky. "But God said 'Thou shalt have no other gods before me,' so even He knew they existed."

Meinwen nodded. "Well reasoned. You remind me of a friend of mine. He was very open-minded too. He taught me a lot."

"Is he still around?"

"He hasn't died, as far as I'm aware, but I haven't seen him in years. Tell me something. You must know everyone in the town."

"Pretty much." The priest raised his eyebrows. "Why?"

"Do you know someone called Richard Godwin? I was asked to look out for him and have a bit of a chat."

Simon looked surprised. "I know Richard. He's the stepson of Robert Markhew at The Larches. Who told you to look out for him?"

"Robert Markhew. He asked me if I'd have a bit of a chat with him."

"You know Robert?" He stared at her. "From where? He's never mentioned you."

"I met him online when I decided to move to Laverstone. I did a search for all the people here and he was one of the only people who was willing to chat to a lonely Welsh girl. There were a couple of others but they weren't the sort of people you'd want to meet in real life, if you know what I mean." She emphasized the statement with a grimace. "I'm not surprised he didn't mention me though. Would you tell a priest you'd been talking to a witch?"

Simon laughed. "I suppose not. What did he want you to talk to Richard about? Perhaps I could help."

Meinwen studied him. If you couldn't trust a priest, who could you trust? "Robert wants this Richard to marry a girl called Mary. His niece, I think. Richard doesn't seem to be interested, though, and that's where I come in. I've already met Mary. She seems like a nice-enough girl."

"She is, or will be when she gets over this craze for looking like a zombie. How do you fit in, though? Does he want you to magic them together?"

Meinwen laughed. "I'm not that kind of witch. Never cause harm, I say, though Mr. Markhew thought I might be persuaded to cast a little magic over the couple."

"Witchcraft? Not in my parish you won't."

Meinwen laughed. "Nothing of the kind, no. I wouldn't bend someone's will like that. He just wants me to get to know them both and smooth the way for them so that it happens naturally. Besides, I do a lovely trade in natural aphrodisiacs." She winked.

"Fascinating." The priest had an easy smile the women of his flock probably adored. "Look, I have to go out shortly on my rounds, but perhaps you'll have dinner with us sometime next week."

"Us?" Meinwen glanced at the rectory.

"Jennifer and me. She's a fabulous cook." He paused. "You're not a vegetarian, are you?"

"Not at all, I drink goat's blood every full moon." Meinwen managed to keep a straight face for several seconds before she burst out laughing at Simon's expression.

"Oh, very good." Simon patted his chest as if to re-start his heart. "You had me going there. Shall we say Thursday at seven?"

"Lovely." Meinwen nodded a goodbye and watched him return to his patio table and laptop. He looked back again, then up at the sky. "I'll let you know if it looks like thunder bolts."

Meinwen laughed and turned back to her digging. The soil was very flinty and she began making a mental list of things she'd need from the garden centre.

* * * *

"Mr. Markhew?" Jennifer touched the arm of the gentleman perusing the special occasion cards. He turned around and smiled, his beard thankfully clear of any crumbs and, to Jennifer's surprise, kissed her cheek.

"Ms. Brande." He pumped her hand. "You're just the person I wanted to see."

"I am?" Jennifer smiled and fanned away a blush. "I'm flattered."

"Which of these cards do you think would be appropriate?" He waved his hand toward the rack of white cards.

"Congratulations on your engagement?" Jennifer frowned, the corners of her mouth pulled upward quizzically. "Who's getting married?"

"Richard, of course. He proposed to Mary at last."

"Oh? Is he back then? From London?"

"No, he did it over the internet. Proposal by webchat! It sounds like a science fiction novel, doesn't it? I cracked open the champers of course, though he hadn't got any, being in an internet café. When are they going to invent a gadget to send that over the internet, eh?"

"I really wouldn't know." Jennifer grinned as she began reviewing the cards for something suitable.

* * * *

"Richard?" Mary trailed the end of a crop across his cheekbone. "Are you ignoring me?" She reached out and plucked a stray hair from his oh-so-neat locks.

"Ouch!" Richard grabbed the end of the crop and twisted it, spinning around to face her and raising his arm. "Don't try those games with me, dear. This isn't some trivial drama for your amusement, you know."

Mary's face creased as she blinked back tears. "Stop it, Richard." The nerves in her arm felt like they were on fire. "You're hurting my arm."

"Let go of the crop then."

She released her grip and he pulled it away to examine it. "Where did you get this?"

Mary pouted. "My mother's room." She rubbed her arm wondering if she could get away with slapping him. He had perfect cupid-bow lips when he wasn't stretching them into a cruel smile. "Give it back or I'll change my mind about the engagement."

"I don't think so." Richard tapped his thigh with the crop.

"Why not?" Mary's gaze was drawn to the twitching leather. She wondered what it would be like to be helpless, feeling the sting of that little loop across her naked bottom and other, more intimate places.

"It's my stepfather's."

* * * *

Jennifer took a short cut home from town, where she'd had coffee with two of her friends at the White Art, hoping to catch a glimpse of Richard Godwin. The woods below Laverstone Manor, while not actually a public footpath, were well enough used by the locals. The owner, Harold Waterman, turned a blind eye to walkers using it.

She was admiring the sea of wild garlic edging the path when she reached the high boundary wall between the woods and the park. A voice on the other side sounded just like Richard Godwin. She crept closer, pushing through the garlic to press herself against the cold granite blocks.

"You must be patient," he was saying. "You know I can't afford to make him angry at me."

"But I was so surprised." The second speaker was a girl, although Jennifer didn't recognize the voice. Someone young, she thought.

"I know. I'm sorry." Richard sounded anxious. "Don't worry, though. It's only until my inheritance is settled. I can't afford to risk Robert taking me out of his will."

"I understand, Richard, but how do think it makes me feel, hearing of your engagement to that woman?"

"Mary's all right," Richard said. "You'd like her if you got to know her properly."

"I didn't think you liked her very much either," the girl said. "You never said before."

"Let's not quarrel." Richard's voice was soothing. "Let's go back to the hotel and I'll give you something to warm you up."

Jennifer stayed where she was until the voices faded completely, bursting to tell someone the news.

* * * *

Jennifer got to the house just as Simon was pulling on his overcoat. "I'm glad I caught you." She dropped her shopping bags on the old pew in the hall. "I saw Robert in town and guess what?"

"How should I know?" Simon checked through the contents of his briefcase. "Look, did you put the communion wafers and wine in here for the housebound old dears?"

"Of course. Don't I always? Never mind that though. What about my news?"

"What about it? It can't be all that important or he'd have told us yesterday."

"Think again." Jennifer was all but shaking with excitement. "Richard and Mary have got engaged!"

"What? They can't have done. Richard doesn't even like her."

"Well, he does now." Jennifer clutched his arm. "There's more, too. I was walking home through the woods at the bottom of the manor when I heard him talking."

"Heard who? Robert?"

"No, silly, Richard. I couldn't see him because he was on the other side of the park wall, but it was definitely him."

"So?" Simon closed his briefcase. "Do hurry up, Jennifer, I have to go."

"He's got another girl on the side," she said. "I wasn't far wrong about the Markhew harem after all. Like father, like son."

"Stepson," Simon corrected. "That's ridiculous, though. Why would he get engaged to Mary if he's already got a girlfriend? What was he saying to her?"

"He told her to be patient. He didn't want to upset Robert in case he took him out of the will. Do you think that he doesn't love Mary at all and is only agreeing to marry her for the inheritance?"

"I hope not." Simon's expression darkened. "I couldn't allow a marriage like that to go ahead. It augers too much trouble for all those concerned, let alone the whole question of the sanctity of marriage."

"Who do you think his mistress is?"

"How should I know? There are dozens of girls in the town." Simon looked at his watch. "I've got to go. I'll drop in at the White Art on my way back. See if I can talk to Richard about all this."

"Good." Jennifer straightened his lapels. "It's about time you got some gossip for me."

"It's not gossip when it's straight from the source." Simon checked his hair in the mirror. "You know I don't hold with gossip."

* * * *

At The Herbage, Meinwen was begging for release. "Please?" She clenched her pelvic muscles in an effort to prevent her orgasm, twisting against the bonds in the effort. Ropes dug into her skin, the momentary pain bringing her back from the crest before building the anticipation higher.

"Not yet." His voice was a monotone, almost menacing. "Wait."

"Oh God!" Meinwen tried to think of mathematics? Plumbing?

Anything to take her mind off it. "The bathroom tap is dripping," she said, more to herself than with any intent of him hearing her.

"Is it?" At least she had elicited some emotion from him. "Then you'll fix it…"

She groaned.

"Before I let you reach an orgasm."

She looked up to see the same half-smile she'd fallen in love with over the internet.

* * * *

The White Art was beginning to fill as the locals finished work and dropped in for a pint on their way home. Father Brande was respected enough to be granted an easy passage through the throng, reaching the bar without difficulty.

"Good evening, Father." Mike Chapman had owned the hotel for ten years and knew everybody. "What can I get for you?"

Simon grinned. "Nothing actually, Mike. I was wondering if you'd seen Richard Godwin."

"Have you come from his stepfather?" Mike leaned in closer. "Only I can't remember if I've seen him or not."

"Robert doesn't even know he's in town," Simon said. "I'm here as a friend."

Mike nodded. "I'll ring his room then. Can I get you a drink while you wait? On the house."

Simon smiled. "That's good of you Mike. I'll have an Earl Grey."

* * * *

Meinwen checked her email over a soothing cup of chamomile tea. Her hands felt chapped and raw from the physical labor and she mentally kicked herself for not asking Dave to stay over for a day or two, just while the donkey work needed doing. There was no way she could afford a gardener and her blisters already had blisters.

She yawned as she glanced out of the window at the gathering clouds. Was six o'clock too early to go to bed?

* * * *

"Father Brande?" Richard slipped into the nook seat opposite Simon. "Mike said you wanted to see me?" He reached across and shook hands with the priest. Simon had a firm grip.

"I do. What's all this about you getting engaged to Mary Markhew? You're too young to get married yet."

"I thought you'd approve." Richard grinned and hunched forward, resting his elbows on the desk. "I thought all good Catholics were supposed to get married as soon as they could?"

"Supposed to, yes, and expand the glory of the Church." Simon laughed. "It's not so likely these days, though, is it?"

"Maybe not." Richard drew circles in the coffee spill on the table. "Will you promise not to tell my stepfather that I'm here and not in London?"

Simon nodded. "I was a friend of your mother's for many years, Richard. You can trust me."

"Aye, I know that." Richard's phone beeped and he glanced at the incoming message before dismissing it. He dropped his voice. "Robert and I have had a lot of problems lately. Fights and that. I'll do anything for a quiet life."

"Even marry Mary against your better judgement?" Simon asked. "Or carry on with someone else at the same time?"

Richard shook his head. "You've known me all my life. You should know I'm not the kind of man to cheat on the woman he loves."

Chapter 9

"They'll be here soon." Robert Markhew trailed his fingers down the rigid body, taking delight in the wild-eyed panic of the submissive woman bound in hemp rope before him. "What do you think they'd say if they found you like this?"

She grunted through the ball gag, the leather strap so tight the skin of her cheeks was white underneath it. Her breasts stood pert and hardened, confined within twin whorls of rope.

"What's that?" Robert smiled. "I couldn't quite hear you." His fingers ran across her nipple and down over the bound torso, trailing over her mound. He could go no farther, for to prolong her agony and force himself to be patient, he had bound her legs, preventing access to that most precious area of her body.

She grunted again.

"It is indeed." Whether Robert could distinguish her meaning remained unclear but he gave the appearance he had. Acceding or denying any request she might make was part of his enjoyment.

The alarm on his cellphone rang and he smiled.

"Time's up," he said. "We'll continue this at another time." He circled the woman, taking a last moment of pleasure from her discomfort before pulling out the thick rattan cane holding the ropes in place. They fell off her, pooling around her feet like a shoal of eels.

"Get your clothes on." He straightened his bow tie in the mirror. "You need to be serving aperitifs as soon as they arrive. I need to get a bit more work done."

* * * *

"They'll be here any minute." Jean said as she opened the study door to leave. "You don't have time for any more playing on your computer."

"I know. I'll be out shortly." Robert Markhew tapped his status to "away" and pulled another photograph onto the graphics program. Robert considered himself old school and composed his work in the camera but was not averse to digitally cropping and enhancing the colours of his masterpieces. His last show at the Downstairs Gallery had been an acclaimed success and he'd sold forty thousand copies of his book Palimpsests after the review of it in The Times.

He zoomed in to ten-times magnification and edited out a slight blur on the ink used to write page thirteen of Joyce's Ulysses across the naked torso of his model for the day. All in the best possible taste, of course, soft lighting and sepia filters and close-up shots of tonal skin.

He pressed a short-cut for his voice recorder. "Nicole, please remind me to talk to Amanda about inking the models. Today's page had bled. Check what ink he's using. She's using, I mean."

He zoomed out again and saved the file. "Page thirteen stored and completed with file name jay-jay-you-oh-one-three-see. Mark up and transcribe. Single plate, left." Nicole Fielding, his secretary could access his dictation files on the network and transcribe his notes in the morning. He turned off the recorder just as the doorbell rang.

"Time's up," he said to himself, disconnecting the camera, and standing. "Be pleasant to the parish priest and his lovely sister." He crossed to the mirror and adjusted his bow tie, brushed off his beard and rubbed a spot of ink from his cheek.

* * * *

"Here we are."

Jennifer indicated to turn into the wide drive of The Larches, waiting for the approaching car to pass. She was a careful driver, having treated herself to a new Mercedes when her first book topped the million sales mark. At seven years old it looked as good as it did when she'd bought it.

"It was kind of you to drive." Simon adjusted his tie in the passenger vanity mirror. "It means you can't have a drink."

Jennifer smiled. "I'd rather stay teetotal than turn up to The Larches in that battered old thing the church lets you drive."

She turned into the driveway but had to slam on the brakes as a blue Vauxhall shot out of the drive and into the road, heedless of either the Mercedes or any other traffic that might have been passing. Simon caught a glimpse of a tear-stained face at the wheel.

"That was Susan Pargeter." Simon stared after the car. "I'm sure she was crying."

"Really?" Jennifer's mind was racing. "Perhaps Robert's kicked her out of his harem." She slipped back into gear and eased forward.

"That's not very kind." Simon returned his attention to the gravel drive. "I don't think I've ever seen her quite so upset. I wonder what's happened."

Jennifer parked the car in the wide turning circle and stood back while Simon knocked on the door, waiting several minutes for a reply.

"We have got the right day, haven't we? Robert did say tonight?"

"Of course he did." Jennifer leaned past him and hammered on the door until it was opened by a flustered young woman.

"I'm so sorry." She stood to one side to let them pass into the hall, decorated with paintings on either side of a panelled door. "I heard you knock but I was up to my elbows in entrails. I hope you haven't been waiting long."

Jennifer smiled. "Long enough to feel the chill. It's purgatory out there."

"Jennifer!" Simon's feigned outrage was sufficient admonishment.

"Good evening, Father, Miss Brande." Mary trotted down the stairs with a smile almost wide enough to reach her eyes. "Amanda! Don't just stand there! Take their coats."

"Hello there." Simon shrugged off his mac and handed it to the maid. He turned to Mary. "I hear you have some good news."

"You've already heard!" She grinned even wider. "Isn't it wonderful? I can hardly believe it myself."

"I'm so pleased for you." Jennifer kissed the blushing cheek and threw a glance at Simon from behind Mary's back. "You must tell me all about it."

"I admit I was surprised when Richard asked me." She looked from Jennifer to Simon and back. "I didn't think he had much interest in marriage, at least not with me. Since we'd known each other for so long I assumed he just thought of me as a sister or something."

"He certainly seems to think more of you than a sister now." Jennifer folded Mary's hand into the crook of her arm and led her into the sitting room. "When's the big day?" She left Simon in the hall, aware he'd take the opportunity to look at the Victorian paintings.

* * * *

"There you are, Father. I thought we'd lost you." Robert Markhew appeared from the direction of the kitchen, wiping a spot of grease from his beard with a napkin. "I saw Mary talking to Jennifer and wondered where you'd gone."

"I was just looking at this Pieta." Simon indicated a large oil depicting Christ on the cross, a tearful Mary Magdalene washing his bloody feet with her tears. "Our Lady of Pity."

"It's been in the family for years." Robert put an arm around Simon's shoulders and guided him toward the sitting room. "I'll leave it to you in my will, if you like."

"Ah, I'm flattered but I couldn't accept. Vows of poverty, remember?"

"I'll leave it to the church, then. Pity for St. Pity's."

"Splendid. Thank you." Simon twisted to look back at the painting. "It'll hang in the Lady's Chapel."

"As you wish." Robert sighed. "You've heard the news, I suppose? Richard's engagement?"

"Indeed I have." Simon smiled. "Congratulations are in order, I believe."

"I expect so." Robert nudged Simon's arm. "Sly little bugger, eh? Still, it keeps everything in the family. Shall we go in? I believe dinner is ready."

* * * *

Nicole knocked softly on the door to Peter's cottage. As the gardener and handyman he had the place to himself, a cottage built originally as an adjunct to the main house for visitors to occupy. It served Peter very well, leaving him free to work at any hour without disturbing the rest of the occupants.

It served Nicole well, too. No noise carried from Peter's cottage to the rest of the house, leaving them free to pursue a relationship outside that of Sir Robert and the rest of the family.

He knew about it, naturally. Little went on at The Larches without Robert knowing the details, but as long as their activities didn't impinge on either their work or his demands he allowed their relationship to flourish.

After no reply to her knock, Nicole tried the handle. The cottage was empty, Peter's coat missing from the hook on the back of the door. She kicked off her shoes and went into the bedroom, switching on the two wall lights to bathe the room in a soft glow.

She pulled off her dress and put some music on, selecting a book from the shelves to read. Peter wasn't one for fiction, preferring instead to acquaint himself with the intricacies of whichever cars the house owned or the complexities of maintaining a large garden for year-round colour and cut flowers. Between the manuals for the lawn mowers and the Jaguar, though, was a slim volume of poetry. She took it out and sat on the bed in the uniform stockings and underwear Robert Markhew dictated his female staff should wear and began to read.

Much of the book comprised haiku, each one a glimpse into the life of the writer. Nicole flicked back to the cover, where the author was listed as Paul Oldman. She flicked back to the page she'd just read:

> *secretary smile.*
> *she takes down all he dictates--*
> *silk stocking, torn.*

Nicole frowned. It sounded like her. Could Peter have written this under a pseudonym?

She read through several more of the poems. Here was one about Robert, one about love, one about sex between two men...

The minutes ticked by into an hour. The CD she'd put on had begun to repeat the first song and she realized she hadn't heard the other tracks. She'd read the entire volume by the time she heard the outer door open and Peter's gruff baritone.

"Who's here?" He came into the bedroom, his smile when he saw her creasing the corners of his eyes. "Did we have an arrangement tonight? I must have forgotten."

Nicole held up the book of poetry and his face fell. "Did you write this?"

He nodded, crossing the gap between the door and the bed to sit next to her. He fumbled for her hand. "Don't tell anyone. We're not supposed to profit from our positions here."

"That depends how good you are." She reached back and unhooked her bra. "Let's make haiku together."

* * * *

The dinner was a quiet affair if you discounted Mary's constant monologue about her engagement. Jennifer was sick of hearing about it even before the main course was served. There were only so many times one could feign interest.

"Have you met Amanda?" asked Robert, when the girl who'd opened the front door came in to take away the remains of the soup course. "She's staying with us for a little while for some training."

"Briefly, at the door." Simon half stood and held out his hand. "How do you do? I'm Father Brande and this is my sister, Jennifer."

Jennifer smiled, noticing the maid's honey complexion. "Where are you from, Amanda? Spain?"

"No, ma'am. Basingstoke. My mother's Spanish, though." Amanda had a soft, lilting voice and was clearly nervous in front of guests. She gathered up the bowls with an efficiency any restaurateur would envy.

"How long have you had her?" Simon asked when Amanda left the room.

"What?" Robert seemed startled by the question. "Oh. A month or two. Not long. She's quite good, isn't she?"

"Quite."

Jennifer raised her eyebrows but Simon seemed to be deliberately looking away. This at least was a piece of news and she wondered how to work Amanda into her web of Robert's theoretical harem.

Simon busied himself with his napkin. "Is Susan all right? She was leaving just as we arrived."

"Was she?" Robert looked around the table. "I hadn't noticed she wasn't here, to be frank. Her duties are fairly light with Richard away."

"Talking of which, how did he propose?" Simon addressed the question to Mary, who was only too happy to discuss the unexpected web chat that initiated such a change to her life.

Jennifer had memorized the details by the arrival of the main course and watched as Simon tucked into the beef and vegetables as if he hadn't eaten for a week. Robert merely picked at his, pushing the plate away before it was even half finished.

The one-sided conversation from Mary died out by the time they were served cheesecake and coffee. Jean had remained as silent as her brother throughout the meal and even Jennifer, usually so eager to gather gossip, had seemed subdued.

When Amanda had cleared away dessert, Robert looked up. "Would you care for brandy and a cigar in the library, Simon?"

Jennifer pursed her lips, knowing this was an opportunity to gather information she wouldn't be privy to. Simon would be insufferably smug about it afterwards. "I'd be delighted," he said, rising. "If you'll excuse us, ladies."

The moment they'd gone, Mary left the table too, her heels clattering as she dashed up the stairs. Jean watched her daughter until she was out of sight, a smile on her face.

"It's lovely to see her so happy."

"It is." Jean looked at her with narrowed eyes and Jennifer felt she was being judged. "I wonder if I could ask you a favour." Jean leaned forward to close the gap between them. "Would you mind talking to Robert for me? I'd ask your brother but Robert has a soft spot for the ladies."

"I'll try." Jennifer held her hand. "What about?"

"Mary. She doesn't really have anything of her own. Anthony, my late husband, didn't leave us much and it was good of Robert to take us in."

"So?" Jennifer filed away the titbit of information. "How can I help?"

"Would you mind asking what sort of settlement he's going to make on her? I know he's not really obliged to give her anything, but it would help to get them off to a good start."

"I'll do my best." Jennifer grasped the older woman's hands. "I promise."

* * * *

Robert led the way back to the study, unlocking the door and ushering Simon inside. While the priest looked at the huge array of books on the shelves he poured two large measures and sank into a wing chair by the fire. "Do sit." He waved at the matching chair. "I don't often get the chance to talk man-to-man with someone. Cigar?"

"Not for me. I don't smoke." Simon sat and picked up the brandy, cupping it in one hand. "Thank you, though."

"I thought all priests smoked." Robert took one for himself. "Part of the job description, like knocking back the communion wine and deflowering the nuns."

Simon laughed. "Only in sitcoms and tabloids."

Robert did his best to smile back but feared it looked polite but strained. He lit his cigar, deep in thought. After a minute or two he looked up, holding Simon's eyes with his own. "It's been a rough couple of days. Hell, in fact, if you'll pardon my use of the expression."

"I'm not surprised." Simon leaned forward. "We've all been hit hard by Grace's death and now you have an engagement to deal with."

"You don't understand," Robert interrupted. "There's more to it than that. Far more." His voice softened. "You're a priest. I know I can trust you. Over the last year, Grace and I became very close, close enough that we began to share our personal thoughts."

"Go on." Simon nodded.

"I'm not sure that there's a polite way to say this," Robert continued, "so I'll be blunt. The day before she died, Grace told me what had happened with her husband."

"Henry's unfortunate demise?" Simon sat back, resting the glass of brandy on his leg. "It could have happened to anybody." He blushed. "Well, almost anybody. The accident…"

"...was no accident." Robert put down his glass and held his head in his hands. "Grace planned it all. She murdered him."

"You can't be serious." Simon sat up in his chair. "Why?"

"There were...things...in that marriage that were not right," Robert said. "Things that would have driven a saint to murder. He was abusing her terribly. I saw the marks he left on her when he was alive. One day she'd had enough." He threw up his hands. "While he was asleep she altered the knot in the rope he used for his...activities. When he...er...spilled his seed it wouldn't come loose again afterwards. The police ruled the whole affair an accident."

"That's horrible." Simon shook his head.

"There's more, though. Someone found out about the murder and was blackmailing her for large amounts of money. She was at her wits' end. She had to tell me because her bank account was almost dry. Another couple of months and she would have had to sell The Herbage. If she'd managed to let it earlier..." He let the sentence hang.

"Who?" Simon sat forward again. "Who was blackmailing her?"

"I don't know." Robert hung his head. A line of ash from his forgotten cigar dropped to the ground. "I asked her to give me twenty-four hours to think of what to do to help her before I took any action. Of course, she used that time to kill herself."

"So Jennifer was right."

"What?"

Simon looked up. "Jennifer was sure that Grace had killed Henry. I pooh-poohed the notion. I owe her an apology."

"Not yet. I still don't know who was blackmailing her. It's my fault. I shouldn't have left her alone."

Simon reached across and touched his knee. "It's not your fault, Robert. A suicide is nobody's fault but their own. Leave any recriminations to God."

"She'd still be alive if it wasn't for that blackmailer," Robert said. "I have to find out who it was. It's the last thing I can ever do for her."

"How will you manage that? A private investigator?"

Robert bit his lip. "That's an idea. I could certainly afford to." He leaned forward and dropped his voice. "Grace said she'd write me a letter explaining everything. Something I could take to the police." He frowned, standing. "Wait a minute." He went to the door and opened it. "Amanda?"

The trainee maid came from the kitchen drying her hands on a tea towel. "Yes, sir?"

"Was there any post this morning?"

Amanda looked around. "No, sir." She crossed to the sideboard in the hall. "But this was hand-delivered this afternoon. I put it on the side for you." She handed Robert an envelope.

He looked at the handwriting. "Yes." He closed the door and tore it open. "This is from Grace." He scanned the opening paragraph.

My dear friend,

It grieves me to write this but I fear for my life. You may be aware that Father Brande has been visiting me regularly. At first he was a great comfort after the passing but lately I am discomfited by his presence. He--

Robert folded the letter back into its envelope.

Simon put down his glass. "What did she say?"

"Nothing of importance. A suicide note, nothing more. Perhaps if I'd read it sooner..." He tucked it into his jacket pocket. "Thanks for the talk. I appreciate you listening to my ramblings." He opened the study door and stood to one side waiting for the priest to leave. "I'm sorry. This is one of those times I should keep her confidence."

"It was no trouble at all. I quite understand." Simon skulked past and Robert closed the door behind him.

* * * *

"Who's that?" Jennifer nodded toward a man on the side of the road. "He's waving at us."

"I've no idea." Simon laid his hand on her arm. "Better pull over and see what he wants."

Jennifer indicated and stopped the car next to the man. Simon rolled down his window. "Can we help you?"

"Cheers for stopping, mate." The man smiled as he leaned down to the height of the window. "Magic. Can you tell me where The Larches is?"

"The Larches?" Simon's voice raised in surprise. "Of course. Go to the end of the road and turn left into Cherry Tree Road and the house is past the first bend on your right."

"Cheers mate. I owe you one." He stood, rapping on the roof of the car and leaving nothing but the impression of aftershave and an odd accent. Simon craned his neck to look behind the car.

"What an odd fellow. I wonder who he was."

"You should have asked him." Jennifer indicated and pulled out again. "He might have been Grace's lover or something."

"Don't be ridiculous, Jennifer. He's probably a friend of Richard's from college." He looked at the time on the dashboard clock. "It's early yet. How about a nightcap at the White Art?"

"Are you sure?" Jennifer was dubious. "You've had several already."

"A little one won't hurt. Come on. You know you want to."

"Very well." She accelerated toward Laverstone's only hotel. The internet could wait another hour for her presence.

The White Art was a rambling old building on the corner of Lovatt Street and Taunton Road. Several men stood at the open doorway smoking cigarettes but Jennifer pulled into the car-park at the back and followed Simon into the lounge. She glanced up at the sign as she passed beneath. It depicted a full moon bisected by the lines of a pentagram. "You ought to complain about that sign."

Simon laughed. "Why should I? It's been like that since before I was assigned the post here."

"It's not right. They should go back to being called the White Hart instead of all this witchery nonsense."

"It's good for the tourists. Mike makes a mint when they come to see the village stones. He gets quite a bit of trade in the summer from the folks doing the Stonehenge and Glastonbury tour."

The lounge was quiet, though a fair amount of noise filtered through from the bar. Jennifer stood at the bar and removed her gloves while Simon flagged down the barman.

"Father Brande. This is a pleasant surprise." Mike Chapman jerked his head toward the bar. "You any good at darts? We're being thrashed by the team from Morley Croft."

Simon shook his head. "Sorry, Mike."

"No matter. What can I get you?"

"A small scotch for me and..." He looked at Jennifer, his eyebrows raised.

"I'll have a port and lemon." Jennifer looked at the other guests. There was no one she recognized.

"There you go." Simon took out his wallet and laid a five-pound note on the bar. "Is Richard upstairs?"

"I don't know offhand." Mike glanced into the bar. "I've not seen him, though he might well have come in and gone straight up."

"Mind if I check?"

Mike shook his head. "Help yourself."

"Splendid." Simon touched Jennifer's arm. "I'll only be a minute. You go and sit down."

* * * *

"So what did you find out?" asked Jennifer when they got home. She was already seething from the silent car journey. "You were gone for ages when you went to see Richard and then just swallowed your drink in one gulp. It must have been something important."

"Actually, no. Richard wasn't there so I left him a note to come and see me. The trouble was I had to go and find a pen and then needed a piece of paper." Simon looked at her as she took his coat to hang up. "I have to think." He kicked off his shoes and put his slippers on. "Robert told me some disturbing news. I need to pray for guidance."

"Tell me something, at least." Jennifer put the discarded footwear onto newspaper. "You and Robert were cloistered in his study for over an hour."

Simon headed up the stairs. "You were right all along. I'm going to bed."

"Right about what?" Jennifer shouted, her exasperation with her secretive brother reaching boiling point, but he gave her no reply.

* * * *

Jennifer was engrossed in an online conversation about Margaret's dog when the phone rang. She looked at the clock in the corner of the screen. Eleven-fifteen. The ringing stopped, answered by Simon in his bedroom. Minutes later he came thundering down the stairs pulling his clothes on as he went.

Jennifer ran into the hall. "What's happened?"

His face was grim. "That was Amanda, the maid at The Larches. Robert's been murdered."

Chapter 10

Jennifer pulled up onto the gravel drive, avoiding scraping the other parked car by a finger's width. "That was close," she said, turning off the engine.

"Close? You could have wrecked Robert's Jaguar." Simon was breathing far too heavily for the simple drive. Jennifer put it down to the drinking. It always made him tetchy.

"Anyway, what would it matter if Robert's dead? He's hardly going to complain is he?" Jennifer pulled off her leather driving gloves and stowed them in the glove box. "And if he comes back from the dead to moan about it, I'll apologize, okay?"

Simon scowled and got out of the car, forcing Jennifer to hurry after him toward the dark house.

She caught his arm. "It's all closed up for the night. If there's been a murder here, why isn't it bustling with activity and the police? Are you sure it wasn't somebody's idea of a joke?"

He scowled. "It's in very bad taste if it is." He stepped back, looking up at the darkened windows. "Perhaps they're all at the back. You wait here and I'll go and check."

Jennifer wrapped her coat more tightly around her as he disappeared around the side of the house. She could hear nothing but the *tink-tink-tink* of the engine cooling and the hiss of traffic in the distance. She was just debating calling out when the crunch of gravel announced Simon's return.

"There's not a light on anywhere." He half-ran up the steps and banged on the door. "Better to wake the house than ignore the call, though. Imagine if Sir Robert were lying bleeding to death in his bed?"

It took several minutes for lights to come on and the door to be opened. Amanda was pulling a red silk kimono closed. "Father Brande? Did you forget something?"

"What?" Simon tried to look behind her. "You phoned me about the murder."

"No, I didn't. I was in bed." Amanda rubbed sleep from her eyes. "What murder?"

"Robert Markhew, your employer. You phoned me a few minutes ago."

Amanda shook her head, a few locks of hair falling from her tight braid. "I assure you I did no such thing, Father. As far as I know, Mr. Markhew is perfectly fine."

"Someone's playing a joke on you, Simon." Jennifer pulled at her brother's sleeve. "Let's leave these good people to their beds."

"No. I must insist upon speaking to Robert." Simon looked from Jennifer to the maid, wide eyes reflecting the light from the hallway. "Someone phoned me and I can't take the risk that Robert is lying dead or injured somewhere. Wake him up, please, if he really is asleep. If I am just the victim of a cruel prank I will happily apologize afterwards."

"Best do as he says." Jennifer pressed Amanda's arm. "There's no dissuading him when he gets like this."

Amanda shrugged and opened the door wider, standing to one side to allow them passage. There was none of the activity one would associate with a murder evident.

"Amanda? What's going on?" Nicole Fielding stood at the top of the stairs, frowning at the unexpected activity. For such an attractive woman during the day, Jennifer thought, she made up for it at night with her hair in curlers and a dressing gown that looked to be a hand-me-down from her grandmother.

"It's Father Brande." Amanda closed the door and went to the bottom of the stairs. "He reckons Mr. Markhew's been murdered and won't leave until he sees him."

"Nonsense." Nicole did up the cord of her dressing gown. "Come back in the morning."

"I must insist on seeing him forthwith." Simon glared up the stairs. "Good God, woman, this is a matter of life and death. Would you wake him, please?"

Nicole grimaced. "Very well but I shall blame you for the inconvenience. Sir Robert doesn't take kindly to interruptions."

"Please do." Simon looked back at Jennifer, who nodded encouragement.

She guided Amanda to one of the high-backed chairs. "Let's get all this sorted out and get back to bed." Amanda said nothing, merely covering her mouth with her hand to yawn.

"He's not in his room or his studio." Nicole returned to the landing. "Why isn't he there?"

"How should I know?" Amanda asked. "He was in the study, the last I heard."

"Then let us check." Simon stepped to the door and rapped on the old wood. "Robert? Are you in there?" When there was no reply he tried the handle. "It's locked."

"Break it down," Nicole urged, having come downstairs at last. "If something's happened to him…"

Simon threw himself against the door but the oak didn't budge. He tried again with the same result.

"This is ridiculous," Nicole said. "Amanda? Go and fetch Peter."

"Yes, ma'am." Amanda hurried off.

"Peter Numan?" Simon rattled the doorknob one last time and stepped away. "I didn't know he was here as well."

"Yes, he looks after the cars and the grounds." Nicole bit her lip as she looked toward the kitchen. "Mr. Markhew took him on when he left school. He was a good friend of Richard's at the time and didn't have the qualifications for university. It seemed an apt solution."

"I see." Simon nodded.

"I told you all this at the time." Jennifer took the seat vacated by Amanda. "Head like a sieve, you. That's what Mum always used to say. I don't know how you passed your exams."

They looked up at the sound of footsteps. Amanda returned with the young Peter Numan, clad only in his jeans.

"Father." Peter nodded a greeting.

Nicole clasped his arm. "Will you bash this door open, Peter? Father Brande here hasn't got the muscle to manage it. He thinks Robert has been murdered."

"Murdered?" Peter grimaced and landed a side kick to the lock. Wood splintered. He kicked twice more until the wood around the lock gave way and the door lurched with a resounding crack. He pushed it open and entered the room, the others following on his heels.

"Oh my Lord." Simon made the sign of the cross.

Robert Markhew was slumped half across his desk, one hand trailing the sea of woollen carpet. His glassy eyes stared at the door, specks of blood peppering the pages of the book beneath his head. The dagger protruding from his back had allowed blood to run down his arm and pool on the floor.

"You were right." Amanda pressed her fist against her teeth. "He has been murdered."

"And burgled." Peter pointed to the open window. "We'd better call the police."

* * * *

Jennifer looked across at her brother, spotting the tell-tale signs he was over-tired. He rubbed his eyes, yawned and pinched himself on the arm. "I've already gone over all this with Sergeant Davies." He was talking to a plain-clothes policeman taking notes in front of him.

Detective Inspector White nodded. "I appreciate that, sir, and I'm very grateful, but I like to hear the events myself. It helps me form my own opinion, you see. Besides, you might think of something else with the re-telling."

"Very well." Simon took a long draught of the sweet tea Amanda had served earlier. Jennifer hoped it was warmer than hers had been. "I was woken by a phone call from Amanda at a little after eleven." He nodded toward the maid. "At least I thought it was her, although when I got here she said she knew nothing about it and that as far as she knew, Robert was alive and well."

"What time would this be, sir? How long was it between you receiving the phone call and arriving here?"

"It was about half-past eleven when we arrived."

"We?"

"My sister had to drive. I'd had too much brandy."

Jennifer nodded and the inspector scowled. "Was it a cellphone or a landline you received the call on?"

Simon frowned. "It was the house phone. Does it matter?"

White raised an eyebrow. "It might, sir. You can never have too many details. How did you know it was Amanda calling?"

"I recognized her voice. We'd had dinner here so it was still fresh in my mind."

"I see." White made a note in his book. "What happened when you got here?"

"Amanda answered the door and said he was alive, but I insisted upon seeing him. When I got inside, Nicole called down from the top of the stairs to find out what the commotion was. Amanda told her I thought Robert had been murdered and she went to check his bedroom. He wasn't there."

"So you checked the study?"

"That's right. Amanda said that was where she'd seen him last. The door was locked so she fetched Peter to break it down. That's when we found the body."

"Did you touch the body at all, sir? Any of you?"

Simon shook his head. "No. Peter and Amanda were going to, but I told them not to. That's when we called the police."

* * * *

"Tell me in your own words, love." Sergeant Davies sat at the table, his notebook open and his pencil poised. Jennifer thought he looked more professional than the inspector. She squeezed Amanda's hand.

"I don't know anything about it." Amanda leaned forward showing more than an ample amount of cleavage for a decent girl "The first thing I heard was Father Brande hammering on the door. I thought he'd forgotten something."

"Wait." Davies looked up. "He'd been here earlier?"

"Yes," said Amanda. "He and his sister had dinner with Mr. Markhew. They talked in the study after I cleared away the dishes."

"I see." Davies made a note. "Any idea what about?"

"No. It was none of my business." Amanda tugged at her earlobe. "After Father Brande left I didn't see him again until Peter bashed the study door open, though I know Mary saw him after me."

"Thank you." Davies referred to his notes. "Was the study window open when you saw him last?"

"No." Amanda rubbed her eyes. "I closed and locked the windows myself before I did the bedtime drinks round. Since Mr. Markhew was in the study I left that one, but it was closed and locked before dinner."

"What time were your bedtime drinks?"

"Around ten. I couldn't give Mr. Markhew his, though. Mary asked me not to disturb him. I went to bed afterwards."

"All right, Miss Jones. Thank you." Sergeant Davies looked at her. "We think it might have been an aggravated burglary. We found this in the earth under the window." He showed her a cellphone in a plastic evidence bag. "Do you recognize it?"

"It looks like Richard's." Amanda pressed the screen through the bag and it lit up with a picture of a motorbike. "I couldn't swear it's his, though."

"Is that all? You can see how upset she is." Jennifer put her arm around Amanda's shoulders.

Sergeant Davies nodded, the motion making his chins wobble. "I suppose so." He flicked back a few pages of his notebook. "And you are?"

* * * *

"Is there anything else you can remember about the evening?" Inspector White looked at the priest. From what Jennifer could see, her brother looked close to breaking point. Any minute now and he'd be ranting about sinners and hellfire.

"I don't think so." Simon shook his head.

"There was that man on the road." Jennifer felt it her duty to interrupt.

"Man on the road?" Inspector White stifled a yawn.

Simon glanced at his sister, nodding. "That's right. How could I have forgotten? When we were on our way home last night, someone asked us the way here."

"What time was that?"

"We left here at quarter past nine according to the clock in the car. It would have been about five minutes later."

"Who was this man? Can you remember what he looked like?"

"It was no one we knew." Jennifer spoke on her brother's behalf. "The voice was familiar, though."

"In what way?"

"It was a Birmingham accent, but he said 'Lurches' rather than 'Larches.'" Simon tapped on the table to emphasize the point. "I know I've heard it before, though I can't for the life of me remember where."

"I see, sir." Inspector White made another note. "Could you describe this man?"

"Not really." Simon shook his head. "It was dark and I only caught a glimpse of him. All I can remember was he was unshaven and fairly young. He had one of those hoodies all the kids wear these days."

"He had a rucksack." Jennifer grinned, happy to remember the detail. "A black one with a yellow stripe."

"I see. Thank you, sir."

* * * *

"You are Miss Nicole Fielding?" Sergeant Davies started a fresh sheet of paper. "You were Mr. Markhew's secretary, I believe?" He smiled at her. She looked almost lost in the bustle of policemen and scene-of-crime officers.

"That's right." Nicole had removed the curlers from her hair and now it fell in ringlets past her shoulders. "I got up when I heard the commotion downstairs."

"Could you tell me your perception of the events of the evening?" He looked up into her eyes, surprised by their sharpness in contrast to her body language.

"Father Brande and his sister left a little after nine and Mr. Markhew went into his study. I heard him talking to someone in there at nine-thirty."

"Any idea who?"

She shook her head. "I'm afraid not."

"Did you hear what was said at all?" He studied her face. You could tell a lot from a face but Nicole Fielding kept her gaze levelled at him.

"A bit," Nicole admitted. "Someone was asking him for money."

"What did Mr. Markhew say to that?"

"He shouted a bit." Nicole glanced around the room and lowered her voice. "He said 'Do you think I'm made of money? You can ask all you want but you're not getting a penny from me.'"

"Interesting." Sergeant Davies wrote it down. "Do you have any clue of the identity of this petitioner? Man or woman would be helpful."

Nicole shook her head. "I'm sorry."

* * * *

Inspector White rapped on the bedroom door and waited. After a few moments he heard a moan from inside.

"Who is it?" The voice was languid, as if its owner had just been awoken. "Do you know what time it is?"

White glanced at his watch. "Two forty-six AM. Would you mind opening the door, Miss Markhew? It's the police."

Mary opened the door, rubbing her eyes. White looked at the purple-haired girl clad only in a t-shirt depicting kittens and managed not to raise an eyebrow.

"The police? Has something happened?"

"There's been an incident downstairs. Someone broke into your father's study."

"Did they?" Mary blinked hard, steadying herself against the door frame and blocking White's view of the interior. "You mean Robert, though. He's not my father, he's my uncle."

"My apologies, miss." White looked away from her cleavage. "Could you tell me your perception of the events between Father Brande leaving and the household retiring for the night?"

"I suppose so." Mary's brow creased. "I said good night to Uncle Robert at quarter to ten and came up to bed."

"Is that all?" White flipped a few pages backward in his notebook. "You didn't happen to see anyone else about at that time?"

"No." Mary gave a bark of laughter. "Apart from Amanda, of course. She was on her way to give Uncle a cup of tea and I stopped her because he didn't want to be disturbed." She lowered her voice. "He keeps porno magazines in his desk."

"Does he indeed?" White smiled. "That doesn't really concern us. What time did you speak to Amanda?"

"After my uncle, so about ten to ten, and then again at five to."

"Again? Why?"

"She came back out of the kitchen with another drink. I had to tell her to leave him alone."

"She was persistent then?"

"Yes. I came upstairs then, though. I don't know if she tried a third time."

"Thank you." White closed his notebook. "If you don't mind me asking, isn't it a little early for a girl of your age to be in bed by ten?"

"It's the house clock," Mary said. "Everyone goes to bed early. Besides, I didn't go to sleep straight away. I watched a film first and then...er...thought about Richard."

"Richard Godwin? Your fiancé?"

"That's right. He's in London at the moment."

"I see. Thank you, Miss Markhew. It's probably not important, but what film did you watch? I don't remember there being one on telly last night."

"It was a DVD." She dropped her voice. "Lovers in Latex. Do you want to borrow it for evidence? I won't tell anyone if you don't."

White coughed. "That won't be necessary, thank you." He turned to go back downstairs.

"What was taken?"

He turned back. "I beg your pardon?"

"You said there'd been a burglary. What was taken?"

"Ah. I wasn't entirely clear with you there," White explained. "I said that someone had broken into your uncle's study. You'd best prepare yourself for a shock, miss. I'm afraid that your uncle's been murdered."

He was not expecting Mary to swoon. He thought women only did that in black-and-white films, or if their corsets were too tight, not that he saw many women in corsets since he'd left the obscenities division. The thud as the amply built Miss Markhew hit the floor made him wince.

He walked to the top of the stairs. "Miss Markhew has just fainted," he called. "Someone get her a glass of water." He looked back at the open door and dropped his voice to barely a whisper. "And a carpenter to fix the hole in the floorboards."

Chapter 11

Inspector White waited on the landing while Jean Markhew and Nicole Fielding fussed over Mary and got her back into bed. Downstairs, the forensics team had arrived, and were causing more chaos by taping off whole sections of the hallway. It was fortunate the house had so many people here to clean up after them, he thought, glancing at the two officers dusting for prints.

The murder scene was off-limits to all but the tech boys and White took a few minutes out with a cup of lukewarm coffee to consult his notes. A whole chunk of the evening was unaccounted for between after Father Brande leaving and the discovery of the body. He looked up to see several of the house occupants watching him. Although subdued, the house was taking on a festive air and the buzz of conversation in the living room as the residents discussed their theories about the murder was beginning to interfere with his thoughts.

He stepped inside and the conversation ceased as fast as a Conservative club meeting when a woman walks in. Simon Brande was seated on the edge of the sofa, sipping tea from a china cup. White beckoned him. "Can I have a word, Father?"

Simon nodded and looked for somewhere to put his cup, settling with the floor at the side of the sofa. It was an accident waiting to happen but White made no move to alert anyone to the precarious position of a cup half-full of tea on a cream carpet. "We'll use the dining room, I think." He allowed Simon to lead the way. "There's less likelihood of our being disturbed."

"If you like." Simon opened the door and took the seat nearest the door. White sat at the head of the table in Robert's chair.

"Do you recall anything further about that the gentleman who asked for directions?" he asked. "You stated he was in his early twenties with an unshaven face and a hoodie. Is there anything else you can add? It's not much to go on for an investigation."

Simon shook his head. "Nothing. It was dark and all I could see of him was by the dashboard lights. He did smell of beer and cigarettes, if that's any help, and he had a bag with him, a small rucksack, as if he'd travelled for some distance."

White nodded and made another note in his book. "If that's the case and this is our man, then he came here with the intent of seeing Markhew. This was no aggravated smash and grab."

"That does seem likely," Simon agreed, "assuming the lad is our murderer. I don't see who here would have a motive."

"Don't you?" White sat forward in his chair. "What about blackmail?"

"Blackmail?" Simon shook his head. "Sir Robert didn't need to blackmail anyone. He was comfortably off in his own right. Old money, I think, and a portfolio of investments as long as your arm from what I've heard, and that's not mentioning his books."

"I didn't think he was a blackmailer," White said. "But it's certainly possible that he was being blackmailed. The secretary, Nicole Fielding, stated that she overheard him telling someone that he couldn't afford to give them any money."

Simon shrugged. "It's possible." He lowered his voice. "Jean asked my sister to talk to him about a settlement for Mary now that she's engaged."

"I heard about that," White said. "To Richard Godwin, I believe, Markhew's stepson. Any idea where he is? I was told 'somewhere in London' which isn't terribly helpful."

Simon smiled. "Try the White Art in town. You'll find that Richard has been staying there for the best part of a week, just to avoid his stepfather."

"Has he indeed?" White made another note. "He'll be the main beneficiary, I suppose. That gives him the oldest of motives."

"Not Richard. He wouldn't hurt a fly." Simon sat back in his seat, stretching his legs under the table. "I've known him since he was an infant."

"Do you really know anyone, I wonder?" asked White. "Everyone has something to hide, especially from a man of the cloth."

"I can't deny that." Simon laughed. "I only recently found out something interesting about Grace Peters that she never confessed to me herself."

"Oh?" White raised an eyebrow. "What might that be?"

Simon lowered his voice. "I suppose it can do no harm now that she's dead. Robert only told me yesterday, but she was being blackmailed for the murder of her husband."

White let out a whistle. "Henry Peters? The sly old bag. She had us convinced. We had it down as an accidental death."

"We all did," Simon said, "except for my sister. She was sure he'd been bumped off."

"Why didn't she come forward with that information?"

"No proof. She has this group of friends on the internet. They're all into conspiracy theories, though if you ask me all they seem to do is gossip like old women."

White looked down at his notes. "You were discussing it with Mr. Markhew this evening, you said."

"Yes." Simon leaned forward in his chair. "Robert asked me my advice about it. Grace Peters had asked him for help because of their closeness and because she'd run out of money. He was torn between turning her over to the police and helping her out. While he thought about it she killed herself. He was racked with grief and thought that the only thing left for him to do was to bring the blackmailer to justice. He asked me if I'd any idea who the blackmailer was."

"You didn't know?"

"Why would I?"

"You're the parish priest." White played with his pen. "You're in a unique position to spot if someone is unexpectedly flashing the lucre about."

"No one comes to mind, Inspector. Perhaps it wasn't a churchgoer. If someone had confessed to me I would have been hard pressed to offer absolution."

"It's an avenue of enquiry, anyway." White smiled. "I don't really know much about confession, I'm afraid. I'm Church of England myself."

Simon smiled back. "I won't hold that against you."

White looked down at his notes. "So let me get this clear. Grace Peters killed her husband, someone found out about it and blackmailed her, so she eventually confesses it to Robert Markhew and kills herself. Then last night, after dinner with you and your sister, Robert has an argument with someone who asks him for money and is murdered." He looked up. "Have I missed anything?"

"The letter." Simon leaned forward. "Just before I left he received a letter from Grace, sent before she committed suicide, obviously. He read it but said it was nothing pertaining to the blackmail. I'm sure he was covering it up. Someone in this house, perhaps."

"Then we must find this letter," said White. "It must be the key to the murderer." He got up from his chair and crossed to the door. "Davies!" he called.

The younger man came running. "Yes, sir?"

"Tell them to look for a letter," he said. "It's important."

"It was delivered by hand," Simon added.

Sergeant Davies nodded. "Yes, sir." He headed toward the forensic experts in the murder room.

White returned to the chair. "What about the maid, Amanda James? She looks a bit suspicious, don't you think?"

"In what way, Inspector?" Simon sat back again and crossed his legs. "She hasn't been here long, I understand. I hardly know her. You're surely not going to declare 'the maid did it' are you? That's almost as clichéd as the butler."

"She tried to get in the study to see Mr. Markhew at least twice during the evening. Mary told her that Robert was not to be disturbed, yet found Amanda trying to see him again after that."

"It's possible." Simon made a steeple with his fingers. "Do you think she's the blackmailer?"

"If she'd gone in again after Mary went upstairs to watch her film, she could have killed Robert, left through the window and come back in through the side door."

"Perhaps," Simon agreed, "but that could be true of anyone in the house."

"It could." White stood. "Let's go and have a look." He led Simon back to the study, where the forensic team were just finishing. "Any sign of that letter?" he asked.

"No guv," replied the older of the pair. "Not a trace."

The other snorted with suppressed laughter.

"What's so funny?" asked White. "This is a murder you're laughing about."

"Sorry, sir." The man composed himself. "It was just the pun on 'not a trace.'" He paused, seeing the blank look on White's face. "Being forensics, you see."

"I do." White sighed. "Look, can you give me any details of the killer? Man or woman? Big? Short? Have you found any prints?"

"A few, sir." The second technician indicated a line of numbered cones. "We've got a spatter pattern here, indicating that the knife was inserted, removed and re-inserted." He stood behind the body and mimed stabbing the victim. "The murderer was right-handed and between five-feet-four and five-feet-ten. That's all I can say at the moment."

"What about the footprints outside?" White asked.

"We've got an impression of them," the first said. A man's size eights. I couldn't tell you what, though, until we can do a comparison check."

"All right." White nodded toward the evidence bags. "Let's have a little look."

"Yes, sir." The second technician handed over the cast.

White held the footprints under the light. "It's a lead, I suppose," he said, running his finger across the treads. "You don't think it's a tad convenient, though? The killer leaves so little evidence in the room yet plants his feet carefully in a damp patch of earth underneath the window."

"Perhaps it didn't occur to him, sir."

"These are high-quality shoes." White pointed at the pattern. "Now, if they were work boots or Doc Martens like the gardener's, you might not notice stepping in mud but this fine footwear? You feel every drop shift under your weight."

"Drop, sir? Shouldn't that be blob? Blob of mud?"

"Don't be facetious, Constable."

"Even if this is a genuine lead, it doesn't rule out any suspects."

"No." Simon stared at the corpse. "Average height, average shoe size."

"Give me a couple of photographs of the weapon," he said to the technicians. "Let's see what I can find out about it."

They handed him a pair of Polaroid photographs. "It's quite distinctive," said the first. "It's a fantasy weapon rather than a practical one."

White glanced at the trails of blood. "It looks practical enough from here."

* * * *

"Nicole Fielding, please?" White looked into the living room where the secretary was now fully dressed, her hair tucked up into an efficient loop at the back of her head.

She stood and followed them to the dining room. "I've already told you everything I know."

"That may be so, Miss Fielding." White treated her to a rare smile. "We want to ask you about this, though." He gave her the two pictures of the knife.

"That's Mas--" she corrected herself. "Mr. Markhew's. It was a gift from Peter."

"Was Peter in the habit of giving his employer gifts?"

"Not often," Nicole said. "This was special, though. He got it from an exhibition he went to. Mr. Markhew kept it in the glass case in his study."

White looked at Simon. "Give Mr. Numan a shout, would you? Let's ask him as well."

Simon left the room, returning moments later with the gardener-handyman.

"What can you tell me about this knife?" asked White, taking the photographs from Nicole and giving them to Peter.

"It's the one I gave to Mr. Markhew." Peter tapped the photograph. "It's only for show, though. It wasn't meant to be used."

"I'm sure Mr. Markhew would agree with you, sir." White took the pictures back. "Are you in the habit of giving deadly weapons as gifts? Has your aunt received an Uzi, perhaps, or your grandmother a Gatling gun?"

Peter laughed. "Heaven forbid. This was a special gift. Robert...Mr. Markhew...and I were supposed to go to an exhibition together. Something came up at the last minute and I went on my own. I brought him this back as a souvenir."

"What exhibition would this be?"

"The Star Trek exhibition in London a couple of years ago." Peter smiled. "It's a Klingon *Daqtagh*. We were both really into it see, though we used to argue who made the best captain." He faltered. "Nothing serious, you understand, nothing I would have killed him about."

"Miss Fielding here tells me that it was kept in the glass case in the study." White collected the photographs again. "Is that correct?"

"That's right." Peter nodded. "It has a drawer thing that slides out. It makes a terrible racket, though. I keep meaning to oil it."

"Is it a high-pitched shriek?" asked Simon. "As if someone trod on a cat's paw?"

"Sort of," agreed Peter. "Though I've never trodden on a cat."

"I heard that noise," said Simon, his face lit with excitement. "When Jennifer and I came to dinner."

"What time would this have been?" Peters asked, making a note in his book.

"Seven o'clock?" Simon suggested. "Give or take five minutes. No later than ten past, certainly. I was studying the crucifixion painting at the time. Jennifer was talking to Mary in the sitting room."

"That could be helpful," said White.

"It couldn't have been Robert, though," Simon said. "He wasn't in the study. He was with me admiring the Pieta and made a point of telling me he had the key in his pocket."

* * * *

White watched the coroner, Dr. Eric Chambers, and his assistant remove the corpse of Robert Markhew on a wheeled stretcher then turned to the people in the sitting room. "Right then, ladies and gentlemen. One last task and we'll let you rest in peace." He frowned. "Er, in a manner of speaking." He called to the forensic technicians. "This way if you please, gentlemen."

"What's going on now?" Mary had managed, with the aid of a coffee and a small glass of something medicinal, to come downstairs.

"We just need to take everyone's fingerprints. For elimination purposes."

She pulled her dressing gown more tightly around her. "What if I refuse?"

White raised his eyebrows. "Why should you if you're innocent? I could get a warrant for them tomorrow if you prefer."

"I was just asking." She sat again. "I don't mind, really."

White looked at the two technicians setting up a piece of glass attached to a laptop. "What are you doing? Get the dabs kit out."

The second technician grinned, polishing the glass with an alcohol wipe. "This is it, sir. The latest thing. There's no need for all the purple ink and dab sheets any more, this does it all for you and no mess for the people being tested."

White grunted. "I don't trust these modern gimmicks."

"You're just behind the times, sir." The first technician pulled on latex gloves. "You've got to get with the groove."

White scowled. "I'll give you a groove if you're not careful." He looked around the room. "Father Brande? You and your sister can go now, if you like. I know where to find you if I need to ask you anything further."

Simon looked disappointed. "Are you sure there's nothing else I can do, Inspector? Give solace to the bereaved, perhaps?"

White shook his head. "Get off to bed, sir. We can handle it from here. Good night." He turned back to the room. At least the list of interviewees was almost finished. "Susan Pargeter?"

* * * *

Jennifer slid into the driver's seat and started the engine, switching the interior heat to full and setting the windows to demist. "Come on, Simon," she said aloud as she watched her brother pause to say something to a policeman on the doorstep. She switched on her headlights to hurry him. It worked. He waved goodbye and trotted across the gravel.

He opened the passenger door and leaned inside. "You go on, Jennifer. I'm going to walk back."

"At this time of night? You'll freeze."

He laughed, causing the policemen to glance over. "I'll be fine. I need to clear my head and talk to the boss for a while."

"You're mad, Simon." Jennifer's smile betrayed the lie. "Very well. See you at home."

* * * *

"So what happened?" Jennifer stood by the kettle, waiting for it to boil. "You were with the inspector for hours and then you took twice as long to get home as you should have done. Have they any idea who did it?"

Simon lowered himself into the kitchen chair. "Not yet. Can you believe it? A knife in the back, no less." He glanced at the clock. "Will you look at the time! I've got to be up in four hours!"

"Never mind that." Jennifer made two cups of tea. "Who do you think murdered him?"

Simon took his drink, holding it in cupped hands. "I've no idea. Amanda seems the favourite suspect. She tried to get into Robert's study several times, even after she was told Sir Robert wasn't to be disturbed. She's also the right height to have killed him and the right-sized feet to have left the footprints they found."

"*Pfft.*" Jennifer snorted. "It wasn't Amanda. She's far too nice to be a killer. Even if she did want to kill Robert, she's too much of a lady to use a dagger. She'd have poisoned him or strangled him. Something that doesn't leave a mess."

Simon laughed. "Because she'd be the one cleaning up afterwards? What makes you so sure she didn't do it? Not that I think she did, mind. My bet is on the chap that stopped us for directions."

"I just know her too well, that's all."

Simon frowned. "How could you know her? We hadn't met her before last night."

"You hadn't, anyway." Jennifer smiled into her tea.

Simon twigged. "She's one of your gossip cronies, isn't she?"

"So what if she is?" she said through pursed lips. "I was right about Grace Peters, wasn't I?"

Simon nodded, lost in thought. "You were indeed." He was silent for a moment then looked up, his forehead creased. "That's how you knew about the dagger as well! I never mentioned it."

* * * *

With the police gone, the household had a chance to look over the scene of the crime, despite the yellow police tape over the door and Inspector White's warning not to disturb anything.

Amanda pointed at the spatter markers and the red stain. "How am I supposed to get that out of the carpet? That's the stain from Hell that is."

Nicole loosened her hair from its tight pins. She couldn't help herself. "How about Jesus soap-on-a-rope and holy water?" She grinned at the expression on Amanda's face as she crossed herself. "And don't give me that Catholic girl rot. I've known you too long."

Peter grinned. "Don't let our esteemed police confidant Father Brande hear you say that. He'd have you excommunicated."

Chapter 12

Mary watched the priest pull up at the side of the White Art and jump out of his car, leaving it running on a double yellow line. With a perverse and somewhat guilty hope, she wondered if a policeman would come along and give him a ticket. She didn't like Simon Brande much. He was too much the ladies' man to be a proper priest.

He tried the door handle several times and resorted to banging on it. Was he really that much of an alcoholic that he was so desperate? She tucked herself behind a tree and took her phone out, opening the lens cover and setting it to video. At the very least an irate priest should earn her some page views on YouTube.

Simon pulled on the handle again, giving it one twist too much for tolerance. Mary had to clamp her hand over her mouth to stifle the laugh as the brass broke and, with the force of Simon's tugging, flew back and banged him on the head. She'd never heard a priest swear before.

The door opened from the inside to reveal Mike Chapman the landlord, wearing grease-stained butcher's apron. "Don't you know what time it is?" He snatched the handle from the priest's hand. "We're closed. I haven't even begun to serve breakfast yet."

"I need to speak to Richard Godwin urgently." Mary was gratified to see Simon's attempt to just push his way into the hotel was met by an immovable landlord. "It's about his stepfather."

Mike shook his head. "No can do." He rubbed his eyes with the heels of his hands and yawned. "He checked out last night. You could try his phone."

Simon pulled out his phone and dialled. He waited a minute and scowled. "Straight to voicemail."

Mike's face creased into a frown. "I thought you were friends with him?"

"I am." Simon put the phone back in his pocket. "What time did he leave?"

"Sometime in the early hours, I think. I didn't see him go." Mike glanced into the bar behind him. "Is there anything else? I am busy, you know."

Simon took a step backward "No, I suppose not. Thanks for your time, Mike."

"Any time, Father." Mike grinned. "If it wasn't for your sermons I'd lose half of my Sunday trade."

Simon returned to his car with a face like thunder. He glanced once more at the hotel as the door closed and roared off.

Mary ended the recording and played it back. The camera on her phone wasn't brilliant and lent the audio a booming quality but it was clear enough to make out every word of the exchange. She tried Richard's number on her own phone again. Just as it had done four times already, it dropped her straight to voicemail. Richard was not taking calls.

"Arse." Mary stuffed the phone back into her pocket and turned away. It seemed Richard really wasn't here after all. Mike might cover for his residents but he would never lie to a priest.

* * * *

Jean Markhew opened her eye at the slight rattle of china and raised herself onto one arm. "I'm the mistress by default now, am I?" she asked, looking at the bowed head of the semi-naked girl at the side of her bed. Amanda made a slight inclination of her head sufficient to answer the question.

Jean looked at the cup of steaming tea, plate of toast and copy of the morning's Laverstone Times on a silver tray. She made no indication Amanda should put the tray down. "Hmm?"

"You are, ma'am." The maid bowed her head in acknowledgement and respect. "Though I wish it were in better circumstances."

Jean reached out with her free hand to stroke Amanda's hair. "As do I," she said with a chuckle, "though beggars can't be choosers and I'm sure he'll have left me very comfortable. I shall be happy when all this business is done with and they catch whoever did it." She sat up, pulling the pillows vertical so she could lean against the headboard. "Pass the tea, there's a dear."

She took the proffered cup, leaving the saucer on the tray, and flicked open the paper. "Murder at The Larches" proclaimed the headline with a shot of the outside of the house, obviously taken early this morning for there was a policeman standing at the gate but no vehicles other that Robert's Jaguar on the drive. "Have you seen this?" she said. "How do they get the news so quickly?"

"I really couldn't say, ma'am." Amanda still stood bolt upright and Jean glanced up.

"I appreciate the formality but do relax, dear. Massage my feet while I breakfast, would you? Your other duties can spare you a few minutes, surely?"

"Of course." Amanda put the tray on the side table and sat on the bottom of the bed, raising the covers until Jean's feet were exposed. She began to massage them, her thumbs kneading the pressure points on her new mistress's soles.

Jean glanced up from the paper and smiled. "Much better."

She read the lead story and followed it to page five. Much of the article was stock background on Robert and his books and political work. One phrase stood out. "Listen," she said. "'Police are looking for a member of the household to assist them in their enquiries but are unwilling to release any names at present.'"

"Richard, I suppose, ma'am, though he's not been here all week."

"I doubt the boy would have the balls." Jean folded the paper and took the plate of toast. "Robert never wanted me to be his submissive. Being Anthony's widow made it too close for comfort, too much like a hint of incest, though we were never even slightly related. I didn't even know him very well before Anthony died, though I recognized that look in his eye." She glanced down the bed, catching Amanda's eye. "You know the one."

She finished the tea and replaced it on the tray. "I shall have to put on a show that I'm upset by his death." She began buttering the toast. "Set out the black for today. It will at least please Father Brande that I wear mourning black for a while."

"Yes, ma'am." Amanda rose to stand, the single movement graceful and obviously well practised.

"Did you kill him?" Jean asked.

Amanda looked up, her bright eyes glistening in the single ray of sunlight that danced between the closed curtains. "No, ma'am, I did not."

Jean nodded. "We'll see. Though I'm inclined to believe you."

* * * *

"I'm back." Simon's voice echoed from the hall as the door slammed.

"There's tea in the pot." Jennifer went to the kitchen doorway and watched as he dropped his coat and briefcase on the pew in the hall. "We have a visitor."

He strode into the kitchen and stopped, a look of surprise on his face. "Mary? What are you doing here?"

"I come to ask you for your help, Father." Mary twisted a paper napkin in her fingers. "I want you to come with me to The Herbage."

"Next door?" Simon sat. "Whatever for?"

Jennifer got up to fetch him a cup. "Now don't have a coronary but she wants to ask the witch who killed Robert." She patted him on the arm as she set the cup down, "She's afraid you'll excommunicate her for it."

Mary blushed, which clashed terribly with her hair.

Simon reached out and patted her hand. "I chatted with Miss Jones yesterday and she's actually very nice. We may have opposing theologies but she's an intelligent woman who can put forward a convincing argument."

"She's psychic as well." Mary's eyes were wide, her words breathy. "She can find out everything and tell us who the killer is."

Simon laughed. "I'm not sure I'd go that far. If she was, though, would you be willing to hear the truth? What if it turns out that Richard is guilty? How would you feel then?"

Mary smiled. "Richard is no saint but he's not a killer. He wouldn't hurt a fly if it didn't beg him first."

"I don't understand." Simon frowned. "What does that have to do with anything? This was a crime of passion. Men do strange things in a fit of passion."

"Not Richard." Mary shook her head. "He might like it rough, but he would never be violent. Especially not with his stepfather."

Jennifer poured the tea, trying to be unobtrusive but relishing every moment. Wait until she told the girls.

Simon glanced at her before turning back to Mary. "I'm not saying I think Richard did it, just that there's the possibility. He did stand to inherit the estate, after all."

Jennifer frowned. "Did he? I thought Jean…"

Simon interrupted. "He'll have left her a generous stipend but the bulk will go to Richard, surely? He is Sir Robert's stepson, after all. He'll be a very rich young man."

"If you don't suspect him," said Mary, "why did you go to warn him this morning?"

"You saw me?" Simon shook his head. "That wasn't to warn him. That was to tell him the bad news before the police did."

Mary held the napkin to the corners of her eyes. "I went to see him as well. He stopped answering my phone texts and his cell just goes straight to voicemail. He left last night, didn't he?"

Simon nodded. "In the early hours. He's made it worse for himself by leaving. It looks as if he's fleeing the scene of the crime."

"I know." Mary clutched his hand. "Susan Pargeter told me the police went looking for him after you went home but he'd already done a runner."

"They did," Jennifer watched the swirl of her tea as she stirred it. "They searched his room as well." She grinned at their expressions. "I have my sources."

"You and your internet cronies." Simon reached for the sugar. "Who's favourite for the deed, then?"

Jennifer shrugged. "Actually it's even-stevens between Richard and Jean. The figures will change when the will is read out, though, depending on who was named as his beneficiary." She noticed Mary's face and squeezed her hand to reassure her. "I don't believe either of them did it. Richard is such a nice boy and Jean is comfortable as she is. She had no reason to rock the boat."

"All the more reason to go to the witch." Mary took a deep breath. "So we can clear his name before the police lock him up for good. I don't for one moment think my mother did it. She wouldn't have the guts."

Simon sighed. "Very well. We'll ask Miss Jones for help, though the police won't like us interfering."

"They should thank us." Jennifer squeezed Mary's hand again to chivvy her on. "I bet they don't have a network like ours to help them get to the bottom of things."

* * * *

Meinwen happened to glance out of the window as the trio opened her gate. Mary Markhew, the priest from next door and a woman she assumed to be the priest's sister were already striding up the path.

She opened the door before they reached it. "Good morning. I felt you coming."

"Saw us out of the window, more like." Simon grinned. "We have a favor to ask, or at least Mary does. I'm not entirely certain I approve."

"You'd better come in." Meinwen stood back. "Enter freely, and of your own will."

"Isn't that for vampires?" Mary asked.

Meinwen laughed as she went past. "Perhaps. It is more a request that you accept what you find inside without judgement. I am stating I have not coerced you into entering."

Simon nodded, his hands clasped at his chest. "Judge not, lest ye be judged."

"Matthew seven, verse one." Meinwen closed the door behind them. "But yes, that's more or less it."

"Stating to whom? The police?" Jennifer wrinkled her nose. "That's an odd smell Have you been smoking pot?"

"No." Meinwen led the way into the lounge. "It's just incense on the altar of Kali."

Mary looked at the statue of the six-armed goddess and shuddered. "Isn't she the goddess of vengeance?"

"Sometimes," Meinwen admitted, "though she is a mother as well. She gives aid when harsh tasks are to be performed, though she often demands a high payment."

"What sort of payment?" Simon peered at the statue, noticing the stains on the brass. "Blood I suppose."

"Sometimes," Meinwen elaborated no further. "May I offer you something to drink?"

"Tea would be nice," said Jennifer.

Simon nodded. "Everything seems brighter over a cup of tea."

"Nothing for me though." Mary was looking at the shelves. "This place is really cool."

"I've not been here long, so mostly the coolness is the taste of the owner." Meinwen headed to the small galley kitchen to brew tea. "Make yourselves at home."

"I meant to ask you about that." Simon sat on a high-backed dining chair. "I was surprised The Herbage had been let, bearing in mind that Grace only died the day before yesterday. When was the rental agreement set in motion?"

"Last month." Meinwen brought in the drinks on a tray and sat. "It took me this long to get organized and order stock for the shop." She began handing out cups. "I hope you like chai. I generally have it at this time of day. It clears the chakras."

Simon sniffed. "It smells like aniseed. Foreign."

Meinwen forced what she hoped was a pleasant smile. "All tea is foreign. Now, what can I do for you? More love potions?"

Simon glanced at Mary, who nodded at him. "We'd like to ask you to help us with a murder."

Meinwen's face darkened. "I don't do that sort of magic. Too much negative karma."

Mary giggled. "Not perform a murder. Help solve one."

"Whose?"

"Robert Markhew. He was stabbed last night in his study."

"Sir Robert, murdered?" Meinwen put down her tea. "Oh." She sank back in her chair remembering the feel of his hand against her cheek then choked back a tear. "I only met him once but I liked him. He was a very charismatic man."

"He was my uncle." Mary put her tea down. "Now my fiancé has disappeared as well. The police probably think he did it."

"Why?" Meinwen could feel a headache coming on. "This is Richard Godwin you're talking about, isn't it?"

"Yes." Mary smiled. "Your potion worked perfectly."

Meinwen didn't contradict her. "If you want me to get involved then I must be involved fully. You might not like what I find out."

Simon raised his palms. "I don't have any secrets."

Meinwen turned to him. "We all have secrets. Just be sure you won't regret asking me to find them out."

"We won't." Jennifer clasped her hands as if in prayer. "Does that mean you'll do it?"

"*Mae'n debyg felly.*" Meinwen stood and crossed to the statue of Kali, then pressed a finger to the goddess's forehead. "I suppose so." She turned to face them. "Why not tell me the story from the beginning?"

"This is exciting." Mary's eyes were wide and shining. "It's like having our own Miss Marple."

Simon began to relate what they knew, with many interruptions from Jennifer and Mary. When he ground to a halt he found his tea had gone cold. He waved away Meinwen's offer of a refill.

"Let me get this straight." Meinwen snatched up a ribbon and tied back her hair. "Robert Markhew was stabbed between nine forty-five and midnight with a fantasy dagger Peter Numan had given him that was, up until seven o'clock, kept in a metal case in the study."

"That's the long and the short of it." Jennifer looked at the other two but there was nothing they wished to add.

"The study was locked but the window was open with shoe prints below it. The chief suspects are the maid, Amanda, Richard and the mysterious stranger who asked for directions."

"That's right." Jennifer avoided Simon's eye. "And Jean Markhew. She might have done it to inherit the estate."

"It's not likely." Meinwen considered it. "It's more likely to be whoever blackmailed Grace Peters. They will have been afraid this letter incriminated them." She looked at Simon. "Who else knew about the letter, besides yourself?"

"Robert, obviously, and Amanda. Perhaps one of the other staff? He seems to have an awful lot."

"We think he has a harem." Jennifer giggled.

"I can assure you he doesn't." Mary scowled at her. "I think I'd know."

"Sorry." Jennifer looked down at her hands. "It was only idle speculation."

"Susan Pargeter is the housekeeper, yes?" Meinwen turned to Simon for confirmation. "And she was asking about drugs and poisons in church?" She tapped her temple as she sorted through the information Jennifer had related. "Why was she hurrying away before dinner?"

Mary spoke up. "I didn't know she had. I'll ask her if you like."

Meinwen nodded. "Please do. Why did you both go to the White Art this morning?"

Simon glanced at Mary. "I went to tell Richard his stepfather had been murdered."

"And I went to give him some womanly comfort." Mary looked directly at Meinwen. "I knew he was in town although Uncle Robert thought he was still in London."

"Was that your only reason for going there?" Meinwen asked Simon.

"Of course." Simon looked affronted. "Have you got any aspirin? That incense is giving me a headache."

"Certainly." Meinwen went through to the little galley kitchen and took a bottle from one of the shelves. "I thought you High Church people used incense." She emptied two tablets into Simon's hand.

"We do, but that's in a draughty church, not a cosy sitting room. "What are these? They're not aspirin." Simon swallowed them.

"They're willow bark. It's where aspirin comes from." Meinwen winked at Jennifer. The older woman hid her smile behind her hand.

Meinwen drank her chai, not caring it had gone cold. "Now we must go to the police," she said. "I don't want to be arrested for obstructing their investigation."

* * * *

"No. I will not have you intruding on my case. If I find you asking questions I'll have you up for obstruction." Inspector White was not pleased with their request. "If the papers got a hold of this, they'd have a field day and I'd get demoted to a beat copper." He shook his head. "I can't imagine what the super would say if he found out I'd hired a psychic."

"It's not like that." Meinwen frowned. "Think of it more as 'integrating with the local community to further the investigation.'" She dropped her voice. "Now there's a sound bite for you. I'm not looking for any publicity, here. I just want this town to get back to normal."

"Hmm." White pinched his lip, thinking. "That could work. An integrated, grassroots investigation. I like the sound of that." He looked at Meinwen. "All right, but you must tell me anything that you find out and leave any arrests up to me."

"Deal." Meinwen held out her hand and he shook it.

"You haven't been smoking any funny cigarettes, have you?" White sniffed cautiously. "I'd have to arrest you if I catch you with any."

Meinwen shook her head. "It's just incense. Who's chief on your suspect list then?"

"Richard Godwin." White pulled out his notebook. "He was in Laverstone and staying at the White Art without his stepfather knowing. Why was that, do you think?"

"He was having problems with Robert. He told me that himself. He wouldn't have mentioned it if he was about to go and kill him." Simon pulled out his notebook. "Will this take much longer? I have an appointment."

"Maybe, maybe not. He left in a hurry without paying his bill, he's the right height, he's right-handed and he knew where the dagger was kept." White turned a page and picked up the phone. "Peters? Have you done that match on the shoes we found in Godwin's room yet?"

He paused to listen to his sergeant and put the phone down. "The shoe prints that we found are the right size to have been Richard Godwin's. Although we won't know for certain until we find the shoes that made the prints."

"That looks bad, Inspector, but I know Richard." Simon stepped forward. "He wouldn't have killed his stepfather. He's a good lad."

"He's wanted for questioning at the very least." White returned to his notebook. "Then there's the maid, Amanda. She kept trying to get into the murder room. There's something fishy about her."

"Fishy or not, you'll have to manage without me this afternoon." Simon pulled on his overcoat. "I have to perform Mass at the hospital."

"As you will, sir. We'll just pray we find our murderer."

* * * *

Nicole groaned.

The windowless room was hot, her skin hotter still from where the candle wax had dripped onto it, making it redden under its new layer. Her hair, freed of its usual neat twist, hung limp with sweat and spit, trailing the floor. Her knees were twin fires of agony from supporting her weight for so long, though she couldn't have moved them if she'd tried. Leather straps encased her wrists and ankles, each one attached to a spreader bar, and another ran up the centre line of her body, forcing her to maintain a kneeling position.

She shrieked as the whip pulled off a piece of wax. "Who killed Robert?"

"I don't know."

The whip struck again, taking off another piece of wax and leaving a long welt in its place.

"Who killed Robert?"

Nicole shook her head. "I don't know."

The whip struck again and again, each blow eliciting a squeal of pain from the bound girl. "Who killed Robert?"

The twelfth strike made Nicole scream. "Yellow!" Tears streamed down her face. "Yellow."

The cool of an ice cube replaced the heat of the wax and the Jean's leather-clad hand brushed the sweat-matted hair from her eyes. "Drink." Jean held a straw to her lips and Nicole sucked in cold water. "Good girl."

* * * *

Later, after a shower, Nicole groaned again.

"What?" asked Jean. Nicole twisted the laptop around so she could see the screen.

"These are Sir Robert's accounts."

"What about them?" Jean put on her glasses and studied the figures. "Twenty thousand pounds withdrawn?"

"This morning. Only Robert, Richard and I had access to it and it wasn't me."

"Which makes my future son-in-law a thief at the very least," said Jean.

* * * *

"So this is the murder room?" Meinwen closed her eyes and turned in a small circle. "It's cold."

"Can you feel the spirits?" asked White. "I think the heating's off."

"No, the window's open." Meinwen stepped over the stained carpet as she crossed to the casement. She avoided touching the glass. "Which way were the shoe-prints facing?"

White consulted his notebook. "Inward. The intruder stood looking in for several minutes, to judge by the even depth of the tread. The window wasn't forced."

Meinwen crossed to the glass-topped cabinet. "This is where the knife was kept until seven o'clock?"

"That's right, yes."

Meinwen squatted to look more closely at the sliding drawer. "Just because Simon heard the case open doesn't mean the knife was being removed. When a door opens it could be to let someone in or let someone out."

"The knife was removed, though. It was the murder weapon."

"It was certainly removed at some point," Meinwen agreed. "Would you call Amanda, please?"

White crossed to the door and spoke to his constable. Amanda arrived within moments and Meinwen stared at her powerful build before shaking her hand. "You're Amanda James?" she asked, watching her face.

Amanda nodded. "That's right, ma'am. I look after the house and guests."

"Do you look after the heating as well?"

"That's right. Robert--Mr. Markhew was quite particular about having a warm study."

"Was the heating on high or low last night?"

Amanda shrugged. "It was just normal. Same as it always was."

"Was the study warmer than the rest of the house?"

"Of course. Mr. Markhew didn't like to be cold."

Meinwen nodded. "Whether the room was hot or not will tell us if Mr. Markhew opened the window for air or to let someone in. If the room was no warmer than usual, it seems the latter is likely. That may or may not have been Richard." She turned back to Amanda. "Was there anything else unusual that night?"

The maid raised her eyebrows. "Such as?"

"I don't know," said Meinwen. "I'm not familiar with this room. Were there any books missing from the shelves, pictures taken down, that sort of thing?"

"No." Amanda pointed at one of the wing chairs. "That's back in position, though."

"The armchair?"

"Yes." Amanda looked down at her. "Sir Robert generally used it for reading, last thing at night. When we found him..." She faltered and took a deep breath. "When we found the body the chair had been pulled up in front of the desk, like someone had sat in it, talking to him. It usually faces the other one across the fireplace. I was going to put it back when the police had left, but I remembered they said not to touch anything in here. Someone has, though."

"Someone with something to hide, I'll warrant." White examined the floor around the chair.

"Everyone has something to hide." Meinwen looked at the maid. "Don't they Amanda?"

She cocked her head to one side. "I expect so. Is there anything else?"

"I thought you were supposed to be psychic." White tapped his notebook with his pencil. "Haven't the spirits told you what happened yet?"

"The spirits help those who help themselves," Meinwen replied. "What's the old saying? You can give a man a fish and feed him for a day, or you can teach him how to fish and feed him for a lifetime."

"Very philosophical." White led them out of the murder room and helped her take off the disposable foot coverings. "That doesn't answer any questions, though, unless you're offering to buy us all dinner."

"If I solve the case, you owe me a dinner." Meinwen went into the sitting room to speak to Mary. "You were the last person to see your uncle alive."

"Apart from the killer."

Meinwen gave her a tight smile. "Obviously. Was the window open when you saw him?"

Mary's forehead creased in thought. "I don't know. I don't think so."

"Was there a draft? Did you hear anything?"

Mary bit her bottom lip. "Wait! I heard the church bell striking the quarter hour."

"Is that usual?"

Mary shook her head. "No, but the window must have been open for me to hear it."

"Excellent." Meinwen looked at the inspector. "Then we know Mr. Markhew was alive after the visitor he let through the window had been and gone."

White's cell rang with a garish modern pop song. "Excuse me." He covered the mouthpiece with his hand. "I'll have to take this."

The others waited while he discussed something in a low voice. After a few minutes he put it back in his pocket and turned. "That was my sergeant. We've traced the call made to the rectory at eleven fifteen last night. It came from the platform two of Laverstone station."

"What train runs from there at that time of night?" asked Meinwen.

"The night express to Glasgow, which departed at eleven twenty-three."

Chapter 13

Mary gave a bark of laughter, covering her mouth when the others stared at her. "It couldn't have been Richard then. I don't think he knows anyone in Glasgow."

Meinwen patted her shoulder. "It does stop en route. Milton Keynes, Coventry, Birmingham, Carlisle…"

"Birmingham?" Jennifer clutched at Inspector White's coat. "Do you remember the strange chap who asked Simon and me for directions? He had a Birmingham accent."

"You said it seemed familiar at the time." White took out his pocket book. "I'll make a note but it's not much help at the moment. It's not like I can check who got off the eleven twenty-three at Birmingham Station."

Mary shrugged. "If it had been Richard he would have gone to London, not any of those northern places."

"Is it possible he phoned from the northbound platform and took a southbound train?" Meinwen happened to glance upward. "Why is there a hook in the ceiling, Amanda?" she asked.

She followed her gaze. "It's been there since before I came here. Perhaps it was to hang a projector screen up with."

"Not in front of a gas fire, surely?" Meinwen stood under the hook and tried to reach it. Even with her arms stretched above her head she was a foot too short. "The light would show through the screen and ruin any slides or film that was showing."

Amanda shrugged. "Your guess is as good as mine."

Mary walked back to the study and returned with a collection of Robert's photography, a folio edition fifteen years old. "I've never seen that hook used." She leafed through the book until she found the print and turned the book around for them. "But it used to be." The full-page photograph portrayed in monochrome a naked man hanging from the hook, his flesh partially stripped away and pierced with dozens of thorns. Mary trailed a finger down the image. "Uncle's books were supposed to be locked away when I was little but I knew where he kept the key."

White frowned and leafed through several more pages. "Mind if I hang on to this?"

Meinwen raised her eyebrows. "Latent homosexual urges, Inspector?"

White scowled. "Nothing of the kind. There may be a connection between these photographs and the murder. Perhaps it was one of the men in here who did him in."

Mary shook her head. "I doubt it, Inspector. This book is ancient and, besides, he always had his models sign release forms." She brushed back her hair with one hand and glanced at her watch. "Would you mind if I left you to it? It's gone two already."

"Has it?" Meinwen pulled out her cell to check. "I've missed lunch." She looked at White. "I don't need her for anything else. Do you?"

"Not at all." White smiled at Mary. "You run along then. I think we're about done here."

Meinwen's phone slipped from her fingers and landed with a thud on the soft carpet.

"Allow me." said Amanda, reaching down. Her hair fell forward, obscuring her face, and Meinwen stared. On the back of the maid's neck, where it would normally be obscured by the hair, was a small tattoo, no more than an inch high.

Meinwen leaned forward to examine it. "Stay there a moment."

Amanda paused as Meinwen pushed the rest of her hair forward.

White leaned in over her shoulder. "A tattoo? Nothing to get excited about, Ms. Jones. What young girl doesn't have one these days? That's an unusual one, though, I'll admit. It's normally dolphins and butterflies."

"Body art is about empowerment." Meinwen ran her finger over the design. It looked like a pair of letter Rs drawn back to back and sharing a central stalk. "People have been performing body modifications for centuries. They found a mummy in ice dating back to the fourth century BC with scarification, and Julius Caesar wrote about the Celtic tribes tattooing themselves with woad." She motioned Amanda to get up again. "Three of the warriors in the Water Margin were described as having full-body tattoos as well."

"I used to like the Water Margin." White gazed into space, as if his childhood was being replayed on a screen. "It was on every Friday night at tea time. My mum always made fish and chips and, as a treat, I was allowed to watch that with a pineapple cream cake."

Meinwen stared at him, her mouth open with astonishment. "I was referring to the book. It was based on the activities of Song Jiang, who died in eleven twenty-seven. The television series was hardly accurate."

"I just liked the design." Amanda handed Meinwen her phone. "Something a bit different, you know?"

"Heathens, according to the Bible." Meinwen lifted the sleeve of her blouse to display a tattooed armband. "It's a good job Father Brande isn't here, he'd have a fit. God specifically denounces the use of tattoos in Leviticus chapter nineteen, verse twenty-eight, which states 'Ye shall not make any cuttings in your flesh for the dead, nor print any marks upon you.'"

"That's hardly adhered to now, though, is it?" White sketched the design of Amanda's tattoo in his notebook. "If you kicked all the people with tattoos out of the church you'd have no congregation left."

"They have to accept the penitent back into the fold. The Old Testament is pretty much overruled by the New Testament, anyway, not that is stops it being used politically." Meinwen rubbed her eyes. "Those fire-and-brimstone preachers scare me."

"Me too, actually." White closed his note book. "There are precious few of them in England, I'm glad to say."

"Even Jesus had a tattoo according to the Revelations of St. John. The modern church tends to ignore Leviticus." Meinwen patted his hand. "Apart from the bestiality." She turned back to Amanda, who was smoothing her hair back and took her phone from the girl's hand.

"What does it mean?" she asked.

Amanda put a hand to her neck. "Nothing much. I had it done for an old boyfriend."

"It's unusual." Meinwen took the girl's hand. "Is it his initials?"

"Yes." Amanda pulled her hand back. "Is that everything? I'm neglecting my duties."

"Do you still have duties now Mr. Markhew is dead?"

Amanda frowned. "Of course. There are still seven other people living here. Life must go on." She looked at the heavy boots both White and Meinwen wore. "Especially with you lot tramping all over the place. Have you seen the hallway after last night? It looks like a herd of pigs has been through."

"Now now," said White.

Amanda blushed. "I meant it literally. Mud from the garden, fingerprint powder, that sort of thing. It'll take a month just to get the house clean again after so many people have been tramping about."

"Isn't there anyone else to help? The housekeeper?"

"Susan?" Amanda dropped her voice to a whisper. "She wouldn't stoop to housework."

"Oh?" White lowered his, too. "There's no love lost between you then?"

"Not really. She thinks she's above the likes of me." Amanda checked her watch. "Can I go now?"

"Of course." White stepped to one side. "We'll call you if we need you again."

"Thanks. I hope you find him soon. The killer I mean."

"Him, Miss James? How do you know the murderer is a man?"

Amanda shrugged. "It stands to reason, doesn't it? Sir Robert was a very charismatic man, at least to the ladies. None of the women would have killed him, so it had to be a man."

"That's what we're endeavouring to find out."

"Good." Amanda stalked out of the room.

Meinwen rubbed her temple with her fingers. "If she'd had that tattoo to honour a boyfriend, wouldn't she have had it somewhere more prominent? Have you come across anyone else with a neck tattoo?"

White shook his head. "Not that I know of. Is it important?"

"It could be." Meinwen felt the back of her own neck. "The placement. It's like a cattle mark. What about the woman who committed suicide?"

"Grace Peters? White raised his eyebrows. "She was an upstanding member of the church. I doubt she'd have a tattoo done but I can find out. Her autopsy report will be on the computer." He took out his phone and dialled. "Peters? Are you at base?"

He listened for a minute then spoke again. "Pull up the report on Grace Peters, will you? Does it mention a tattoo anywhere?"

White put a hand over the mouthpiece. "It won't take a minute. Everything's on the intranet now. There's no need for him to go searching for case files." His phone bleeped. "Yes? There is? Can you describe it to me?"

He closed the connection a few minutes later. "Here's one for the books. I don't know how you knew, but you were right. She had the same tattoo as our Miss James. They couldn't have had the same boyfriend, surely? I mean, Amanda's a young woman and Grace was into her sixties."

"They might well have had, but I still don't know how it fits into the murder, if it does at all." Meinwen rubbed the back of her neck. "Can we have another look in the study before we go?"

"If you like." White led the way and nodded to the constable as he took another two pairs of disposable bootees. "What are you looking for?"

"I'm not sure yet." Meinwen bent to cover her shoes and went in, pausing for a moment then crossing to the desk. "Was there a computer here? The desk is awfully bare for someone who spent so much time at it."

"There was." White consulted his notes. "A *Magelight* brand laptop. We've taken it in to have a look at his files."

Meinwen nodded, thinking back to one of the conversations she'd had online before she moved here. It had been a Thursday night and the shop had been closed all day. She'd wanted to go out, but there weren't many places to go on a wet Thursday night in Aberdovey, not if you didn't fancy sitting in the pub watching the darts players holding their bellies in and pretending to be virile. She'd stripped down to her undies and logged online instead. The conversation had gone on for an hour.

Scribe: What if I wanted more than this? More than a few words on a screen every now and then?

Sir Real: Are you talking about a real-world meeting? That's a big step. It's a big pond full of little fish.

Scribe: I'm not just a little fish, though am I? I have you to protect me.

Sir Real: Not in Wales you don't. I don't know anything about the scene in Wales, other than what goes on in Bristol and Cardiff.

Scribe: Bristol isn't in Wales.

Sir Real: Don't be pedantic.

Scribe: What if I came down to see you? Where do you live?

Sir Real: A little west of London. You would be welcome. I have one or two girls already, though. You would be a small fish in a very small pond here. You might stir up a few jealousies. My girls don't like change.

Scribe: Do you play with both of them?

Sir Real: Of course. That's what they come here for. They live the life that they want to. It costs them nothing and they live under my protection. I'm well enough off to support myself in the manner I most enjoy.

Scribe: I could come if you wanted me.

Sir Real: The question is more would you want to take that step? If you want to be mine in real life there are certain rules you must adhere to.

Scribe: What sort of rules?

Sir Real: Persistent, aren't you? For one, I insist upon absolute obedience, no matter how much you protest at the work I give you to do.

Scribe: I can do that. What else?

Sir Real: Feel the back of your neck, just above the hairline. Locate the spot where your neck feeds into your skull. Do you feel it?

Scribe: Yes.

Sir Real: I require all my girls to have a tattoo there.

Scribe: I want it.

Sir Real: That's just desire talking. Remember that this is a permanent mark that would be with you for the rest of your life. Think about it carefully. You can ask me again in two weeks.

Scribe: Any other rules?

Sir Real: I also share my house with my late brother's wife. She can be…difficult. If you're serious about moving here I'll find you a place to live in town. I know someone who has a vacant house not far from here. You'll have to cultivate a friendship with Jean before you could ever think of moving in.

Scribe: I'll do my best.

White coughed. "Are you all right, Ms. Jones?" He put his hand on her back. Meinwen could feel it, cold and hard like a lump of ice against the heat of her memory. "I lost you there for a minute."

"I was meditating." Meinwen turned away to cover her blush. Robert Markhew and her Sir Real were the same person. If the police had his computer, there was a good chance they would find her conversations with him. Should she should tell Inspector White now or hope to uncover the murderer before he found out she was implicated?

Chapter 14

"May I offer you a lift back into town?" Inspector White paused before getting into his car.

Meinwen shook her head. "I prefer to walk. It puts me in tune with nature and allows me to organize my thoughts."

He looked up the street. "I'm not sure I can let you walk alone, Ms. Jones. There is a killer on the loose."

She touched his arm. "Thank you, honestly, but I'll be fine. I'm happy to walk on my own. If nothing else it will give me a sense of the town."

"Well, if you're quite certain I can't persuade you otherwise…"

"No. Go." Meinwen made shooing motions and he climbed into his car, grinning. She waited for a moment but he pulled out his phone.

She set off, her feet crunching on the gravel drive as she admired Peter's work on the garden. At the bottom of the drive she turned left at into the leafy avenue that led back to the town.

* * * *

Jean Markhew watched them go from the upstairs window, tapping a finger absently against her lips. "What horrors will your meddling cause?" she asked, her voice low.

"I beg your pardon, ma'am?" Nicole looked up. Lines of rope above her breast snaked under her armpits and around the back of her neck, forcing her head down. Other coils fastened her arms together behind her back from her elbows to her wrist, a neat line of knots running down the centre. The position of her arms thrust her chest forward. She kept her feet apart to maintain balance.

Jean looked up at the ceiling, spotting a thread of dust-encrusted spider silk. "Nothing for your ears, girl. Who killed Robert?" She trailed her crop across erect nipples.

Nicole held her gaze. "I wish I knew, ma'am," she said. "I'd tell you in an instant."

"Would you?" She gave the secretary three sharp strikes across her breasts. Nicole gasped. "Hurts twice, doesn't it? The strike itself, the pressure of which forces blood away from the welt and the afterburn of the blood returning, such a simple toy but it can be so painful."

Jean allowed her to regain her breath before striking her a further six times, each one heavier than the last. Nicole winced with each blow, her gasps running together until she was snorting. Tears of pain mixed with mucus. "Please, ma'am." She whimpered as blows rained down upon her thighs and bottom. "Yellow."

The blows stopped instantly and Jean bent to kiss her, feeling the secretary's tense muscles relax under her touch. "Good girl." Jean's kisses were feather-light over Nicole's cheeks, drying away the tears. "I know I can trust you now." She began to undo the bonds and, as soon as her arms were free, Nicole dropped to her knees, pressing her lips against the soft leather boots Jean wore.

Her new mistress lifted her face up and gazed into Nicole's cornflower eyes. She could bewitch anyone with those. "Why did you come here?" Her fingers left red marks on the pale skin. "Why did you want to work for my brother-in-law?"

"Money at first, ma'am." Nicole said through the older woman's hold. "I was out of college and out of work. I saw Sir Robert's advertisement for a live-in secretary in The Lady and applied. He offered me the job and here I am."

"And now that he's gone?" Jean could pick out the smattering of freckles under Nicole's foundation. "Do you want to leave?"

"Oh no." Nicole's throat bobbed as she swallowed. "This is my home now. The people here are like family."

"Will you stay and be mine? Serve me as faithfully as you served Robert? Will you provide as many…services? Now your master is dead you may leave freely if you wish. I will provide excellent references."

"I will serve you, ma'am." Nicole's voice was the whisper of a lover.

* * * *

Meinwen pulled out her copy of Folklore of Laverstone and looked up Cherry Tree Road, discovering the existence of a gap in the stone wall that led through the park and into the woods at Laverstone Manor. From the map she determined she could follow the path through the wood into Vicarage Road and the church of St. Pity's and home. She went through the gap which led, once she was past the hawthorn hedge that grew against the back edge of the wall, into a thin meadow already bursting with wild flowers. She bent to stare at the intricate tracery of vetch and cowslip. "This is beautiful," she said. "I would never have guessed that an upmarket area would allow something like this to flourish."

She checked the guidebook.

Pettin Lane. This patch of land once belonged to Owen Pettin (1736-

1769) and formed his portion of a field. When he died he bequeathed everything to the church under the promise that his wife and child were allowed to remain on the land and work it. The rest of the field was sold during the nineteenth century but the Catholic church retained the portion that became known as Pettin's Acre and later, Pettin Lane.

There are a number of orange-barked Silver Birches on the pasture. This is due to the high concentration of copper ore in the earth beneath. It was mined extensively by the Victorian entrepreneur Sir Harold Lauder (1798-1874) who later built the park which now occupies the site. There is a statue of him at the western entrance to the park

Beyond the birches the path led directly into the park itself, a regular route for locals if the width of the trail was anything to go by. Meinwen walked past the still-dormant rose garden and took her bearings from the just-visible spire of St. Pity's.

She sat on a bench overlooking the bowling green and phoned Simon, hoping he'd finished his Mass at the hospital.

"Hello?" He answered after the fourth ring and sounded out of breath.

"Simon? Meinwen. Is this a bad time?"

"No, it's okay. I've just left the hospital. I was on my way to the car. What can I do for you?"

"Who inherits the Markhew estate? It might well have a bearing on the case, though I doubt that the beneficiary would be the murderer."

"Why not? It's served as an incentive for murder before."

"Yes, straight out of an Agatha Christie." Meinwen laughed. "Nobody is that foolish any more. You can't benefit from murder."

"What if that stranger I saw was an assassin hired by the beneficiary?"

"It's highly unlikely." Meinwen reached to pluck a few fresh hawthorn leaves from the hedge bounding the green. "Besides, how many assassins would ask the way to their target? They'd plan their route meticulously and back it up with a Sat Nav." She began eating the leaves, savouring their peppery taste. "It's almost a pity, really. If someone had hired an assassin there would have been a trail leading back to him."

"Or her."

Meinwen merely grunted.

"I wish I'd thought to ask about the will. Jean would know if Robert had a copy. She would have told me." He cleared his throat. "There's Jean herself, of course, Robert's sister-in-law. Even if she's not a beneficiary she would probably have leave to remain in the house. Then there's Richard.

Although he and Robert had arguments--"

"What family doesn't?" interrupted Meinwen.

"Exactly. I can't see Robert not giving him the bulk of the estate. Then there's his niece, Mary. She'll come away with a tidy sum I'll bet."

"Anyone else?"

Simon drew in a sharp breath. "That's all the immediate family. He might have left a stipend for the staff, but I can't see it being worth enough to kill him for."

Meinwen nodded. "That leaves the blackmailer then. I wonder what happened to the letter you saw Sir Robert open."

"The murderer must have taken it."

"Which would indicate that he and the blackmailer are one and the same."

"I thought that was obvious."

Meinwen could hear an engine starting. "Nothing is obvious. Where are you?"

"I told you. St. Pity's. You?"

"By the bowling green in the park."

"I have to go. See you later?"

"Isn't that Mary Markhew up ahead?"

"How should I kn--"

Meinwen closed the connection and stood. Mary was dancing at the edge of the boating lake. "She's young and in love." Meinwen smiled, shading her eyes against the slanting light as well. "Why shouldn't she be happy, even if her uncle has died?"

* * * *

Mary felt the note in her pocket and couldn't help smiling. Her feet skipped without her even thinking about it as she neared the pond, scattering the geese that ran squawking back into the water.

"You look happy." Peter, the gardener from the house, caught up to her and she blushed.

"I know I shouldn't, what with Uncle Robert being murdered and all." Mary grinned and swung herself around a lamp post. "I can't help it, though. I'm engaged to be married and I've inherited a big bucket of dosh."

"Oh?" Peter smiled and walked along with her. "From your uncle, I suppose. He was rather well-off, wasn't he?"

"More than I thought." Mary pulled out the note to show him.

"Mother found a copy of his will. I shall be getting a quarter of a million pounds! It means I won't have to lie any more."

"I didn't think you did." Peter sounded surprised. "Look, perhaps I'd better leave you alone. It wouldn't be right for an engaged woman to be seen with a single bloke."

"Don't be silly." Mary took hold of his arm. "You're practically family. I only meant I can stop grovelling for pocket money and won't have to spend hours scouring second hand shops and pretending the things I've bought are new."

"Oh, I see." Peter smiled and patted her hand. "You should have said. I'd have bought you new clothes. You smell lovely, by the way."

Mary laughed. "That's very sweet, but I doubt you earn much as a gardener."

"I will one day." Peter stopped, his smile radiant. "Richard said when he inherits he'll invest in a garden centre and have me manage it. They're all the rage now, garden centres. Everybody goes. It's like a national institution."

"That will be wonderful, Peter." Mary smiled for him. "You'll be an instant hit. You might even get your own television program. You've got the looks for it, and the muscle."

It was Peter's turn to blush. "Do you think so? That would be my dream."

"Then you should follow it. You know Richard will keep his promise."

"Where is Richard? I heard that he'd vanished."

"He'll be back." Mary skipped a few steps. "Everyone thinks he did it, but he'll be cleared when Meinwen finds the real killer. She's a psychic."

"A psychic?" Peter smirked. "You're having me on."

"No, really." Mary squeezed his arm. "I've seen her do things." She looked ahead. "Shh! Don't say a word. That's her." She waved. "Meinwen!"

* * * *

Meinwen walked the remaining few yards to catch up. "Hello Mary. Who's this Adonis?" She smiled up at Peter.

"Peter, this is Meinwen. Meinwen, this is Peter Numan, the gardener and handyman at the house."

"Ah." Meinwen smiled again and shook his hand. "I've heard about you. You were one of the party that found the body, I believe."

"That's right. Along with Father Brande and his sister, Nicole and Amanda. I was taken aback and no mistake. Who would have wanted to kill a nice man like Master Markhew?"

"Master?" Meinwen raised an eyebrow.

"Mister, I mean." Peter blushed. "I didn't do very well in school."

"That's all right." Meinwen smiled at them both. "What are you so cheerful about? You look like you've won the lottery."

"I almost have." Mary grinned and pulled out the note she'd shown Peter. "I had three good pieces of luck this week. I got engaged to Richard and Mother found the will. I'll be getting a quarter of a million, look!" She held out the scrap of paper.

"And the third piece of luck?"

"I found a ring." Mary dug into her pocket and pulled it out. "It's gold, look. I was going to take it to the jeweller's in Cheap Street."

"May I see?" Mary passed it to her.

"How odd," she said. "Someone will be bemoaning the loss of this." The ring had a Celtic design Meinwen recognized as a lover's knot, a continuous line twisted into triangles to represent the three faces of the Goddess--maiden, mother and crone--and a promise to love the wearer in all three phases of their life. It was more than that, though, it was a wedding band, its thin width suggesting a woman's finger. She held it up to the light. "Where did you find it?"

"In the fountain at home." Mary held out her hand to get it back. "A bird must have dropped it."

Meinwen frowned. "Why do you say that?"

"Well, it's a wedding ring, isn't it? Nobody at The Larches is married except my mother, and it's certainly not hers. Can you tell whose it is?"

Meinwen shook her head. "Of course not. Why would I?"

"I thought you were psychic? Don't you get a sense of the owner when you touch something?"

"Oh, psychometry, you mean." Meinwen patted her arm. "I have to set out candles and things before I can attune myself to an object. That, a scanner and a good internet connection."

Peter squinted at the band of gold. "Why would anyone throw away a ring?"

"Lover's tiff?" Meinwen passed it to him. "You don't recognize it either?"

Peter shook his head. "Should I?"

"Not really. It just seems very serendipitous finding it now, the day after a murder. What's the betting we know the owner? Have any of the girls in the Markhew household been married?"

"No." Peter half-laughed. "Sir Robert preferred his staff single."

Meinwen took the ring back off him. "Would you mind if I hung on to this for a little while?"

Mary bit her lip. "I suppose so. As long as I can have it back afterwards. It's got to be worth a hundred at least."

"Of course." Meinwen tucked it into her wallet. "If nobody claims it, it's yours." She looked at Peter. "Did either of you hear or see anything prior to the murder that might help with the investigation?"

Peter shrugged. "Nothing that will help. I heard…Mr. Markhew talking to a woman about some papers. I assumed it was Nicole."

"When was this?" Meinwen leaned in close. Peter's breath smelled of cigarettes and beer.

"About half-past nine?" The rise in Peter's voice sounded as if he were asking her. "I'd been to the White Art and was on my way home. I live in the little cottage at the back of the house."

"I see. Anything else?"

"I saw a woman leaving the gate just as I got back. I couldn't tell who it was, though."

"What did she look like?"

Peter held his hands up, his face a tight-lipped expression of hopelessness. "I don't know. It was dark and I only saw her for a moment. I only know it was a woman because she was wearing a skirt."

"All right, Peter. Thank you. You've been very helpful. Mary, enjoy the rest of your day." Meinwen clasped both of their hands then walked on, picturing the ring and trying to imagine it on the fingers on the Markham household. She was sure she'd seen the design before.

Chapter 15

When Meinwen reached the northern gate to the park, where two life-size terracotta lions guarded the black iron gates, she found Simon sitting on a bench beside the winter-dormant fountain. "I thought I'd walk you the rest of the way." He proffered a cardboard cup of coffee, the companion to one in his other hand. "I wasn't sure what you drank so I got you a soy latté. Was that all right?"

"Perfect." Meinwen sipped it, unaware of how cold she'd become until that moment despite her walk under the watery sunshine. "I saw Mary and Peter Numan earlier. Mary's getting a substantial disbursement from the will. She was celebrating."

"I can't say I blame her." Simon stood and gazed at the fountain. The bronze swans were etched with verdigris, the water beneath thick with plastic bottles and empty beer cans. "It's not like they were particularly close. What were you talking to Peter Numan about? Is he a suspect too?"

"Everyone's a suspect, Simon, but no, I don't think he did it. He did hear Robert talking to someone he thought was Nicole after you had gone, though. Did Robert usually have that many visitors to his study in an evening? It seems like the whole household wanted to speak to him."

Simon drank the last of his coffee and dropped the container in a bin. "I've no idea. I know he was feeling mortal after the death of Grace Peters. Perhaps he was calling them in. Did he hear what was said?"

"No, or he wouldn't tell me if he did. He did tell me he saw a woman leaving through the gate, though."

"Good heavens! The place was busier than Piccadilly Circus! Who?"

"He didn't know, but it's another knot in the puzzle string that needs to be unravelled."

"Could it have been Susan Pargeter?" Simon held out his arm and Meinwen took it. "I saw her leaving in a car earlier." He led her toward a small path and a wooden gate.

Meinwen stopped and took out the ring. "Here's something else. Meinwen found it in the fountain at The Larches. Any idea who was married?"

Simon held it up to the light. "Celtic. Not a proper wedding ring." He passed it back. "I've no idea. Sorry."

Meinwen consulted her guide book. "Where are you taking me?"

"Home, the pretty way." Simon led her out of the park and along a short path into the woods that belonged to Laverstone Manor. She stopped at the threshold, her heart hammering.

"What is it?" Simon paused and turned back.

"I'm not sure." Meinwen looked up at the beech trees, last year's tired brown leaves just beginning to drop as the copper-hued buds began to open. "It feels a little oppressive here, as if dark deeds were performed."

"Nonsense." Simon held up a low branch of elder for Meinwen to walk under. "It's just a wood. I thought you people liked woods?"

"You people?" Meinwen plucked up courage and stepped onto the trail. The feelings washed over her and settled. Her heart ceased its hammering and she compared it to visiting the dentist, where the smell of antiseptic and chlorine washed over you as you opened the door, only to fade into the background after a few breaths.

"Witches, pagans." Simon smiled. "I thought you were all into the forest as a primeval metaphor for growth."

"Cernunnos, the Lord of the Forest," she said. "And Herne, his English counterpart." She caught up with the priest. "There's no calling to them here. Let's hurry, please."

"If you insist." Simon led the way along the path. "I don't understand why you're so skittish."

"You know that feeling when you walk into a cathedral and you feel so peaceful you could just lie on the floor and sleep?"

"I do, yes."

"This is the opposite." She stopped stock-still. "What's that noise?"

Simon cocked his head to one side like a dog. "It's the river. We'll cross it in a minute. There's a waterfall farther up, where the Laver leaves the High Chalk. They call it Lover's Leap, a romantic bastardization of Laver's Leat."

"A waterfall?" Meinwen stared into the woods.

"Yes. Would you like to see it?"

Meinwen shook her head. "No, thanks. Not today. I'd rather get out of the woods, please."

"As you like." Simon pointed at a patch of light through the trees. "Look! There's the edge of the wood, just past the bridge."

"Thank goodness." Meinwen picked up her pace, forcing out a laugh. "I hope there are no trolls here."

Simon chuckled and followed her out, nearly bumping into her when she stopped to pick up something from the path. "What now? Another wedding ring?"

"No." Meinwen paused, deep in thought. "It's a raven's feather." She looked up into the trees, trying to spot the bird.

"Ugh." Simon grimaced. "Put the filthy thing down."

"Why?" Meinwen turned to him, her anxiety about the woods forgotten.

"They're unclean." The look on Simon's face was sheer horror at the blue-black feather in Meinwen's hand. "Ravens represent impurity, destruction, deceit and desolation."

"Also wisdom, knowledge and protection." She ran the feather through her fingers. "*Tha gliocas an ceann an fhitich.*"

"What?"

"It's Gaelic. It means 'There is wisdom in a raven's head.'" Meinwen smiled. "In Irish folklore Raven is associated with the Triple Goddess, the Morrigan, who took the shape of Raven over battlefields as Chooser of the Slain. She was a protector of warriors, such as Cu Chulain and Fionn MacCual."

"And it was cursed by Noah for not returning to the ark with news of the receding flood." Simon stomped past her. "It's an ill omen, I tell you."

"Yet, conversely, the Bible also says that ravens were the protectors of the prophets." Meinwen tied the feather into her braid and caught up. "They fed Elijah and Paul the Hermit in the wilderness and helped St. Cuthbert and St. Bernard."

"That was an exception." Simon stepped out of the wood onto Lew Road. "Ravens represent evil. For centuries both witches and the Devil have been able to take the shape of a raven."

"And why shouldn't they? It's a pleasing shape to take." Meinwen looked up at a tall man in an expensive grey suit carrying a furled umbrella. He wore sunglasses even in the shadow of the trees, the edges of the glass all but invisible against his dark skin. The feeling she'd had when she entered the wood returned so fast it gave her a headache.

"Mr. Jasfoup." Simon's smile was so fake he could be selling used cars. "What a lovely surprise. We were just admiring your wood."

"Harold's wood, really. I'm just staying at Laverstone Manor between contracts." Mr. Jasfoup was tall with the elegance of someone who knew how to make the best of his assets. His skin was darker than Daffyd's, the colour of rich Belgian chocolate. "But I am remiss in my etiquette. Introduce me to your charming companion, Father Brande."

"Oh, this is Meinwen. Meinwen Jones. She's just moved into the town."

"Oh, the new tenant at The Herbage?" Mr. Jasfoup bowed, his Italian suit creasing in exactly the right place. "I'm delighted to meet you, my dear."

"Thank you." Meinwen could make out a shadow around the

gentleman as if his aura was shifting. She decided on the spot she didn't trust him.

"Well, I won't keep you." Mr. Jasfoup nodded to them both. "Father Brande, please pass my condolences on to Mrs. Markhew and the family. I heard about the unfortunate incident."

"I will. Thank you." Simon nodded, his voice guarded, and the gentleman walked past them into the wood, heading toward the mansion at the other side of the wood.

"Who was that?" Meinwen asked when he was out of earshot. "He gives me the willies."

"That was the companion," Simon managed to sneer through the word, "of the lord of the manor, Mr. Harold High-and-Mighty Waterman. I don't know that much about him, he tends to keep himself to himself."

Meinwen shuddered. "I hope I don't run into him very often."

They crossed Lew Road and Simon motioned her through an old iron kissing gate into the cemetery beyond. The gate clanged closed behind her and she waited while he caught up. "You don't like this Waterman chap very much, then?"

"I'm sure he's a fine gentleman, and I'll admit he gives generously to the church," said Simon, "but he's very standoffish. He has a way of talking with a sneer as if he's tolerating you about as much as a ground beetle. Good for the community but not something he wants to spend any time with."

"Not a Catholic, then?"

"Good Lord, no. I'd be surprised if he wasn't struck by lightning if he set foot in St. Pity's."

Meinwen laughed. "It's a beautiful building." She paused to gaze up at the spire. "How old is it?"

"Mostly nineteenth century." Simon pointed at a section built from a different shade of stone. "Though St. Mary's Chapel goes back to the sixteenth and the catacombs below even further."

"Catacombs?" Meinwen raised an eyebrow. "That's unusual for a town."

"It is. They're all blocked off, I'm afraid. They used to connect the town with the Long Wynd."

"Long Wynd?"

"The barrows to the east. You should visit them. Bronze Age, I believe."

"I will." They walked under the lychgate into Church Lane. Meinwen looked up the road. "I know where we are now. My house is just up here."

"Indeed it is." They walked side by side up the road.

"Tell me about Grace Peters," Meinwen said. "How did her husband die?"

"We all thought it an accident at the time. He had an accident while Grace was playing bingo at the Women's Institute. I only found out recently she'd planned it." Simon shook his head. "There's one soul that I couldn't save."

"I see." Meinwen looked at the priest, his face drawn in genuine sorrow. She touched his arm. "I'm sorry. What relationship did she have with Robert Markhew?"

Simon shrugged. "Just friends, I thought."

"I was surprised she had the same tattoo as the maid."

"A tattoo?" Simon frowned. "Grace didn't have a tattoo. I'd have known. What tattoo did Amanda have?"

"A double-R, like a monogram. Grace did have one on her neck, under her hair. The inspector checked. It was on the coroner's report."

"Well I never saw it. And Amanda has one too? How curious. If that was Robert's it would point toward something more…intimate."

"We don't know it was Robert's design." Meinwen pressed her palms to her cheeks. "That's only supposition at present. We don't even know what it means. It could be the mark of a secret society or a cult."

"A cult?" Simon clenched his teeth. "What's the betting that they've all got them? Jennifer said all along he had a harem. I'd rather she was right than find there was a cult under my very nose."

"I wouldn't go that far." They reached the house and Meinwen opened the gate to hide her blush. "Can I offer you a cup of tea?"

Simon checked his watch. "A quick one, perhaps, and then I must be on my way. I still have a sermon to write."

Meinwen unlocked the door and led the way inside, leaving Simon perusing her bookshelf while she made tea. A few minutes later she returned with a tray. Simon looked at it dubiously.

"Don't worry," she said. "This is just a breakfast blend."

She sat in the wing-backed armchair, the only heirloom she possessed. Whenever she used it, she could still smell the tobacco her grandfather had used in his pipe, though the chair had been professionally cleaned long since.

"Do we know how Anthony Markhew died?" she asked.

Simon tore his gaze away from the bookshelf, crammed with books like *The Use of Fetishes in Long-distance Spellcraft* and *Blood Rituals:*

How to Avoid the Interest of the Lower World. "Jean Markhew's husband? If I recall correctly he died of a stroke accompanied by massive internal bleeding. I never actually met him, though. They lived up north, somewhere in the God-forsaken wastes. Leeds, I think. Why?"

Meinwen steepled her fingers. "If Robert Markhew had a relationship with his sister-in-law is it possible he had something to do with his brother's death?"

"I doubt it, though these books--" He gestured to the shelf. "--have made me think of long-distance fratricide by witchcraft. I don't think Sir Robert and his brother were on speaking terms at the time." He picked up a bag of white, knobbly objects. "What are these?"

"Human knuckle bones, used for divination." Meinwen smiled at the speed with which the Catholic priest dropped the bag. "Why? Had they fallen out?"

Simon shrugged and picked up a piece of stone, holding it to the light where the blue and white marbled texture glimmered. "I've no idea. Perhaps Robert really was fornicating with Jean." He laughed and tossed the stone from hand to hand.

"Be careful with that." Meinwen clenched her teeth. "It's a dried gallbladder."

"Eww. That's disgusting." Simon replaced it and sat, taking his tea from the tray. "I've been racking my brains trying to imagine who might have been blackmailing Grace. She pretty much kept herself to herself. Apart from Susan, I was the only one who visited her regularly."

"And you had no suspicions?"

Simon shook his head. "None. You could have knocked me down with a feather when Robert told me about the blackmail."

"What sort of feather?" Meinwen twirled the one in her hair. "A raven's?"

* * * *

Jean Markhew was waiting for him when Simon returned home. "Oh, Father Brande. At last." She broke off from her talk with Jennifer. "Would you be a dear and talk to the blasted solicitor?"

"Jean." Simon put down his briefcase and shook her hand with both of his own. "I almost had a heart attack when I saw Robert's car in the drive. What solicitor? What about?"

Jennifer left the room, heading toward the kitchen. Jean watched her go "The one dealing with the will." She crossed her legs, treating Simon to a flash of leather-heeled boots. "Robert only left me fifty thousand pounds, and he's left Susan Pargeter twice that."

"The housekeeper? Why?"

"You tell me. They weren't very close. I don't know what he saw in her."

"Perhaps you could contest it after the inquest," suggested Jennifer, returning with a cup of tea she handed to Simon. "If all the beneficiaries agree, a will can be changed."

"Inquest?" Jean narrowed her eyes. "There isn't going to be an inquest."

Simon sipped at the hot brew. "There must be, Jean. Robert was murdered."

Jean waved a hand "I'm sure no one meant to murder my brother-in-law. It may well have been an accident. Someone slipped while holding the knife, I expect."

"Why do you think that?" Simon collapsed onto one of the dining chairs. "It looked to be a deliberate murder to me."

Jean shook her head. "It doesn't matter. An inquest isn't going to bring him back, is it? All I want is for all this to be done with and we can get back to normal. Then Richard can come home from wherever he is and marry Mary."

* * * *

"Miss Markhew?" Nicole Fielding knocked on the door of the girl's room. The noise of the melancholy music that had grated on her nerves for the past half an hour abruptly ceased.

"Yes?" Mary's voice sounded thin and reedy. "What is it?"

"It's Nicole, miss. I have a small problem, if you'd be so kind."

The door opened a crack, just wide enough for Mary to peer out. Her hair was mussed, as if she'd been rubbing it against a pillow. "What problem?"

"It's the petty cash, miss. I need to send someone down to the supermarket but I've no house money left. Mr. Markhew always used to give me the housekeeping on a Friday, but with him gone…" Her voice trailed off.

"Can't you ask my mother?" Mary rubbed her eyes. "I don't deal with that sort of thing."

"I would, miss, but your mother's gone into town."

"Oh. very well. Where does he keep it?"

"In his bedside drawer, miss. I saw him put it there the night before he was murdered, but I don't like to just take it without a witness."

"Come on then." Mary led the way to her uncle's bedroom. "Where does he keep it?"

"That drawer there, miss." Nicole pointed and watched as Mary took out a sheaf of bank notes. "Thank you." She leafed through the stack. "Wait. This can't be right, it's a hundred short."

"Are you sure?"

"Yes, miss. It's always three hundred pounds. Never more, never less. There's only two hundred here."

Mary frowned. "Who else knew about it?"

Nicole counted on her fingers. "Mrs. Markhew, of course, and Catherine. She normally does the shopping but she's put her notice in."

"Really? Why?"

"She had an argument with Mr. Markhew before he died. She wants to leave right away."

"Let's go and ask her." Mary led the way downstairs to Catherine's room where she rapped on the door. Nicole could hear a few thumps before Catherine replied and she was able to follow Mary inside.

Catherine was sitting on her bed with a novel in her hand. A photograph in a frame had been turned face down on the table and Nicole longed to look at it.

"I hear you're leaving us." Mary could sound as cold and impassive as her mother at times.

"That's right." Catherine stood, her face red and blotchy. "Mr. Markhew shouted at me because I shifted some papers on his desk without permission and he asked me to leave."

Mary pressed on. "Do you know about the housekeeping money?"

Catherine nodded, twirling her pendant through her fingers. "Of course. I used to do all the shopping. That's today, isn't it? I'd forgotten with all the upheaval."

"You didn't take any of the housekeeping early, then?" Mary's voice dripped with suspicion.

"No, of course not. I always wait for Sir Robert to give me what I need."

* * * *

Mary leaned back against her headboard. The business with the missing money had been upsetting and she'd retreated to her room after imploring Nicole to "be a bit frugal this week." At least they wouldn't have to shop for Richard's expensive tastes. The old man would happily pay more for an ounce of pâté than Mary's whole weekly allowance. On the other end of the phone, Meinwen rabbited on about the murder.

"So you've no idea what she and Mr. Markhew were arguing about?"

"No." Mary fingered the silk of a dress she'd found in the thrift shop. It was so pretty she hadn't been able to resist buying it, even if it had been four sizes too small. "She said that it was over moving some documents but I don't think that was the whole truth."

"What was she doing on the night of the murder?"

"I don't know." Mary tried to remember. "I think she said that she went to bed early."

"That's not much of an alibi!"

"But would an argument be enough reason to kill my uncle?"

"I wouldn't have thought so." Mary could imagine Meinwen laying out tarot cards to divine the murderer's identity. "But then, people are killed over the loss of a parking space these days."

Chapter 16

Peter felt the hood go over his neck, the holes fitting snugly over his nostrils. His breathing slowed and his heartbeat, hammering since he was called to the house, calmed until he was no longer aware of it.

"Good boy." Jean's voice filtered through the leather of the hood. "Be calm. Be still."

The cold steel tip of a blade caressed Peter's exposed lips, running down over the fabric of the mask and into the fabric of his shirt. There was a tug as she cut through the stiffened collar, then the icy touch of the edge as it followed the line of his spine, cutting the shirt from his back. He knew how sharp the knife was, having sharpened every one of Mr. Markhew's toys. This, he could tell from the way it moved, was the stiletto.

His shirt fell to the front and was yanked off his arms, exposing his torso to scrutiny.

"He did play hard with you, didn't he?" He could feel Jean's fingers following the tracery of old cuts and scars Robert had taken pleasure in applying--every cut deep enough to bleed, and shallow enough to heal with nothing more taxing than a wash with warm water and a line of antiseptic cream.

His hands were twisted behind his back and he gripped each elbow with the opposite hand. No need for bondage, Peter was more than willing to take whatever she offered. Even through all of Robert's attentions he had called yellow only once, and that was when he had become faint from blood loss and had to be helped to a seat.

Robert had taken great care of him that night, bathing his wounds personally and kissing each one better before laying him down on freshly laundered linen sheets as he slid his penis into Peter's accepting arse, his hand reaching around to assist Peter in his own orgasm until they both came together and lay still, entwined in each other's arms for the rest of the night.

"I said kneel." Her voice broke his train of thought and he dropped to his knees, splaying his legs as Robert had preferred. She ignored his cock, running the blade once more down his spine. "I could sever this with a single stroke. One slip of the blade and you'd never walk again, forever dependent upon me for your needs." He felt the trickle of blood as the tip dug into the skin. "You wouldn't be able to stop me. You wouldn't be able to complain. The police might have something to say but we all know there's a killer on the loose. He must have struck again."

Peter began to shake.

"You're connecting the dots, aren't you?" She leaned in close and whispered again. "Robert liked to be on both ends of the blade. I bet you didn't know that. His skin was a myriad of cuts, just like yours. Where do you think I learned to use a knife? Why do you think he knew just where to cut you for the effect he wanted? It's because he'd felt them all himself."

She switched sides, trailing the blade across his shoulders. "Now you have doubts, don't you? Now you're wondering if Robert's death was murder after all or if I was playing with him, trying to find the perfect spot for a non-lethal thrust. I was wrong that time, but this time I know just where to drive the knife home."

The steel left his flesh and pricked him just above his lumbar joint. "Who was Robert talking to the night he died? Who did you hear through the open window?" She pressed harder. "Was it Nicole?"

A thin trickle of blood slid under the waistband of his jeans, channelled into the crack of his arse. "I don't know." His buttocks tightened. "It could have been anyone."

More blood and his heart began to hammer anew. The steel slid farther into his anus, travelling deep into his body. Any moment now and he would be crippled for life.

"Who?" Her voice was insistent. "Think! You remember the voice. You've heard it before. Whose was it?"

"I don't know!" His cheeks were wet under the leather. "Please? Yellow?"

"Good boy." The hood was torn away, leaving him blinking in the bright light of the library. Jean smiled and showed him the teaspoon she'd exchanged for the blade. "The end of a spoon and warm lube. The rest of it was in your head."

Chapter 17

Scribe: Jennifer? This is Meinwen, next door.
Cacoethes: Clever. How did you trace me?
Scribe: *laughs* I asked Simon what your username was.
Cacoethes: LOL. Fair enough.
Scribe: You know a lot of what goes on in this town. Can I ask you a question?
Cacoethes: Sure. Is it about the murder?
Scribe: Perhaps. I'm looking into backgrounds. The police seem to have ground to a halt.
Cacoethes: OK. What do you want to know?
Scribe: Who was Catherine Latt's employer before Markhew?
Cacoethes: brb
Scribe: OK
Cacoethes: Back. It was Harold Waterman at the Manor.
Scribe: Oh, great. That place gives me the creeps.
Cacoethes: Want me to go up and ask him about her?
Scribe: You'd do that?
Cacoethes: Sure. I've wanted a reason to get inside there ever since he inherited it. I don't know where he got the money from. One minute he owned a second-hand furniture shop and the next he owns the Manor. Not only that, but the place gets fixed up. He must have spent a fortune on it. The place was in ruins when the old man died.
Scribe: Old man?
Cacoethes: Frederick Waterman. He'd had the place since his parents died as a kid. Harold was his nephew. His sister--the mother--is still alive. She lives in The Terrace. Works for the other side occasionally.
Scribe: Satan?
Cacoethes: No, silly. St. Jude's, the C of E church.
Scribe: Oh. *laughs* Where do you think the money came from?
Cacoethes: That kind of money? It had to be drugs.
Scribe: Ack. I've changed my mind. I'll ask White to do it.
Cacoethes: Don't you dare. I'm gone already.
Scribe: Be careful then. What time will you go?
Cacoethes: First thing in the morning, as soon as S leaves.
Scribe: Ring me as soon as you're back so I know you're safe.
Cacoethes: Thanks. I'll talk to you tomorrow.
Scribe: Good night.

"Not playing with your witchy friend today?" Jennifer smiled as she helped Simon on with his coat.

"Professional acquaintance." Simon smiled back. "Perhaps later. I rather neglected my duties yesterday. I need to check on the church first. The accounts need to be submitted by next Friday and I haven't even made a start on them."

"I might drop by later then, and bring you a cup of tea."

"Make it a double mocha coffee from the deli and I'll love you forever." Simon grinned. "In a spiritual, fraternal way, obviously. I don't want to commit an irredeemable sin."

Jennifer laughed. "It's a deal. I'll see you later."

She waved him off before throwing on her own coat, backing her Mercedes into the road and heading up to the manor where she was forced to stop. The gates were opened by means of an electronic key she didn't have. On the gatepost was an intercom terminal.

"Yes?" It was a woman's voice and Jennifer could hear a child in the background.

Jennifer pressed the intercom button. "Hello. I'd like to see Mr. Waterman, please."

"Elder or younger?"

"Er," Jennifer recalled the details. "Harold Waterman."

"Right. Of course. What is it about?" The baby in the background giggled.

"I'm chasing up a reference for a previous employee? Catherine Latt?"

"Okay. I'll buzz you through."

The gates opened inward to leave a gap Jennifer could drive through. The suspension on her car handled the cattle grid with barely a vibration. In the mirror Jennifer could see the gates closing behind her.

She pulled up in a wide gravel turning circle. The manor was bigger than it looked on Google maps, a Georgian-style building with two wings leading off the main house and a stable block to the left hand side, all painted white. The top of the central block – which looked older than the wings – was crenellated in the style of a fortified house and a domed cupola rose from the centre. There were at least a hundred windows on four floors. She was glad she didn't have the job of cleaning them.

"Coo-ee." Jennifer recognized the voice as belonging to the woman on the intercom. She looked to be in her late twenties or early thirties, with skin the colour and texture of the mocha she'd promised Simon later. Her hair was braided into corn rows and she wore a t-shirt, jeans and a wide, easy smile. The child on her hip looked to be about eighteen months old, one hand clutching the trailing ends of his mother's hair and the other balled into his mouth. "We only use the front door for weddings and funerals." She pointed to the side of the house. "Come 'round the back."

The back turned out to be a stable yard with several outbuildings and a half-glazed door to the west wing of the house. The woman led the way into the kitchen.

Jennifer held out her hand. "Jennifer Brande. You must be Mrs. Waterman."

"Hell, no." The woman laughed. "Do I look sixty? Mrs. Waterman is Harold's mum. I'm Latitia Campbell."

"Are you and Mr. Waterman…" Jennifer let the question trail off.

"I'm just the interior decorator and this--" She heaved the child farther up her hip. "--is Levin."

"He's adorable. Hello, Levin." Jennifer smiled at the baby, who dribbled.

Latitia led the way inside and plonked him on the floor where he promptly climbed onto the small two-seater sofa and reached for the remote. Latitia frowned. "He doesn't respond to Telly Addict yet." She looked back at Jennifer, her smile fading. "What can I do for you?"

"It was Mr. Waterman I came to speak to." Jennifer glanced around the kitchen. For such a huge house, it was extremely cluttered, with a dining table crammed into one corner and a mini-lounge in the other. Next to the door was an array of outdoor gear--coats, boots, several shotguns and an unstrung hunting bow. "Is he here?"

"Aye. Will you get him?" Latitia spoke to someone over Jennifer's shoulder, but when she turned around there was no one there.

"Sorry." Latitia smiled at Jennifer's confused frown. "That must have looked strange. They have a voice-activated intercom system installed. Would you like some tea?"

"Please. White, no sugar." Jennifer sat at the table. "It's a lovely place. Is there any chance I could look around while I'm here?" She twisted to see a set of Victorian daguerreotypes on the wall.

"Probably not today," Latitia set out a tray. "We're a bit busy with the end-of-tax-year returns."

"I see. Another time perhaps." Jennifer turned back to see a tray with three cups of tea already on the table. "That was quick."

"Harold likes his tea." Latitia pressed a tippy cup of juice into Levin's chubby hand.

"Miss Brande? What a pleasure to have you visit." Harold Waterman was a striking man. Not exactly handsome, he looked like a disgracefully ageing rock star, dressed in leather with his white hair tied back into a ponytail.

"Mr. Waterman." Jennifer stood and shook the man's hand. "I'd like to ask you a few questions about a previous employee of yours. Catherine Latt?"

"What about her?" Harold sat and took one of the cups of tea. "She was an excellent worker. I have no complaints."

"Why did she leave?"

Harold paused for a moment and Jennifer watched his Adam's apple bob as he swallowed a mouthful of Darjeeling. She tried her own, but it was still too hot. "She wanted to work somewhere nearer town, I think." Harold flashed a smile and Jennifer felt herself warm to him. "We're a bit isolated up here, and she didn't really like all the ghosts."

"Ghosts?"

Harold grinned, patting her arm. "In an old place like this? There are several, you know. Most of them are friendly, so don't worry."

Jennifer laughed. "If you say so. Was Catherine trustworthy?"

"Absolutely. She can certainly keep a secret."

"What sort of secret?"

Harold leaned in close, dropping his voice to a whisper. "If I told you, it wouldn't be a secret."

"Did she ever take anything that didn't belong to her?"

"Of course not. We hang thieves, you know."

"He's having you on, love." Latitia was obviously used to her employer's humour. "We haven't hanged anyone in years."

"Yes. Sorry. I got that mixed up. We don't hang thieves. I expect we give them a lollipop and send them on their way." He frowned. "This was all in the reference I wrote at the time. What are you really after?"

"Could you tell me where she came from? How she came to work for you?"

Harold's face darkened and he stood. "I think I've answered enough questions, Miss Brande. I don't know where all this is leading, but I think I've answered sufficiently for a background check."

"Just one more." Jennifer rose as well, the scrape of her chair against the tiled floor loud enough for Levin to turn the television up. "When was the last time you saw her?"

"A few days ago," said Harold. "Now be off with you. I can assure you Catherine is no murderer."

"How can you be certain?"

"I have my reasons," said Harold. "Latitia will see you out."

* * * *

Inspector White checked the details of the autopsy on his printout. Robert Markhew had been stabbed twice between the fifth and sixth rib, puncturing the lung and left ventricle of the heart. Death would have occurred within seconds. There were no defensive wounds on the body, but the skin displayed signs of a huge number of scars from sharp blades.

Other identifying marks included a small tattoo on the back of his neck, similar to a stylized lunar landing pod.

White leafed through the attached photographs. Markhew had sported the identical tattoo to the one he'd seen on the neck of the maid.

He dropped the file onto his desk. Were they all part of some cult?

White dialled his sergeant's desk. "Peters? Have you still got the case file for Grace Peters? I need to have a read of it." A thought occurred to him. "Was she any relation to you?"

* * * *

"That's his shop over there." Jennifer pointed through the window.

"I sort of gathered that." Meinwen handed her a coffee and followed her gaze. "I was going to go in until I met that creepy Jasfoup bloke."

"They're rich." Jennifer shrugged. "They just have different values to the rest of us."

"I suppose." Meinwen put her cup down and began to unpack a box. The shop was due to open at the end of the week and so far she'd neglected it. She'd asked Jennifer to meet her there when she'd called to say that her meeting with Harold Waterman had concluded. "What did you find out?"

Jennifer shrugged. "Nothing really. A little about his living arrangements and his interior designer has the most beautiful little boy. A real angel."

"I meant about Catherine Latt." Meinwen grinned.

"Oh." Jennifer pulled herself away from the window. "Not much about her, either. He said that she'd been an excellent worker and he had no problems at all. She left his employ to get a job nearer town. He said that she was trustworthy but got shirty when I asked him how she'd come to be in his employ."

"That's when he threw you out?"

"Yes. He kept talking about secrets, and how they wouldn't be secrets if he told me about them."

"How odd." Meinwen opened a box of assorted packs of tarot cards and began putting them on display. "You've heard nothing new about Richard Godwin then?"

"Nothing, no. Not since that morning in the park." Jennifer sipped her coffee.

"What was that?"

"Didn't I tell you? He was telling someone to be patient and that he couldn't afford to upset his uncle until he inherited the estate."

"That's interesting. Who was it?"

Jennifer shook her head. "I don't know. I was in the manor woods, behind the park wall. He was on the other side of it. I put out a search on it but no one saw."

"Curious." Meinwen put a black cloth over another shelf and began to fill it. "That makes it look worse for Richard, of course, if he was desperate to inherit."

"He didn't do it." Jennifer picked up a set of cards depicting angels. "He's too obvious. I think someone's trying to pin the blame on him. Why would he get engaged to Mary and then kill his uncle? It doesn't make any sense. My money is still on Susan Pargeter."

"Oh?" Meinwen stopped what she was doing. "Why?"

"She was really upset about Grace Peters's suicide and was asking Simon all about pills and the effects that they had on the body, and whether they could be detected after death."

"That does sound suspicious," Meinwen agreed, "but Robert Markhew was killed with a Klingon dagger." She grinned. "It was not a good day to die."

"Not for him, no."

Meinwen began to open another box. "Who does Simon visit on his rounds? I never knew what a priest actually did on a home visit."

* * * *

"Undo the top two buttons of your shirt, Peters."

Inspector White looked at the paperwork on his desk. "Why didn't you tell me that you were related to Grace Peters?"

"I didn't think I needed to, sir. She was a distant relative. A great aunt, I think. The last time I saw her was twenty years ago. She gave me a packet of chocolate buttons."

"Nevertheless, Peters, it could compromise the case." White stood and moved around his sergeant, pulling down the back of his collar to expose his neck. He was almost disappointed to find there was no tattoo.

"You can button up again," he said.

"What did you expect to find, sir?"

"A tattoo, like the one we found on Markhew, the maid and your great aunt."

Peters shrugged. "I don't even know what they mean, sir."

* * * *

"I spent most of the day with your friend Meinwen," Jennifer said over dinner.

Simon was non-committal. "Oh yes?"

"She's a lovely woman. She knows all sorts of things about religion."

Simon grunted through a piece of lemon meringue pie. "Don't believe everything she says. She'll only corrupt you."

Jennifer nodded and took a sip of her wine. "She asked a lot of things about you as well. Who you visited on your rounds, what a priest did on a home visit, that sort of thing. She said we'd better find Richard soon or it will look bad for him."

Simon looked up. "You didn't tell her about that conversation you overheard, did you?"

"Of course. She's investigating the case. She doesn't think he's guilty though. I think she fancies Susan Pargeter for the murder."

"That's ridiculous. Susan was asking about pills and Robert was clearly stabbed. Look, don't say anything more about Richard. You're just helping to incriminate him. I wouldn't like to see him go down for something he didn't do."

"I'm sure they won't, Simon. Between Meinwen and the police the murderer is bound to be caught."

Simon grunted, reaching for a second piece of pie. "I hope so. Let's just hope she's better at witchcraft than she is at detection. It's almost a pity the Church banned burnings."

Chapter 18

Jean sat nestled against pillows, her bedroom curtains closed against the heavy April rain. Amanda stood once more at the side of her bed, holding the saucer for the cup she was drinking from.

The soft light of twin bedside lamps illuminated the girl standing at the foot of her bed. Jean sipped her tea thoughtfully, admiring Catherine's silent form.

"I don't care that my brother-in-law dismissed you. Do you still wish to leave?" she asked. "Whatever you and Robert argued about can remain between you and his grave. I am perfectly willing to let you start again with a clean slate. A cook like you is hard to replace." She finished her tea and replaced the cup on the saucer. Amanda moved it to the silver tray and waited for further instruction.

Catherine looked up. "I do, ma'am. I was never one of Sir Robert's chosen and I've a bit of a hankering to go back to Bridlington. I miss the sea, ma'am."

Jean rubbed her eyes and inspected the grain of sand lodged under her fingernail. "Very well. I believe the severance terms are a week's wages for every month you have been with us."

Amanda handed her the accounts book and she totted up the sum in her head. "I'll round up it up to fifteen hundred pounds." Her voice softened. "I'll give you an excellent reference, of course. I hope you're happier wherever you find yourself next." She made an entry next to Catherine's name.

Catherine dipped her head. "Thank you, ma'am. It's nothing personal. I just have a different path to tread, I think."

"As you like. We wish you well." Jean nodded a dismissal and handed the accounts book back to Amanda. "Just leave it on my desk. I'll make a bank transfer after the inquest. Set out the black again. I'll be happier when I can discard the mourning black, but I must still play the grieving lady of the house."

* * * *

The verdict of the inquest was that the death of Robert Markhew was by misadventure--murder by a party as yet undetermined.

Meinwen caught up with Inspector White outside the courthouse. "What will you do now?"

"Instigate a full alert for Richard Godwin." White handed the case files to Sergeant Peters and opened his umbrella. "We'll soon have him behind bars. Even if he didn't do it, I'll warrant he knows who did."

"Do you think he saw the killer and is now in fear for his own life?" Meinwen pulled her black woollen coat closed, flipping the hood up to protect her hair from the rain. It always went frizzy when wet.

"Anything's possible. It would explain why he vanished so abruptly if he's innocent." White pulled up the collar of his raincoat.

Simon hurried up to them. "Is there any progress on the case? Has Richard turned up yet?"

"No and no," said Meinwen. "Death by misadventure and the police have begun a search for him."

"The poor lad." Simon was hunched against the rain but White made no move to offer him space under the umbrella. The hem of Simon's cassock was already sodden where it flowed from beneath his coat. "The evidence points to him, does it?"

"Not yet." White increased his pace. "But until we've questioned him he won't be ruled off the suspect list."

Meinwen stayed at his side. "I'm still certain he's innocent. I'd feel it if he weren't. That phone call to Simon from the station is the clue. If we could find out who made that call it would go a long way to solving the crime."

White laughed. "Finding the murderer would go a long way to solving it as well."

"Did that letter that Robert received when I was there ever turn up?" Simon asked. "The one from Grace Peters?"

"No," White said. "I would be very interested to see that. It might shed some light on the fingerprints we lifted off the knife as well."

Meinwen chewed her lip. "They didn't match anyone in the house, did they?"

"Unfortunately not."

"Did you compare them with Robert Markhew's? I wouldn't be surprised if the killer is trying to confuse you."

"What makes you say that?" White paused and looked at her, one eyebrow raised.

"We know that Robert must have held the blade. If the murderer wore gloves it stands to reason that the only ones on there would be his."

"That's partially true." White began walking again. "We did indeed lift Markhew's own fingerprints off the knife, but they were in the wrong position, as if he was holding it to his own chest."

Meinwen nodded. "I think I can explain that."

"Oh? That's interesting. How would you know why he'd held the knife to himself? We have no reason to think he was suicidal."

"He wasn't." Meinwen touched his arm lightly. "My shop is just up that way." She pointed to the alleyway leading off the market. "I can't really show you my theory in a public place."

White gave her a curt nod. "Very well. Lead on."

* * * *

"Imagine I'm Robert Markhew," said Meinwen in the relative privacy of her shop. The floor was fairly clear now, since she had spent so much of the previous day getting the place ready to open. Neither Simon nor the inspector looked too closely at the contents of the shelves.

White frowned and sat back in the hard chair. "You're a little small to be him but I can suspend disbelief for a few minutes."

"Good." Meinwen glanced at Simon, sitting in her grandfather's chair to watch. "Now imagine that you're a woman."

White laughed. "That's a little more difficult. Do you want me to speak in a high voice?" He shared a grin with Simon, like two schoolboys with a private joke.

"Don't be silly." Meinwen picked something up from her desk and approached White's back. "Now don't turn around. Imagine that you're in love with me."

"All right." White sounded dubious. "I'm not though. I'm very happy with my Beryl, thanks."

"Good for you." Meinwen patted his back. "This is just pretend. I'm Robert Markhew, remember?"

"Go on then." White took a deep breath and shrugged twice. "Oh, Mr. Markhew. I'm so in love with you that I want to have your babies."

"That's a little over the top." Meinwen snaked an arm around him. "Close your eyes."

"No funny business." White twisted his head to grin at her. "Remember there's a priest watching."

"Shush. Close your eyes."

"If you say so." White winked at Simon and did as he was asked.

Meinwen changed hands and held a piece of cold steel to his neck. "I'm going to cut your clothes off," she said. "I'm going to cut off the buttons one by one with this knife until you're completely naked."

"Oh yes?" White said. "What then? Assuming I don't break both your arms and have you arrested?"

"You wouldn't because you love me and you'd do anything I asked you to."

"That doesn't include cutting my buttons off," said White. "Beryl would have a fit."

"Okay, that's enough." Meinwen sighed. "Open your eyes. This was supposed to be a sexy bit of foreplay between a virile man and a woman desperate to please him. Look at the knife I'm holding."

White opened his eyes "It's a letter opener."

"Yes," she said, "but look at the way I'm holding it with the blade toward you and my thumb almost touching the butt of the handle. Which way 'round are my fingerprints?"

"Oh yes." The inspector raised his eyebrows. "They're the wrong way 'round. Very clever."

"There." Meinwen put the letter opener back onto her desk. "That's my theory, anyway. The killer wore gloves and the only time this knife was used before the murder was for sex games."

"It certainly looked plausible to me," said Simon. "If I wasn't a priest…" He laughed.

* * * *

"Inspector White, Father, Miss Jones." Amanda answered the front door to The Larches. "Is this an official visit?"

"It is." Meinwen bustled past her. "We need to talk with Mrs. Markhew, if you please."

Amanda led them past the crime scene tape of the study to the sitting room. "I'll inform the mistress of your presence."

Meinwen caught her arm. "We also need to talk to Mary, Peter and Nicole. Could you ask them to come as well, please?"

"Yes, miss. Right away." Amanda hurried upstairs.

Susan Pargeter came in from the direction of the kitchen. "Would you like refreshments? Tea, coffee?"

"That's very kind of you." Meinwen glanced at the Inspector's stony face. "Tea for me, please. Caffeine free, if you have it."

"Nothing for me." White looked toward the stairs

"Father?"

"Oh. Ordinary tea, please." Simon beamed at her. "You are too kind."

"I don't think we've got any caffeine free." Susan frowned. "Would you like coffee instead?"

"A sprig of fresh thyme in water then." Meinwen smiled.

"Hot water?"

"Yes, please."

"Right you are." Susan left, pausing at the door to make way for Jean Markhew. Mary and Nicole followed, with Peter arriving just as Susan returned with the drinks. He took the tray and set it on the table.

"What's this about?" asked Jean, looking from the inspector to Simon and Meinwen.

"We need to know where Richard is. The longer he stays away the more incriminating the evidence against him. At the moment it's only circumstantial but…" She looked at Mary.

"Me?" said the girl. "I don't know where he is. I haven't seen him since before Uncle Robert was murdered."

"Haven't you been in contact with him?" Meinwen indicated the expensive cell phone dangling from her wrist.

"No. He doesn't answer his phone. I told you that." Mary's face creased. "I swear I don't know where he is."

"Does anyone else?" Meinwen looked at each of the others in turn. They all shook their heads. "Does anyone know anything more at all, even if it doesn't seem important?"

"All that I can say is that it's a good thing that we haven't announced the engagement." Jean brushed an imaginary speck of dust from her black dress. "I don't want Mary's good name sullied. He's obviously guilty."

"How can you say that?" Mary asked. "You're talking about the man I'm engaged to."

"She doesn't mean it." Peter put a hand on her shoulder and she clutched at it.

"I certainly do." Jean stood. "Inspector, what will happen to the estate if Richard is found guilty?"

White cleared his throat. "You can't profit from murder. Richard's portion would be divided proportionately between the other beneficiaries, I imagine. The details would be up to the executor."

"Then I shall get on to Ms. du Pointe shortly and tell her the will is being contested."

"How can you be so callous?" Mary clutched at her mother's arm. "Richard and I are supposed to get married. Nicole, will you put a formal announcement in the paper?"

"Er…" Nicole looked to her employer.

"She will do no such thing." Jean very deliberately extracted her arm from Mary's grasp. "It would be imprudent until this murderer is caught and behind bars."

"Meinwen?" Mary turned to her. "Can't you talk some sense into Mother? Richard and I are supposed to be in love."

"I'm sorry." Meinwen shook her head. "I have to agree with Mrs. Markhew. You've been engaged for a while. I doubt that another few days would make a difference. If it is true love, what difference does a formal announcement make?"

Mary gave a deep sigh and slumped. "I suppose so. I just wish everyone didn't assume my fiancé is the killer."

"We don't," Meinwen replied. "But we need to find him to clear his name. I will discover who killed Robert Markhew if I have to summon his ghost and ask him personally. I will find out the truth in spite of you all."

"What do you mean, in spite of us?" asked Nicole. "You make it sound like we're trying to hide the murderer from you."

"Not the murderer, perhaps," said Meinwen, "but each of you has a secret that they don't want exposed. Not just one, in some cases." She looked at each of them in turn.

"I don't know what you mean," said Jean. "I resent your accusations in my own home."

"I don't have secrets," Mary said.

"Nor I," said Nicole. Peter just shook his head, declining to speak.

"Please," said Meinwen. "If one of you tells me, it will save a lot of time and embarrassment, because I will find out what they are."

She looked at their faces. Even Simon averted his eyes.

"I think you should leave now." Jean stood and drew herself to her full height. "I've heard enough."

"Very well." Meinwen held up her hands in a placating gesture. "I'm sorry none of you felt you could trust me."

Chapter 19

Meinwen was halfway down the road by the time Simon caught up with her. "Insufferable people." She glared at him. "They close ranks against outsiders like an arsehole against a finger."

Simon coughed. "I say! I am still a priest, you know."

"Sorry." Meinwen waved her Guide to Laverstone. "I don't want to go through the woods today. Show me a bit more of the town instead."

"If you like, though avoiding the woodland path adds a further fifteen minutes of walking. We'll have to travel right to the opposite end of the park then double back to get to the east gate."

"Are you afraid of a little extra walking?"

"Hardly." Simon led her a different way, pointing out the boat house and the miniature railway station, closed at present, and as they left by the eastern gate, the old Dillon's Fabrication plant, a building left derelict by the steel industry collapse in the eighties.

"They seem a little reticent about helping you with this investigation." Simon fell a step behind when they at last turned into their road and Meinwen's mood brightened.

"More than a little," Meinwen replied. "Each of them thinks that their little secret is important. In normal times it probably is, but against the backdrop of a murder it all pales to insignificance."

Simon nodded. "Unless one of them is the murderer."

Meinwen paused. "Exactly. That's the secret I would understand them keeping, though it will be out in the end. Hugin will tell me."

"Who?" Simon dug his hand into his trouser pocket and pulled out a string of rosary beads. He kept it in his hand as they talked, fingers stroking the jade beads.

"Hugin, one of Odin's ravens, named for thought."

"Oh. Those blasted birds again."

"Of course." Meinwen walked on. "The Goddess gave me an omen to reassure me that I would find the truth. Hugin's feather."

"Omens. What nonsense you believe, Meinwen. There are no omens, just serendipitous occurrences you can interpret to mean whatever you like."

Meinwen laughed. "You're a priest and you don't believe in omens?"

"Of course not. God has no need to give us such things, they are an abomination."

"That old chestnut again." Meinwen smiled. "Deuteronomy this time, I believe?"

Simon nodded.

"I thought we'd established that the Old Testament was outdated? What if the three astrologers from the East had taken that view? The birthday party of Jesus would have been a small affair." Meinwen patted Simon's shoulder. "Admit it. The church changes its mind with the seasons."

"Hardly." Simon clutched the cross on the end of the beads. "I'd be defrocked if I disagreed with doctrine, whatever my personal opinion."

"Can you honestly say you've never had a feeling of impending doom?" Meinwen asked.

Simon shrugged. "I'd be lying if I did, but I think of that as an angel's warning, not an omen."

"Just as I do." Meinwen smiled again. "Angels are supernatural beings in any theology. Just because I don't have the mental image of a winged eunuch in a white robe doesn't make my belief in them any less real."

"I'm glad we agree on something at least." Simon stopped at the gate to Bridge House. "Much as I enjoy our debates on theology, I must get on. I'm neglecting the parish duties."

"And I must get down to the shop." Meinwen walked a little past his gate before turning. "I'll see you later, shall I?"

"Perhaps. If I've got time."

"You must eat." Meinwen glanced at her own house "How about dinner? I'll ask Jennifer too."

"All right." Simon seemed reluctant. "Six o'clock?"

* * * *

The sunlight felt warm on Peter's skin. The glass of the conservatory amplified the heat without the chilling effects of the April breeze and the bench he was lying on had been in the sun for an hour already. His cock stirred as dust mote patterns danced on his closed eyelids.

"You like it here then?" Jean trailed red-tipped fingers across his chest, following the trail to his bare thighs before lifting them at his knees. Peter blushed as he felt his erection grow.

He could hear the bubble of humour in her voice as she stroked the length of his shaft. "You're the only man around here now. I could elevate you to a position of some authority, if you have the mind for it."

He opened his eyes. Jean looked younger when she was relaxed and he felt an attraction to her that was incongruous. "No, ma'am. I could not be your partner. I'm sorry."

She nodded. "I can't say I'm not disappointed. May I ask why? Are you gay?"

Peter grinned. "Not exactly. I would have thought that much was obvious."

"Not necessarily." Jean sat on the edge of the bench by his knees. "You had your eyes closed. You could have been thinking about Robert, imagining him touching you."

"I wasn't," he replied. "I could smell your scent over that of the gardenias. I knew that it was you touching me. I loved Robert dearly, but I'm bisexual rather than gay. I love the person before the gender."

"Then why? Can you not imagine loving me in the same way?"

He rolled onto his side and raised himself on one elbow "I can imagine it but I cannot countenance it. That woman was right when she said I had a secret."

"Would you care to tell me what it is?" Jean stopped touching him and pulled back, watching him with the intensity of a cat watching a canary.

"I love your daughter. She doesn't know and I would never tell her, especially since she's in love with Richard. When Robert died I stayed to look after her. I'll stay for as long as you both allow me to, though she will never know the truth. Not from me, at any rate."

Jean nodded. "She could do worse, though how she would react if it ever came out…" She let the question hang.

Peter reached up and clasped her hand. "She must never know. She has a little of Robert's personality, and it is enough that I can see a little of him when I look at her."

"Very well, you can stay." She lifted a small metal box from the floor and set out some of its contents onto the bench. The tang of alcohol filled the air and the skin of Peter's right thigh went suddenly cold as she swabbed it. "I will give you a symbol to hold on to," she said as the tip of a fresh scalpel blade bit into his flesh. "This is the symbol of Isis, goddess of Egypt. It is from her the myth of the virgin mother came to the West, the one we now worship as Mary. It will be fitting you bear the symbol for my daughter's name in the flesh of your thigh."

"Dionysus was born from the thigh of Zeus," Peter murmured as the scalpel travelled in a series of arcs.

"True." Jean finished the cutting with the sting of alcohol again and wiped away the trail of blood. Peter sat up to look at it. The symbol of Isis was a circle surmounted by an arc like a pair of curved horns to represent the wings of the Queen of Heaven.

"Thank you, ma'am." He drew her hand to his lips for a kiss.

* * * *

Jennifer picked at the lumps of diced meat with her fork. It was certainly an unexpected dish after the leek soup. "I haven't had these since I was in school. I used to think they were made out of brains."

Meinwen laughed. "*Ffagodau* are made of liver with a bit of sage and onion and suet to keep it all together. I used to make them for my da."

"He liked faggots, did he?" Simon raised an eyebrow. "It's not something we go a bundle on, though they do make a refreshing change."

"Thank you." Meinwen grinned as she sliced one in half with her fork and smothered it in gravy. "Actually he hated them, but I didn't like him either."

Jennifer laughed. "Why did he eat them then?"

"It was either that or fend for himself, and that would mean getting up from his chair. I was glad when I was fifteen and I could get out."

"You left home at fifteen? Wasn't that a bit young?" Simon scooped up part of a faggot and chewed slowly as if she might have laced them with hemlock.

"Not really. Youth is a state of mind, I think. By that time I'd looked after the house and hung on to two jobs for best part of three years since my mam died. I couldn't wait to leave. You look at some of the youngsters who leave home today. They're a damned sight younger than I was."

"I suppose." Jennifer took one more mouthful to show willing and pushed her plate away. "I would have thought you'd be a vegetarian with your profession."

"My profession? You make me sound like a prostitute. It's a rare witch who's a vegetarian, Jennifer. What would you do when the farmer calls you in to help birth a difficult pig and offers you bacon in exchange? Say 'no thank you, I'd rather gather some berries?'" She shook her head. "No. Part of being a witch is not to have the pride to refuse a gift. If you refuse the gift of a poor man, you take away his pride."

"That's an interesting theory." Simon used half a boiled potato to scoop up the last scraps on his plate. "Surely it's not the case these days, though. You could ask for money instead and buy your own food, or grow it."

"Then I'd be a merchant instead of a witch." Meinwen put down her cutlery. "Do you expect to get paid for what you do?"

"No, but I'm in the service of God."

"As am I, though my God is a Goddess and I don't limit my services to those who agree with me." She smiled at Jennifer. "So no, I'm not a vegetarian."

"But you don't drink tea," said Simon. "Real tea, I mean. Tea's natural, isn't it?"

"And full of caffeine and tannin," Meinwen countered. "If I wanted to preserve myself like an Egyptian mummy I'd pull my own brain through my nostril, not do it by inches."

Simon pushed his plate away. "If I hadn't finished already I would be now. What about coffee? You drink that."

"Decaffeinated, preferably, but it would have been churlish to refuse the one you bought me, wouldn't it?" She grinned, reaching out to pat his hand. "Sorry. I'm not actually against caffeine but I prefer to avoid it unless I need the boost of energy."

They sat in silence for a few minutes, Jennifer sipping from a glass of Meinwen's apple wine. "It's funny." She stroked away a line of condensation on the glass. "You being here, I mean. A priest and a witch. Doesn't the Bible say 'thou shalt not suffer a witch to live?'"

"I think you'll find the original text says 'poisoner.'" Meinwen collected the plates. "King James had the wording changed so that he could seize land from old women. How were the mushrooms, Simon?"

"Very nice." The priest narrowed his eyes. "They weren't poisoned, were they?"

"No." Meinwen carried the crockery into the kitchen. She raised her voice "Why didn't you mention the conversation Jennifer overheard? It may well be important."

"I didn't think it was." Simon raised his voice as well. "It only casts Richard in an even worse light."

"Inspector White would have thought it important." Meinwen returned from the kitchen with a plate of tarts. "As do I."

"Well, you know now." Simon shrugged and sat back with his glass of wine. "Who do you think he was talking to?"

"I've no idea. Help yourself to the *tarts sioned*," she said. "I'll get you some cream."

"What are they?" Jennifer picked one up and sniffed at it. "They smell like lemon."

"And so they are." Meinwen handed them a dish each and put a jug of cream in the middle. "My mother's recipe. Tell me about Susan

Pargeter."

"There's nothing to tell." Simon helped himself to two tarts and a generous amount of cream. "She's been with Robert for a long time. Very efficient, from what I hear. I don't think there's any reason to suspect her."

"What about the drugs she was asking about in the church that day?" Jennifer pressed lightly on Meinwen's arm. "That was suspicious."

"I told you before, Jen. What does it matter? Robert was killed with a knife."

"Everything matters." Meinwen set a coffee pot and cups on the table and sat down. "Do you remember the stranger who asked you for directions?"

"Of course. What about him?"

"He was at the White Art earlier in the evening. The barman remembers giving directions to a stranger with a Birmingham accent."

"That's a relief." Simon cut into a tart with his spoon and took a mouthful. "I was sure the inspector thought I was making him up. Is he the murderer then?"

"I doubt it. He would not have asked for directions twice if he was intent on killing Mr. Markhew. Also, if the murderer is the blackmailer, he would already know where The Larches was."

"Good point." Simon drew a coffee for himself and Jennifer. Meinwen shook her head at the offer. "Why was he going there then?"

"I think he intended to meet with someone."

Simon sat up. "Who?"

"Susan Pargeter!" Jennifer exclaimed. "It stands to reason, doesn't it? They both have Birmingham accents. I bet she was running away from him and now he's found out where she lives. She was probably married to him and ran away after years of being beaten with a stick."

"It's certainly a possibility," said Meinwen, "though I don't think she was running away from him. It doesn't matter, anyway. If there's a connection there, I'll find it."

"That phone call was from a train that was going north," said Simon. "It may not have been Richard phoning at all, but the Birmingham man."

"I thought it was Amanda on the phone?" Meinwen frowned. "You said that the call was from her, even though she denied making it."

"It sounded like her but I couldn't swear to it," said Simon. "I would have put any accent down to the bad line and the stress of finding out Robert Markhew was dead. It could easily have been a northern accent instead of stress."

"A northern accent, yes." Meinwen took a lemon meringue tart from the plate. "Jean and Mary Markhew both came from Leeds."

"You're not suggesting either of them did it?" asked Jennifer. "They were kin."

"And stood to inherit," Meinwen said. "I will not be happy until I discover what they are hiding."

"What about Catherine?" Simon asked. "She had an argument with Robert the night he died and was dismissed."

"She too has a secret," said Meinwen, "but I'm certain she is not the killer. She could easily have left but didn't."

"I think Richard did it after all." Simon sat back and counted with his fingers. "One, he stood to inherit the house. Two, it was well known that he argued with Robert a lot. Three, he was overheard telling someone to be patient until his uncle died. Four, he wanted to marry Mary and five, he's fled the area."

"I still think he's innocent," said Jennifer.

"Why?" asked Simon. "I wanted to believe him innocent too. I've known the boy all his life, but you've got to face facts. His footprints were in the soil outside the window, he knew where the knife was and had access to it, he was in town but not staying at the house, he hasn't seen Mary since the engagement, hasn't answered any calls and he disappeared after the murder. That was probably his cell that they found at the murder scene. Much as I hate to admit it, it has to be him."

"Has to be?" Meinwen shook her head. "There are too many motives. How often do people come to you for help because they have four things that trouble them? I bet they come to you with one thing or like Job, they carry the burdens alone."

"I suppose."

Jennifer put her coffee cup down with a bang. "I think Richard was framed."

Chapter 20

Meinwen was woken far too early for her liking. She was still in her dressing gown which, contrary to her image, was decorated with paw prints. "Do you know what time it is?" she asked when she wrenched open the door.

"Seven-fifteen." White walked into her house as if he owned it. "I need to ask you a few questions."

"If you must." Meinwen yawned and shut the door. "Do you mind if I make some tea first?"

"Not at all." White smiled. "White and two sugars please."

She left him looking around the living room but he followed her to the galley kitchen. "Did you rent this house furnished?"

"Yes." She put the tea things on a tray and pushed past him. "Why? Is that important?"

"Not really. I just thought that it didn't really look like a witch's cottage, that's all."

"And what does a witch's cottage look like? I tried submitting a design based upon biscuits and sugar cane, but the council rejected it on the grounds of structural stability."

White laughed. "I don't know. I expected to find everything black and lit with tallow candles."

"They're a bugger to read by." She put the tray on the table and poured the tea. "That's why there are so many tales about people getting caught out by the loopholes in the small print. Tallow makes the clauses too indistinct. Give me a good fluorescent bulb and I'll give you a demonic pact to write home about." She smiled. "So what brings you here so early in the morning?"

"You tell me, Miss Scribe."

"Ah." Meinwen sank into the armchair chewing her bottom lip."You've found the files on Robert's computer."

"You should have told me that you were involved. We had the devil of a job tracing those files back to the originating ISPs, then getting warrants for the names and addresses of all the users. He was quite the Jack-the-lad, our Robert Markhew, wasn't he?"

"I should have told you as soon as I realized." Meinwen sat forward, barely supported by the chair. "I didn't want my connection with Sir Robert to colour you against me. Mind you, I'll admit I was taken aback by the number of intimate partners he seems to have had." She took a deep breath. "It was a bit of harmless fun I thought might turn out to be just as saucy in real life." She looked into the inspector's dark eyes. "One odd thing, though. He intimated Jean Markhew was the head of the house and I couldn't move in without her approval."

"He was probably putting you off until he'd met you properly." White sipped his tea. "Was he some kind of sex god? I was tempted to arrest everyone for gross indecency when I read the report on his computer files."

"You can't really." She sat back again, relieved he didn't seem bent on arresting her. "It's all words and no pictures. It could be argued as pure fiction."

"Oh, there are plenty of pictures," said White. "He got up to all sorts, did our Mr. Markhew."

"He was a writer and a photographer, don't forget." Meinwen pulled out two books from her shelf. "He was very well known in the art scene."

"So it seems." White skimmed through the books, his eyebrows rising at one or two of the more extreme pictures.

"You'll find that all the models were volunteers and signed releases, I'm sure." Meinwen smiled as he lingered over one or two of the more artistic shots. "You could check with Nicole Fielding for confirmation."

"I already did after I borrowed a copy from The Larches." White handed her the books back. "I can't say I'm keen on all these art pictures of naked men, though Mrs. White borrowed it to read in bed. There's nothing illegal in these unless I can arrest someone on living off immoral earnings."

"But they don't," Meinwen said. "That's just a normal household where there is a huge proportion of women to men." She shrugged. "If he were alive, the best you'd have got Robert on was being a lucky bastard."

"Not so lucky now." White drank his tea. "Mind if I have a look at your neck?"

"Sure." Meinwen shrugged herself out of her dressing gown, dropping it to just above her breasts and turning her back to him. He lifted her hair.

"Nothing." He sounded disappointed.

"My guess is he only tattooed those he was intimate with on a long-term basis. His permanent lovers, though I'd be interested in knowing how many he had. Not all of them lived with him."

"No." White indicated for her to pull the gown back up. "How did he write? We found complete files on his hard drive, but most writers have a dozen revised drafts and I can't imagine him deleting them."

"I believe he dictated his books and his secretary typed them up. I'd look on her computer for early versions if you need them."

"We didn't find any tape recorders though."

"They're different now. Did you find an MP-three recorder?"

"A what?" White looked confused.

Meinwen went into the next room and pulled out her flash drive. "They look like this only with a few more buttons. They record directly to MP-three format which can be transferred to computer just by plugging it in."

"So this is like a tape recorder?"

"Not that particular one, that's basically just a chunk of removable hard drive, but you get the general principle."

"I see." White smiled and handed it back. "That explains why there were songs on his computer that were just him talking then. They were his dictations."

"Of course!" Meinwen nodded to herself. "That explains a lot."

* * * *

When Meinwen entered the graveyard she could see two figures near the south end of the church. One she guessed was the gravedigger and the other, much to her surprise, was Catherine. She edged closer, careful not to be seen but the two seemed to have eyes only for each other. She worked her way close enough to overhear the conversation.

Catherine leaned back against the tombstone. "I'm sure you're not supposed to do this. Isn't it disrespectful?"

"What can be more respectful than me making love to you on a tomb?" The gravedigger stepped forward to stand between her open legs. "It's a re-affirmation of the cycle of life, isn't it?"

"Birth, death and rebirth? I suppose so." Catherine put her arms around his shoulders and pulled him down into a kiss.

His hand followed the curve of her hip and dived under her skirt, tugging at her knickers and pulling them down. She gasped and fumbled with his pants, unzipping his fly and unbuttoning his waistband before snaking down to free his penis. Her legs folded around his waist, drawing him closer and he raised himself on tiptoe to enter her.

Catherine gasped. "What if someone sees us?"

"Right now?" His breathing grew heavy, his thrusts more urgent. "They'll have to wait until we're finished, because I'm not stopping."

Meinwen ducked down below a headstone, not wishing to be more of a voyeur that she already was. Old Tom didn't seem as old as his reputation, and Catherine seemed to know him very well indeed.

* * * *

Meinwen sat on the tomb next to the gravedigger. She leaned back with her hand supporting her and was surprised to find the tombstone was wet. She glanced behind and, recognizing the sticky white fluid, pulled her hand away and wiped it on a tissue.

"You're Tom, aren't you?"

He looked up from his sandwich. "That's right. Do I know you?"

She shook her head. "I doubt it, I'm new here." She held out her hand. "Meinwen Jones. I'm opening a shop in Knifegate."

"Ah. The witchery place." Tom wiped his hand on his jacket and shook hers. "It's a bit funny you coming to a church, though. I thought you folk were afraid of God."

"Not at all. Your God doesn't like mine, but that's all. What's in your sandwich? It's making me hungry."

Tom chuckled. "You wouldn't like this," he said. "It's ham, cheese and hot chili pepper. It'd burn the roof of your mouth right off."

Meinwen grinned. "You're probably right. I'm used to simple food. We wouldn't have chillies where I come from."

"Whereabouts in Wales is that?" Tom took another bite, crumbs from the bread catching in his stubble. He wiped his mouth with his free hand, a wedding ring flashing in the weak sunlight.

"You could tell I'm Welsh, then?" Meinwen exaggerated her accent and laughed. "I grew up in Aberdovey, on the coast."

"What made you come here? Laverstone is about as far away from the sea as you can get." Tom finished his sandwich and spoke through the bread in his mouth. "I bet it was a man, a lovely woman like you must be following her heart."

Meinwen laughed. "In a way, though it's more of a coincidence. Did you know that this church sits on top of two distinct ley lines?"

Tom nodded. "And another that goes through the manor, yes. Ley lines were a buzzword around here in the nineties. We had all sorts of people investigating them." He pointed. "This one runs from here to Avebury and the other to Stonehenge. Clever folk, these ancients. There used to be a stone circle in Laverstone, they say, but it's long gone now."

"Is there any of it left?" Meinwen watched as he took a long draught from a bottle of mineral water.

"Just Long Mab at the far end of the churchyard and a couple of stones in the woods. The others have either been buried or walked off." Tom offered her the bottle but she shook her head. "Is that what you're here for?"

"Why not?" Meinwen dropped to her feet. "Where is it again?"

"I'll show you." Tom carried his rubbish to a bin. "It's over this way."

Meinwen caught up. "Have you worked here long? I heard you were called 'Old Tom' but you're actually younger than I am. You can't be more than twenty."

Tom grinned. "Twenty-three. There's been an Old Tom digging the graves for decades. I sort of inherited the name along with the job, not that there's that much to do these days. Most people are cremated because of the cost of a plot."

"That's a shame." Meinwen gestured toward the graves. "They give people an ear when they're in the ground. It's not the same when you talk to a pile of ash."

Tom paused and looked at her. "That sounds like experience. You've lost someone close?"

"My mother, when I was twelve."

"I'm sorry."

"Thanks. It taught me a lot about life." They walked on, Tom pointing out interesting gargoyles on the side of the church. "There used to be a Sheela-na-gig, but they removed it just before Father Brande took over the parish. That was a shame."

"Where is it now?"

"Up at the manor. Technically it's still public property and you can ask to view it any time."

"I don't think I'll bother." She gave an upward nod and snorted. "They seem a bit of a funny lot."

Tom laughed. "Mr. Waterman's all right. I've known him for years. He used to run a second-hand shop and would buy our old toys off us."

"Really? He didn't strike me as the altruistic type."

"He was all right. Sharp."

"How so?"

"He used to give us half the money from the toys and put the rest in a savings account. At Christmas we could go to him with our savings books and he'd give it back with better interest than the post office." Tom led them toward the northern boundary of the churchyard, where a pair of ancient yew trees guarded the lychgate. "Here she is." He gestured to a flint megalith. "This is Mab. Legends say she stood here and cursed the church and God turned her into stone." He patted the mossy surface.

Meinwen traced her hand across the pitted surface. The stone towered over her, standing twelve feet above the surface of the earth and probably at least half again below it. There was a hole through it about a third of the way down like an eye staring at the church. "It's aligned with the ley line."

Tom nodded. "The sun shines through it on the spring and autumn equinoxes. Do you feel her?"

Meinwen placed her hand on the stone. It seemed to vibrate through her skin and she stepped back again. "I do. She hums."

"She does that." Tom looked up at the church steeple. "She'll stop chanting when the church falls."

"Local legend?"

He grinned. "Aye. That an' she's resting on the same piece of rock the church is."

* * * *

Meinwen walked back home, making a point of looking at all the gravestones as she passed and saying the names aloud. When she got to the litter bin she stopped. Since Tom was still on the other side of the church she reached in and took the water bottle, careful to only hold it by the base. She took the paper sandwich wrapper, too.

At the tombstone where she had sat talking to him, she pulled out a tissue and wiped the wet area, folding it and tucking it into the sandwich bag.

She left the church and headed into town, her step a little lighter than before.

Chapter 21

Jean Markhew paused at the entrance to the church. Somewhere, Mozart's Requiem reached the Sanctus, the drawn-out violins prompting tears to fall down her cheeks. She followed the music to the vestry, where Father Brande was hunched over some papers, his pen moving rapidly across the page in loops of minute lettering. He looked up when she knocked, the sound barely louder than the music.

"Jean!" He closed the folder of papers and covered it with a half-finished crossword. Standing, he took her hand in both of his own. "What a pleasure it is to see you. Is there something I can help you with?"

"That's lovely music, Father Brande." She held her head cocked to one side, her eyes closed and her right hand lightly beating time. "Where is it coming from?"

Simon gestured toward the desk "There, on the computer. I put some classical music files on it. It's a clunky old thing but it does what I need it to." He lowered his voice. "I'm supposed to be writing my sermon but I was just having a little break and wrestling with the crossword. One of my few vices, you know, but I'm sure the Lord will forgive me."

"The things they think of." Jean stared at the computer screen. "No wonder musicians are busking for breadcrumbs." She rubbed her eyes, guessing how red they must be. "Robert's been murdered."

Simon frowned but took her arm and guided her to the seat in front of his desk. "He was murdered several days ago. You seemed to be taking it well up until now."

"I know, Father, but today is the day that Robert always cooked us a meal. He did it once a week as a sort of appreciation for all the work the staff does in looking after him. They all got Saturday afternoon off and Robert would cook them dinner and treat them as if they were the masters of the house. I woke up this morning wondering what he was going to make--he always made something special--and it hit me he wouldn't be cooking ever again."

"So it's sunk in that your brother-in-law is dead? I'm very sorry for your loss. I'm sure he's gone to a better place."

"Thank you Father." Jean dabbed her eyes with a white silk handkerchief. "What are we going to do without him? He was the linchpin of the house. Everything revolved around Robert."

Simon patted her arm. "It takes a bit of getting used to but you'll cope. It's perfectly understandable to be upset after a death, and even more so when it's unexpected like Robert's was."

Jean dabbed her eyes again. "How do other people cope with it?"

Simon made a steeple of his fingers, resting them against his top lip. "People just carry on. They trust in God to keep their loved ones safe and hope to meet them again in Heaven. Some people put on a stiff upper lip and others ask for help from a grief counsellor. I have the number for the local group if you'd like it." He looked out of the tiny leaded window at the churchyard. "Sometimes it helps to have a special place to speak to them, somewhere you feel particularly close."

"Like a grave, you mean? He hasn't been buried yet."

"I know, but it's scheduled for the day after tomorrow. Perhaps it will begin to get easier after that."

"I hope so. I wish they'd do away with this investigation, though. I can't settle with everything in the air like this."

"It won't be long now, Jean." Simon stood and crossed to the tiny sink. "Inspector White will have the case all wrapped up soon enough. Would you like some tea? I could do with one."

"That would be kind of you. "Not too strong and with one sugar. Make sure you take the tea bag out before you put the milk in."

"Er…right." Simon filled the kettle and switched it on.

"You don't think that they'll arrest me, do you?" Jean sniffed.

"Arrest you?" Simon stopped what he was doing and turned to look at her. "Why would they want to do that?"

Jean paused, gathering her thoughts. "Do you remember that girl saying we all had secrets?"

Simon nodded. "Meinwen, her name is. I remember."

"Yes, I knew it was foreign. Well, she was right in us all having little secrets but what use is knowing them to anyone else?"

Simon returned to the tea. "It depends upon the secret, I suppose. Most secrets are quite harmless. I, for example, have the habit of making sure that my socks are on the right feet. It makes no difference to anyone but I wouldn't like it to be widely known for it smacks of vanity."

Jean chuckled. "Oh Father, you are a treasure. I never thought I'd laugh again."

Simon smiled and passed her a mug of tea. Just for a moment her face creased with displeasure as she had to close her hand around the hot mug to manipulate the handle to her side.

"I can't believe you'd have any secrets worse than that," he said.

"I'm afraid I have." Jean put the mug down on the desk, careful to rest it on top of an old hymn book awaiting repair rather than the bare wood of the desk. "I looked for the will, you know, the day he died."

"Really?" Simon sat again and stirred his tea. "May I ask why?"

"I was worried about what provision Robert would make for Mary and me. He never treated us very well, you know. He was always penny-pinching. We were reduced to buying second hand clothes a lot of the time. Imagine that!"

"Imagine!"

"Robert would give the staff whatever they asked for. Three hundred a week went just on housekeeping, but would he give us a reasonable allowance? No he wouldn't. Fifty pounds a week for me and twenty for Mary. That's all. We felt like paupers."

"That must have been difficult."

"It was." Jean took a sip of the tea and dabbed her lips with the handkerchief. "He didn't understand a lady's needs at all."

"Did you find the will?"

"Not at the time, no." Jean sniffed again. "I was poking about in his study, looking for it when that Catherine came in."

"Catherine? The upstairs maid?"

"*Pfft.*" Jean was dismissive. "She was a better cook than a maid. She wasn't very good at it. She never cleaned my suite properly. There was always dust on top of my wardrobe. I really don't know what she did all day, and she certainly doesn't do anything now."

"I was under the impression she'd given her notice."

"Notice yes. She's still supposed to work it, though. And why has she given her notice in? That's what I'd like to know. She was up to no good."

"When she came into the study?"

"That's right." Jean leaned forward and dropped her voice. "I expect she was looking for something to steal, but was foiled when she saw me. Robert came in behind her and was surprised to find us there."

"I bet he was." Simon glanced at his cell phone. "What did you do?"

Jean shrugged. "I said I was looking for the latest copy of The Lady then went back upstairs to my suite."

"Did you hear anything as you left?"

"She wanted to talk to him about something. She was in a bit of a state. Everyone's talking about her, you know. She must have had something to do with it."

"A little girl like that? Surely not."

Jean scowled. "She scuttles about the place. She startles me with her creeping about."

"Was the glass-topped case usually left unlocked?"

"It might have been." Jean waved the question away. "I'd been watching *Antiques Roadshow* and he had a few pieces that were similar to the ones they'd shown. I was having a look at them to see if they were worth more than he thought. I was going to surprise Robert with the good news. He's got a snuff box in there that's worth six hundred pounds, you know."

"Were you interrupted?"

"Yes. I heard running footsteps in the hall and hurried back to my room. I think that you arrived shortly after that." She took a packet of cigarettes from her handbag. "Do you mind?"

The vicar looked annoyed but nodded. "That would have been Susan Pargeter. We nearly ran into her as we came into the drive. She did seem to be in a hurry."

"Yes. That Inspector White should look at her as well. Perhaps she did it." Jean lit her cigarette, blowing a smoke ring up into the vaulted ceiling. As an afterthought she offered the packet to the priest and he took one, borrowing her lighter.

"I doubt it if she was in a hurry to leave before the murder." He sat back with a smirk as if this were the funniest thing in the world.

"Perhaps you're right." Jean tapped the ash off her cigarette. "Thank you for the talk, Father. It has been helpful to get it all out of my system." She stood and gathered her gloves and handbag but paused at the vestry door. "You won't let them arrest me, will you? I didn't do poor Robert in, even if he was mean to us."

Simon walked her through the apse. "You've done nothing they would arrest you for, Jean, don't worry. Get off home and try to relax. I'm sure all this will be sorted soon."

Jean nodded and shook his hand. "I hope so, Father." She paused in the porch to pull on her gloves then hurried along the path to her car, dropping the cigarette butt at the edge of the graveyard and treading it into the ground.

* * * *

"I wonder if you could do me a favour." Meinwen stood at the door to the rectory feeling somewhat uncomfortable. It was how she imagined Daniel must have felt when visiting the lion's den without a veterinarian's license.

"Of course." Jennifer swapped her oven gloves to her left hand. "Come in. I'm just in the middle of making some jam with the last of the fruit from the freezer."

"My mother used to make jam." Meinwen followed her into the kitchen, marvelling at the orderly lines of jars ready to be heated in the oven.

"Really? I'll save you a jar if you like."

Meinwen smiled "Very much, thank you."

Jennifer returned to stirring the jam. "What was the favour?"

"Could you tell me what cellphone Richard was using? I phoned The Larches to find out but no one there could remember. I know you have a lot of contacts you could ask."

"Sure." Jennifer grinned over her shoulder. "You could have messaged me that."

"I wouldn't have been offered any jam them."

"True. Would you like a coffee? There's some in the pot."

"That's kind of you to offer, thanks." Meinwen sat and drummed her fingers on the table. "Who would I ask to find out about Tom?"

Jennifer laughed. "Simon, of course. As parish priest, he's in charge of the curate."

"Simon wouldn't believe any ill of Tom, though. Who else might tell me about him?"

"Harold Waterman? I think Tom does some work up at the manor on occasion."

Meinwen grimaced. "I'd rather not. His companion has a dark aura. He made me feel dirty just saying hello to him. I dread to think what this Harold Waterman is like."

Jennifer looked up through half-closed eyelids. "Is that dirty in a good way? I write smut, remember?" She waved a hand at the room. "We couldn't afford all these antiques on the stipend that Simon gets from the church. I pay for nearly all of it. He gets a little bit of income from a legacy someone left him and a bit more from his stocks but it's just a drop in the ocean."

"A legacy? I didn't think priests were allowed to have private holdings."

"Oh, he gives any surplus away to the poor," Jennifer said. "It's not like he makes a profit out of anything, more's the pity." She put the spoon on the counter. "Why are you asking about Old Tom? Do you think that he had something to do with Robert's murder?"

Meinwen shrugged. "Not really. He just seems a little odd."

Jennifer laughed. "He's bound to be. He's been the curate and gravedigger for as long as I can remember. You've got to be a bit strange to do that."

"Really? I didn't think he was that old. Quite attractive, I thought."

"You should get out more!" Jennifer gave Meinwen a friendly punch on the arm. "He must be sixty if he's a day."

"Really?" Meinwen raised an eyebrow. "He told me he was twenty-three."

* * * *

Susan put the Jaguar into drive and pulled off. "Did it go well, ma'am?" she asked. "Your talk with the priest, I mean."

"Well enough." Jean Markhew relaxed into the soft leather and pulled off her gloves. "I gave him enough to think that I'm a batty old woman worried about going to prison for stealing trinkets."

"Well done, ma'am." Susan smiled and Jean caught her glance in the rear view mirror. "You didn't murder Master Robert, so they should leave you alone now."

"Exactly." Jean pointed to a lay-by separated from the road by a band of trees and hedgerow. "Pull over in there."

"Yes, ma'am." Susan indicated and pulled into the half-moon section of tarmac. On weekday rush hours there was a sandwich truck that parked here. She drew the car to a smooth halt, switched off the engine and sat with her hands resting palm upright in her lap, waiting for further instruction.

"Help me out, would you?"

Susan climbed out to open the back door. "Is there anything you need, ma'am?"

Jean walked her to the front of the car where she sat on the hood, grateful for the heat of engine against the cold wind. She fumbled in her handbag for her cigarettes and offered one to the housekeeper. "Filthy habit but I feel the need. Did you know Father Brande smoked? You could have knocked me over with a feather when he took one."

"I didn't, actually." Susan lifted a cigarette to her lips and waited for Jean to do the same, cupping her hands around the end when the older woman held out Robert's lighter.

Jean took a long drag in silence, blowing out the smoke through pursed lips. "You're staying with me, aren't you?" She sounded tired.

"Yes, ma'am." Susan stared straight ahead as Jean studied her profile.

"Why did Catherine decide to leave?"

"I don't know for sure." Susan looked into her employer's eyes.

"Some sort of argument with Sir Robert, I think. It upset her."

Jean took another drag of her cigarette and dropped the rest on the tarmac, grinding it out with her heel. "I don't know why he employed her in the first place. She's quite useless."

"He didn't, ma'am." Susan frowned. "It was a favour to Richard, I think."

"Was it indeed? How interesting." She went to the hedge and broke off a straight wand of hazel, trimming off any side shoots with her fingers. "I want you spread-eagled across the hood. She positioned herself to one side, lifting Susan's skirt and pulling her knickers taut to expose her bottom. "Think of this as a reward." Jean ran a finger down the stick she'd just cut then raised it high, her target the crease where Susan's arse met her thighs.

She ignored the hoots of passing drivers.

* * * *

Jennifer jumped as Simon poked his head into the kitchen. She hadn't heard him come in.

"What a lot of jam! No need to tell me what you've been doing today."

"I've been quite the busy bee." Jennifer put down her jam labels and reached for the kettle. "How was your day? Did you get your sermon done?"

"Eventually, once I'd got rid of Jean Markhew." Simon sat at the table. "That woman can whine for England."

"I'll bet. Did she say anything interesting?"

"Not much." Simon shrugged off his coat, leaving it draped over the back of his chair. "She's worried about the will and whether Meinwen would think she murdered Robert."

"Was it?"

"What?"

Jennifer peered through the glass front of the oven. "Was it her who killed him? Dinner will be ready in twenty minutes."

"No, of course not. The idea of her killing someone is absurd."

"She was here earlier. I've promised her some jam."

Simon raised his eyebrows. "Who? Jean Markhew?"

"No, Meinwen. She wanted to know what cellphone Richard used."

"Oh. It was a Nokia, I think. I don't know what one, though. I don't take any notice of other people's phones because I'm happy with the one

I've got. You won't catch me coveting my neighbour's cell."

"Yours is a brick."

"But easy to use." Simon pulled it out of his trouser pocket. "I don't have to remember where all the functions are. I don't need any gadgets."

Jennifer laughed. "As the bishop said to the actress."

Chapter 22

Jennifer scurried out of her office when her brother came home the following evening, to find him stomping about the hall, his coat and briefcase flung untidily onto the hall pew. She half led, half dragged him to the sitting room where he dropped into his favourite easy chair and sat back rubbing his temples. "That's tomorrow's sermon done as well as the end-of-year accounts." He opened his eyes and reached for the scotch. "I loathe that job."

Jennifer switched on the gas fire. "Well, you can forget about them now, at least until the bishop sends them back with a query note attached."

"Don't!" Simon made the sign of the cross. "He's been on at me about my fuel usage as it is."

"Is that why you've started to walk a lot more?"

"Yes, and it's killing me. I shall have to get a bicycle if the diocese funds will allow it."

"I could have a look on *Freecycle*." Jennifer was the local administrator for the free trading group. "I see bikes go up for grabs occasionally. I could even ask for one on your behalf if you like. It's more reasonable than the post that I saw this morning that was asking for a luxury saloon car." She bustled into the kitchen.

Simon raised his voice. "Yes, please. That would be a big help. I'm glad our computer is good for something."

"I couldn't write without it." Jennifer returned, placing a cup of tea in front of him. "It suits me to do all my research at the click of a button instead of spending hours poring over dusty books in the library."

"Thanks." Simon handed her the empty glass and picked up his tea. "The council had a meeting about the library. It seems a lot of people are of the same opinion and they're thinking of closing it."

Jennifer scowled. "We'll see about that. I can soon rally a petition to save it."

"What's the point? If nobody uses it let it close."

"I'll have a word with Mrs. Sedgewick after church tomorrow. She's been the librarian since we were tots."

"Aye. She was a rabid old battleaxe and never changed. When's dinner?"

"Not for an hour yet. You were home early for a Saturday." Jennifer sat on the sofa. "Why don't you go and tell Meinwen about Jean Markhew?"

"I don't want to." Simon kicked off his shoes and began massaging his feet.

Jennifer wrinkled her nose at the smell from his socks. "You need a shower. Preferably before I have to start opening windows."

"It's too early for an evening shower and too late for a morning one." Simon took off his cassock to reveal mundane shirt and pants. He sat back down. "It would smack of vanity to have one now."

"Being clean isn't a deadly sin, you know." Jennifer swapped to the farther end of the sofa. "Though your feet should be declared one."

"I don't care." Simon replied. "I've had a shitty day and I just want to relax for half an hour."

"Isn't that sloth?" She went into the hall to hang his coat up.

* * * *

"We have unfinished business." Jean Markhew trailed the end of her crop across Susan's cheek, causing the younger woman to blush.

"Yes, ma'am." She stood in the "ready" stance--feet shoulder-width apart and arms behind her back, each hand lightly touching the opposite elbow. Her back and head were straight, eyes facing forward.

Jean trailed the crop across her breasts and back. "Go to the dungeon, strip and wait for me."

* * * *

"Nicole Fielding knocked on the door today." Jennifer went into the kitchen, sure he would follow. For all Simon decried gossip he thrived on it.

"What did she want?" He loitered at the door while she put a dish in the oven.

Jennifer straightened. "She was looking for Meinwen."

Simon picked a loose sliver of wood from the edge of the jamb. "What about? Did she say?"

"I don't know. Only that it was important. I sent her over to The Herbage." Jennifer pressed a jar of her mixed fruit jam into his hands. "Why don't you take that over to Meinwen and ask her. You're burning with curiosity just as much as me."

"I'm not. I really don't care any more. Inspector White will sort everything out whether or not I have any involvement."

"Fiddlesticks." Jennifer moderated her language in her brother's presence. "You want to be in the loop but you're too proud to admit it."

"I am not." Simon stared at the jam. "All right. I'll take the jam over and leave it at her door, but I'm not going in."

* * * *

Susan knelt in the dungeon, hands clasped tight and gazing up at the cross on the wall.

Her knees against the hard tiles took her back to hours spent in the church and her mind relaxed as she put aside her daily worries. Finance, chores and commitments melted away until there was only her and the darkness and the scent of frankincense from the incense burner on the mock altar.

She shivered, her bare legs adjusting to the lower temperature, and prayed for peace to come upon the house and Sir Robert's murderer to come to a sudden and sticky end. She had no idea how long Jean would make her wait but it didn't matter. She was one with the solitude and darkness. One with God.

She just wished that her knees were one with the hard floor.

* * * *

Meinwen answered the door, surprised to see the secretary from The Larches on her stoop. "Can I help you?"

"You weren't in, earlier. Miss Brande at the rectory said you'd been out all day."

Meinwen stepped back to allow Nicole to enter. "I was organizing the shop. What can I do for you?"

Nicole stepped into the living room and Meinwen could see the look of surprise as she took in the oak panelling and chintz. She reached for a line of horse brasses.

Meinwen touched her lightly on the arm. "They won't turn into body parts. Try to separate your perception from the ingrained tales of witches you've been fed by the media since you were a child. I don't have green skin and I don't boil children. Not at the weekend, anyway."

Nicole let out a breath and her whole body relaxed. "Was it that obvious? I was expecting…" She shrugged. "I don't know what I was expecting, but it wasn't this."

Meinwen nodded and led the way into the narrow kitchen. "It's a rented house. I can't really festoon it with spider's webs and shrunken heads. Would you like some tea?"

"No, thanks." Nicole looked at her watch. "I have to get back soon. I'm on duty at five."

Meinwen leaned with her back the sink. "So?"

"I'm sorry?"

"What was so important you waited for me to come home?"

Nicole swallowed, her fingertips circling a whorl on the counter-top. Meinwen caught a flash of stocking as she fidgeted. "My skin is crawling like a carrier bag full of kittens. You accused us all of having secrets, and you're right, I do have a secret. I'm up to my eyes in debt. That's why I signed on as Robert's secretary. It saved me having a registered address for a while and got the debt collectors off my back. It gave me a breathing space. The fifty thousand he promised to leave me will go a long way to paying myself clear of them."

"That doesn't sound like a terrible secret. Many people are in debt these days. May I ask what it was for?"

"I told my parents I was working my way through college. What I actually did was party for three years and now I'm paying for it."

Meinwen nodded. "I can't say I approve but you're only young once. I can't condemn you for that."

"There's more." Nicole pulled out a kitchen chair and sat. "Peter and I were writing a book together about our experience in the house. It was going to be published under a pseudonym but our contracts forbade us to publish any details about living there."

"You're having an affair with Peter?"

"Yes. No." Nicole hesitated. "Peter and I are lovers, but it's not really an affair. Everybody knows about it, even Mr. Markhew. Nobody minded. That's where I was at the time of the murder, in Peter's bed."

"I see." Meinwen straightened, reaching for an apple from the bowl on the windowsill. "Is there anything else you want to tell me?"

"No, that's all." Nicole smiled. Her fidgeting had stopped and she looked calm and relaxed. "Thanks for not condemning me. I feel a lot better now that I've told you my secret."

"It doesn't have any bearing on the case as far as I can see. We'll just keep it between ourselves."

"Thanks." Nicole looked at her watch again. "I'd better get back to work or Jean will dock me some time."

"I thought the staff at The Larches weren't paid by the hour?"

"We're not." Nicole grinned. "But we accrue time off and privileges, so I must dash."

* * * *

Meinwen opened her front door to see Nicole out but the girl stopped on the threshold, confronted by the priest holding out a pot of jam.

"Thank you, Father, but we've plenty of jam at the house." Nicole grinned as she skidded past him back to her car.

"Is that for me?" Meinwen gestured to the jam with her half-eaten apple

"Um. Yes." Simon handed it to her and she read the label.

"Mixed fruit? That's what our mam used to call anything she couldn't remember. I'm sure it will be lovely. I'll try it in the morning."

"I'll tell Jennifer." Simon smiled. "Oh, and she asked me to tell you that Richard's cellphone was definitely a Nokia. I wouldn't know the difference, to be honest. They all look the same to me."

"Not to worry." Meinwen opened the door wider. "At least that confirms something. Are you coming in?"

"I won't, thanks. Jennifer will be putting the dinner out soon and I've got to have a shower first."

"As you wish." Meinwen nodded. "I do have something to show you, though."

"Oh?" Simon hesitated for a moment before stepping inside. "Just for a minute then. What did Nicole want?"

"To tell me her secret." Meinwen closed the door. "Although it has no bearing on the case and I promised not to reveal it."

"Isn't that concealing evidence?"

"A witch's house is as sacred as a confessional. People can tell me things in private without fear of my passing them on. As it happens, she also gave me her alibi for the night of the murder."

"Can you at least tell me that?"

"Yes. She was with Peter Numan."

"With?"

"Amorously entwined."

Simon frowned for a moment then his eyes opened wide. "Oh! Can they be each other's alibi?"

"I don't see why not. The killer was only one person."

"But was the blackmailer?"

"The same person as the killer?" Meinwen shrugged. "I've been assuming it was, but you may be on the right track thinking they weren't. We'd have two crimes to solve for the price of one."

"You can rule out Jean Markhew as well."

"Oh?"

Simon sat on the arm of the sofa. "She confessed her little secret to me yesterday. It seems she was in the habit of 'seeing what Robert's little trinkets were worth.' Jennifer looked up her eBay account and half of the contents of The Larches have gone up for sale over the last few months."

"I see." Meinwen sat at her computer and logged on to the auction site. "Do you know her seller ID?"

"It's 'mistressmarkhew,' all as one word. Jean told me it was because she considered herself the mistress of the house."

A few clicks revealed the truth of his words. "Ooh! I like the look of that Kenyan goddess figure. She's got it listed at half its value. Hang on a minute while I place a bid." She entered her details and opened a spreadsheet. "When you talked to Susan Pargeter, did she ask about heroin?"

"She did, actually. Why?"

Meinwen opened her desk drawer and pulled out a folder. "I've got Grace Peters's autopsy report here. She died of a heroin overdose. The suicide by hanging was just a cover."

"That's suspicious." Simon glanced at the report. "Do you think Susan Pargeter did it?"

"I don't know. She doesn't seem the type. Why would she have killed Grace Peters? If she was the blackmailer, she was killing the golden goose."

He handed it back. "It doesn't seem likely."

"It'll need looking into." Meinwen made another note. "It's certainly a tangle of lies and deceit at The Larches. What about the maid, Amanda?"

Simon shrugged. "What about her? She doesn't seem the type though I'll admit to there being something a bit iffy about her."

"Is there a type?" Meinwen twisted her swivel chair to face him. "She's certainly hiding something and if she did it she's going to prison."

"She is?"

"Everybody is." Meinwen stared at Simon for a moment. "Hiding something, I mean. Amanda was the most likely one to find that missing letter, wasn't she? Perhaps she's the blackmailer."

"I suppose so." Simon sighed. "She seems such a nice girl."

"She does. "Meinwen turned and stared at the computer screen. "Something isn't right about the timing of the murder. I think we need to re-enact the evening."

"Like an Agatha Christie!" Simon laughed. "Will they go for that do you think?"

"Let's hope so." Meinwen smiled at him. "Will you phone Jean Markhew and arrange it? She seems to like you better than me."

Simon seemed reluctant to take the phone. "I can't think why. Anyone would think you'd accused her of stealing or something."

* * * *

Jean snapped the single-tail, leaving a thin welt across Susan's back, a match to the seven already there. She had forced the woman past the point where it hurt, her knowledge of biochemistry and the soft moans of her target indicating endorphins were coursing through Susan's body, sending her into a dreamy state of euphoria.

The knock on the door was soft, but her ears were attuned to extraneous sounds and she picked it up instantly. She put the whip down and ran a leather-gloved hand over Susan's back.

"Stay." Jean turned away from Susan, who was strapped to a full-size cross screwed to the wall. "I'll only be a moment." She crossed the room and opened the door just wide enough to see through. "What is it? I said not to disturb me."

"It's Father Brande." Amanda stood in the hallway, holding the house phone with a finger on the silence button. "He insists on speaking to you. He and that Welsh woman want to stage a re-enactment of the night of the murder."

Chapter 23

Meinwen waited at Simon's elbow while he knocked on the door to The Larches, hoping he'd get the better reception.

Amanda's face was tired when she opened it. She just stood back and let them in. "I'll fetch Mrs. Markhew for you. Please wait in the sitting room."

They didn't have to wait for long. Jean soon entered, trailed by Mary.

Jean's face looked drawn and pinched as she sat in an armchair, folding her long black skirt around her legs. "Will this take long?" Meinwen caught the flash of a high-heeled leather boot, but made no comment under Jean's wilting glare.

Simon glanced at Meinwen. "I don't think so. Meinwen and I just want to get a feel of what happened on the night in question."

"I hope this is the last of such intrusions." Jean drew herself upright. "Proceed, then, and don't be too long about it."

"We need Peter and Nicole as well," Meinwen said. "They saw or heard Mr. Markhew before retiring."

An upward nod from Jean sent Amanda to fetch them. She returned a few minutes later with both, Nicole looking like a magazine model and Peter still stuffing his shirt into his jeans, his hair at all angles and the lines of a pillow etched upon his face. Jean glared at him as he tried to tame his unruly hair.

Simon stood. "We just want a recreation of the night. We don't know what happened in the study, so we'll look at what happened out here." He walked out into the hall and with a glance around the room the others followed suit. "Jennifer and I arrived at seven. Amanda answered the door and Mary greeted us, then she and Jennifer went into the sitting room and I studied this painting of the Pieta. I heard a high-pitched squeal then Jean came and greeted me."

"I'd been upstairs in my room," said Jean. "Robert had been working in his study before you arrived."

Meinwen stood to one side with her notes as Simon acted the part of master of ceremonies.

Simon looked at his notes. "We had dinner and Robert and I retired to the study to talk. At nine o'clock Robert came out of the study to ask if any letters had been delivered."

"I said there was." Amanda mimed handing Robert the mail.

"Yes. Robert came back into the study, began to read it, then put it in his pocket and said he'd read it later." Simon mimed coming out of the study. "Jennifer and I left at nine-fifteen."

"Nine-ten I think," said Amanda. "I remember the clock chiming the quarter-hour a few minutes after you'd gone."

"Was it?" Simon looked momentarily flustered. "The clock in the car must be a little fast."

Meinwen raised an eyebrow. "Which makes the stranger asking for directions nearer to nine-fifteen."

"What stranger?" asked Jean. "This is the first I've heard about a stranger."

"The police are looking for him," said Simon. "We don't know if he's connected to the case, or even if he came here at all."

"I would like to be informed of any progress on that," said Jean.

Simon nodded. "Of course." He paused. "Where were we?"

"You were leaving at nine-ten," said Nicole.

"I went straight to bed." Jean looked at Mary. "I had a headache."

"I went to clear up after the meal and wash up," said Amanda.

Peter grinned. "I was still at the pub. I'd have left to come back about then."

"Okay, the next reference on the night we have is at nine-thirty." Simon looked up at Peter and Nicole.

"I heard him arguing with someone from outside," said Peter. "I was on my way round to my cottage."

"Do you usually go around the back of the house?"

Peter nodded. "Of course. I didn't want to disturb anyone by going through the house needlessly. It's quicker to go around the side, anyway."

"You also mentioned you saw someone going out of the gate," Meinwen said.

"I did, yes. That was shortly before I heard Sir Robert. I don't know who it was, but I think it was a woman."

"Right." Simon looked at Nicole. "You heard Mr. Markhew arguing with someone as well, I believe?"

"That's right."

"I didn't see you," said Mary. "I was in the living room, watching telly. I'd have seen you if you were in the hall."

Nicole blushed. "I wasn't here at all, to be honest. I was just repeating what Peter told me."

"So where were you?" Meinwen asked. "In Peter's room, I take it?"

Nicole nodded. "That's right." She looked up at the new mistress of the house. "Mr. Markhew knew about it, ma'am."

Jean just nodded. "I'll talk to you later about that."

Simon coughed. "So Robert was arguing at nine-thirty, overheard by Peter. What happened next?"

"My program finished and I went up to bed," said Mary. "I said goodnight to Uncle Robert through the door at nine forty-five."

"Did he reply?"

"I think so. He was busy working, I think. I could hear him talking into his computer."

Simon made a note of the time on his sheet. "All right. Then what?"

Mary shrugged. "I went to go to bed and asked Amanda not to disturb him."

"I was taking him his bedtime drink," the maid said. "That was at nine-fifty."

"I told her not to disturb him, but she came back five minutes later." Mary shot an accusatory glare at Amanda, who shrugged.

"He never went without his night-time drink," she said. "It helped him sleep."

"Did you try to deliver it again after Mary had gone upstairs?" Meinwen asked.

"No, I gave up," said Amanda. "The next I knew Father Brande was banging on the door saying Mr. Markhew had been murdered."

"I see." Simon looked at Meinwen. "That's all the information I have unless anyone else can add anything."

"No, that sets it clear in my head," Meinwen said. "Does anyone else have anything?"

No one spoke.

"Thank you for putting up with this," said Meinwen. "It's been very helpful indeed."

Jean looked at Amanda. "Would you mind seeing them out? I seem to have developed a headache." She paused and looked at Meinwen. "Perhaps it's an accent grating on me."

"Or a guilty conscience, perhaps." Meinwen smiled. "Just one thing. Peter? When you came back at nine-thirty was the blue Vauxhall in the drive?"

Peter nodded. "Of course. All the cars were there."

* * * *

Mary flinched as Jean turned on Nicole. She couldn't see what the secretary had done wrong but was glad not to be on the receiving end of her mother's ire.

"Upstairs." Jean's eyes flashed with anger. "Right now."

"Yes, ma'am." Nicole hurried upstairs, a lock of hair falling from the tight knit of her bun.

Jean surveyed the rest of them. "Mary, you will go to your room. Amanda, attend to your duties in the kitchen. Peter, I'll see you in the morning. Dismissed." She went upstairs, lifting her long skirt so she didn't trip.

"Were you sleeping with Nicole?" asked Mary.

Peter nodded. "Sir Robert asked me to give her whatever she wanted. There are no emotional ties between us, though."

"Good." Mary stared so hard at him he had to blink back tears. She turned and went up the stairs without a backward glance.

* * * *

"I need a stiff one."

Meinwen looked at Simon in surprise. "I didn't even know you were gay."

He gave a bark of laughter. "A drink, I mean. Will you join me?"

"If you like." Meinwen looked out of the car into the dark street. "Won't people find it a little odd that a priest is going into a pub with a witch?"

He nodded, his eyes fixed on the road. "All we need now is a rabbi and we've got the makings of a good joke," he said.

It was Meinwen's turn to laugh.

* * * *

Jean circled the naked Nicole, a pair of wicked-looking Japanese clamps in her hand. "Your sexual activities with Peter will cease. "You will come to me when you have such needs in future."

"Yes, ma'am." Nicole stood in a relaxed posture, her hands clasped loosely at her back. Jean trailed a finger over her nipples.

"Perhaps this will remind you who owns your arse." Jean fastened a clamp to each of her nipples. "Until you elect to leave, of course."

"I won't, ma'am." Nicole bit her lip to distract herself from the pain in her nipples. "I have no wish to leave. I'm happy here."

"I'm glad to hear it." Jean fastened a chain between the two clamps and pulled.

* * * *

"Jennifer?" Simon pressed the cell brick to his ear against the hubbub of the pub. "We're at the White Art. Fancy joining us?" His face clouded. "Yes, I know I missed dinner. We'll get some chips on the way home." He turned the phone off and gave Meinwen a sheepish grin. "She'll be along shortly."

Meinwen nodded, taking a long draught of the pint of local ale. She put it on the table and wiped away the foam moustache. "It'll do. Not a patch on Bois Bach, though."

"Not a patch on what?"

"The local brew in the Cesail Gwlanog in Dovey," she explained. "Many a night I've been plastered on that."

"I try not to drink to excess," said Simon. "The where?"

"The Woolly Armpit. It's cold in Dovey." Meinwen grinned, the alcohol loosening her reservations. "Were you never young?"

Simon smiled. "Perhaps when I was at university."

"Mind if I join you, Father?" Sergeant Davies leaned over the table. "I could do with a sobering influence on some of the folk in here." He sat without waiting for a reply, dropping a pint of the local brew squarely onto a beer mat. It was followed moments later by a bottle of cola with a straw in the top as a woman sat.

"Ah." Simon touched her lightly on the shoulder. "Meinwen, this is Latitia Campbell…"

"Pleased to meet you." Meinwen extended a hand across the table. Latitia shook it and Meinwen froze.

"…she works up at the Manor."

Meinwen saw the smile in the newcomer's eyes, her hand held a moment longer than necessary.

"I've got the night off," Latitia said. "Since the mistress of the house is at home. You're the new witch, aren't you?"

"Quite an old one, actually." Meinwen grinned and picked up her beer again.

"Found anything new about the case?" Sergeant Davies picked up his glass but found it already empty. He turned to the bar and raised his voice, circling his hand to indicate the whole table. "Mike? Another round over here, please."

"Nothing much," said Meinwen. "How about you?"

"Oh, it's nothing to do with me." Davies shrugged. "Out of my hands, that one. I just get stuck with the road accidents and the like."

"I think it was the daughter what did it," said Latitia. "I saw her with some bloke today and I heard she was engaged to the son. They're a funny lot if you ask me."

"What man?" asked Meinwen. "Who?"

"Search me. I don't know them that well. Probably a close cousin or something." Latitia laughed.

"Am I missing gossip?" Jennifer pulled up a chair next to Simon. "I'll have a gin and tonic. I don't think Mary could have done it, though I'd like to know where her money comes from. She'd be too afraid of getting blood on her clothes."

"Who do you fancy for the deed then?" asked Latitia. "The butler?"

"They don't have a butler." Jennifer took her drink from Mike's tray. "What about Catherine? She had an argument with Mr. Markhew."

"Too obvious." Latitia opened a packet of peanuts, spilling half of them on the floor. Meinwen wondered why the girl appeared so drunk when she was only drinking cola. "You're not going to kill a man just after you've argued with him. I think the little Goth did it, hoping to get at the money once she got married to Richard."

"I wonder where he got to?" asked Davies. "We've got a national lookout for him."

"I think he's in Birmingham," said Jennifer. "I think he's with the stranger who asked for directions from Simon."

"How did you work that out?" asked Meinwen.

"Well, you said there was a train that went there, and he's nowhere to be found."

Latitia laughed. "Birmingham is as good a place as any."

"What do you think, Simon?" Jennifer asked. "You've been very quiet. You must have something to contribute."

"There's the ring Meinwen found," Simon said, ignoring the witch's glare. "That might be a clue."

"What ring?" Latitia and Jennifer asked together.

"I found it in the park," said Meinwen, reluctant to discuss it but forced to by Simon's words. "It was a Celtic design, a lover's knot."

"It was probably Mary's," said Jennifer. "I bet Richard gave it to her and she threw it away because it hadn't got skulls and bats on it. You can tell she doesn't really like him."

"She talks about him constantly."

"That's just a cover. Have you seen her hair? I bet she's a lesbian. She'll have been having a fling with one of the staff, you watch."

"Susan Pargeter!" Jennifer looked shocked. "I bet that's why she drove off on the night of the murder. She'd just found out about the engagement."

"It might have been Catherine's." Latitia leaned forward. "She was always into the Celtic jewellery. It could easily have been hers."

"Why would she throw it away?"

Latitia shrugged. "I still think it was Mary's. Perhaps she's secretly married Richard already and had to throw the ring away to pretend she wasn't."

"Perhaps she married Peter instead," said Simon.

"Why would she? I'm telling you, she's a lesbian and she'll only marry Richard for the money. Why would she want Peter if she can have Richard?"

"She's got a point, you know." Jennifer drained her third gin and tonic. "Everybody knows she doesn't like Richard."

Chapter 24

Inspector White looked at the clock and groaned. Beryl was going to be annoyed and when Beryl was annoyed, White would rather be anywhere than in the range of her sarcasm. The problem was, if he didn't go home soon and suffer the sarcasm, it would turn into silence and that was worse.

He glanced at the phone. One more call before he could leave. Perhaps he'd pick up a Chinese meal on the way. Beryl would like that, and it would offset the pointed comments about burned dinners.

He read the number off a sheet of paper and dialed. "Mr. J Stevens?"

"Yes?"

"Hello, it's Laverstone CID here."

"CID? What's happened?"

"Nothing to worry about, just a routine check. Would you please confirm your travel for the evening of Tuesday the tenth of April?"

"Er…Was that the night I was in Laverstone? I took the late train home."

"You took the eleven twenty-five express back to Chester? Thank you. If I could ask you one more thing… Did you see anyone else on the train?"

"Anyone else? There were a few people. I just read the paper though. Sorry."

"He would have been Caucasian, in his twenties, unshaven and wearing a hoodie."

"A what?"

"Like a hooded sweatshirt, sir"

"Oh, yes. Jack. We met in the pub. Nice enough lad. A student, I think."

"Splendid! Where did he get off the train?"

"Birmingham New Street. I saw him light a cigarette on the platform. You're not allowed to do that, you know."

"Indeed not, sir. Thank you. You've been a great help."

White replaced the phone, grinning to himself for the confirmation that the unknown stranger had indeed been on the train to Birmingham.

He picked up the phone again.

"British Transport Police? This is Inspector White here, Laverstone CID."

* * * *

Meinwen shivered and pulled her coat tight as she stepped out of the pub. "Aren't you cold?"

Latitia laughed. "You get used to it. Parts of the manor are a lot colder than this." She looked up at the sky. "At least it's a clear night. There shouldn't be any rain."

"No." Meinwen left the relative shelter of the doorway. "Mind if I ask you something?" She glanced at the pub door. Simon had gone to visit the gents on their way out and Jennifer had hung back to wait for him.

Latitia followed her look. "Something you don't want your friends to hear, eh? Go ahead then. Fill your boots."

"What do you know about Tom, the gravedigger-handyman at the church? I heard he sometimes does work at the manor."

Latitia shrugged. "Not much. He's not there often. The house staff are pretty handy and can turn their hand to just about anything. We only really see him if we need someone to coach paint the truck. He's a dab hand at that. Used to do it for years until the plastic signs forced him out of business in the eighties."

Meinwen frowned. "Coach paint?"

"You know. Putting the little gold lines on and the shop name."

"Ah!" Meinwen nodded vigorously. "But you're talking about Old Tom. I meant the young one, his son."

It was Latitia's turn to frown. "What are you on about? Tom was never married. Never had a son. He lives on his own in Bank Cottages."

"Oh." Meinwen forced a laugh. "I must have got the wrong end of the stick. Never mind, then. I'll see you again?"

Latitia nodded. "I expect so. It's not that big a town." She headed off toward the manor, turning to wave goodbye.

Meinwen shivered, hugging herself until the door opened and Simon and Jennifer came out.

Jennifer linked arms with her. "Will you join us for supper? Simon promised fish and chips."

* * * *

Jean Markhew carried a silver case into the guest bathroom and gestured for Susan to set a stool next to the sink. "I want an extension cord." Jean set the case on the tiled vanity unit and flipped open the catches.

Susan bobbed affirmation and returned a few minutes later paying out the cable. She set the plugs within easy reach, raising an eyebrow at the sterile pads and pot of black ink.

Jean pointed at the stool. "Sit. Take off your blouse first, though."

Susan pulled it off over her head, folded and draped it over the side of the bath. She sat facing the mirror.

Jean pulled her hair forward to reveal her neck, her hand trailing down over the pert breast. "Lovely. When did you enter Robert's service?"

"Eleven years ago, after his wife died." Susan's voice caught in her throat. "He was kind to me."

"I should think he was. You do a good job." Jean's fingers trailed over a nipple and Susan shuddered. "This is the last time I will offer this. Do you wish to leave my service?"

"No, ma'am." Susan shook her head, her hair falling back over her shoulders. Jean tutted and exposed her neck again.

"Sorry, ma'am." Her voice was barely above a whisper.

"Then that is also the last time you will call me 'ma'am.'" Jean leaned forward and kissed the back of Susan's neck before cleaning it with an alcohol wipe and shaving a small patch. "In private, anyway."

Susan looked up it time to catch her smile in the mirror.

"From now on," Jean said, "You will call me 'Mistress.'"

She smiled as Susan closed her eyes, the buzz of the tattoo gun singing over the white tiles of the bathroom, changing pitch as it dipped into her skin.

* * * *

Jennifer undressed in the darkness, looking through the window. Simon was downing a last scotch downstairs. He claimed it helped him sleep. Jennifer suspected the extra-large helping of haddock and chips would do that.

A flash of brightness caught her eye and she leaned toward the window to see into the garden of The Herbage.

The light flared again in the centre of the circle Meinwen had levelled and by the light of the fire Jennifer could see her pacing, lighting five candles. Jennifer recognized the geometric shape of a pentagram.

She stared, too fascinated to move away as Meinwen squatted next to the small fire she'd built, her back toward the rectory. Every few moments her hands flashed outward, lit by the orange of the fire and the silver of the moon.

Jennifer watched for several more minutes before fatigue overtook her and she drew the curtains, ready for bed.

* * * *

Meinwen's hands flickered over the keyboard. The hour of meditation in the garden had done her the world of good and now her thoughts flew fast and clear as she typed queries into search engines.

It took her until after midnight to find what she wanted. Dating sites and chat rooms furnished her with pieces of a jigsaw puzzle that was itself only a single interlocking piece of the larger canvas of murder.

Alt.sex.org furnished her with the last piece. A three-year-old query from a woman whose husband had completely lost interest in sex led to a mention in the Hampshire Times of a divorce and a three-line paragraph about the sale of a marital home.

Amanda James had been christened Charles Edward James.

Chapter 25

"Dearly Beloved…"

Jennifer looked around the church as Simon's voice rang out over the congregation. It was fuller than usual, the recent murder and her brother's incidental part in its investigation swelling the ranks with the curious and the gossip mongers. Even Jean Markhew had brought her daughter, Mary's presence breaking her four-month absence since the midnight Mass on Christmas Eve.

She wished she'd written his sermon. With the recent events and the accounts to complete it was obvious he'd dashed out a rehash of the parable of the Good Samaritan and called it a day. She was relieved when he got to end and asked them all to stand. Jerusalem was her favourite hymn.

* * * *

Meinwen walked around the church until she found Jean Markhew's Jaguar in the small car park. Susan Pargeter, dressed in a chauffeur's uniform, sat on the stone wall next to it smoking a cigarette in the sunshine. The woman talking to her was just the person Meinwen was looking for.

"Amanda? Can I have a word?"

"I shouldn't without permission." Amanda looked to Susan who nodded and shooed them away, leaning back against the smooth stone. Meinwen led the way to the relative privacy of the tomb of Sir Harold Lauder, 1798 to 1874.

"Are you ready to tell me your secret?"

Amanda smiled. "If you're asking me now you probably already know it. I take it you've spoken to my ex?"

Meinwen shook her head. "Not at all. I respect your privacy."

"Thank you."

"I still need to know what went on that night. I don't care about your past unless it relates to the death of Robert Markhew."

Amanda shook her head. "It doesn't. I was hanging about to speak to Robert about the rest of the surgery I need. He'd been promising to speak to me all weekend and hadn't had a chance."

"You've still got your--" Meinwen raised an eyebrow. "You look so…um…natural."

"Yes. I had an appointment with the surgeon on the Wednesday, that's why I was so desperate to talk to him." She shrugged. "I had to cancel it, of course. It doesn't matter now."

Meinwen nodded. "I'm sorry. Will he have left you anything?"

"I'm not counting on it. I've only been with him since the beginning of the year. Not much longer than Catherine, really."

"At least that explains your persistence in trying to see him."

Amanda sighed heavily and looked directly into Meinwen's eyes. "I didn't kill Master Robert. He was my ticket to a woman's world."

* * * *

Jennifer waited for Simon to finish in the vestry. It was odd she hadn't seen the curate, though his presence was evident by the open grave awaiting the internment of Robert Markhew the next day. Grace Peters, as a suicide, would not be buried on consecrated ground but would instead be cremated and her ashes interred in the cemetery opposite.

Her brother came out at last, holding his coat over one arm. "You needn't have waited. I could have found my way home."

"That's all right. The internet's quiet on a Sunday." She squeezed his arm. "Look! There's Meinwen gathering bones and grave dust."

Simon laughed. "I doubt it. She doesn't strike me as the type to desecrate the dead." They sauntered along the path until they got to where Meinwen waited at the north gate next to the ancient stone, Long Mab.

"I wouldn't expect you to hang about a church on a Sunday, Miss Jones," he said. "Aren't you afraid of all the good Christian vibes?"

Meinwen dipped her head. "Good vibes are never something to be afraid of. No matter what the source, they increase the light in the world." She looked across at the open grave. "Not so with murder, however."

"Anything new to report?"

"We can rule out Amanda. She told me her secret and it's not relevant to the case. She certainly didn't kill her golden goose."

"Robert was giving her money then?"

Meinwen nodded. "He would have done, had he lived. They had an arrangement."

Simon gave a nervous laugh. "Perhaps you'd better keep that to yourself. I am a man of the cloth, after all."

They began to walk back to their respective houses. "I still think it wasn't Richard." Jennifer looked past her brother to Meinwen. "He's definitely been framed. What if it was Mary who did it and then framed Richard to inherit the whole house as the grieving wife of a murderer?"

Meinwen stopped to lean on the graveyard wall. "I don't think it was anyone in the household. For all their minor squabbles they are a tight-knit group of people, each defending the next." She took off her shoe and shook it until a stone fell out.

Simon rubbed his face. "That doesn't rule out the blackmailer, though. What if the blackmailer's a member of the household even if the murderer isn't?"

Jennifer looked back at the church. The sun had almost reached its zenith now, throwing the steeple into dark relief against the blue sky. The silhouette of the minarets at the base of the steeple gave the whole building the look of the Klingon Daqtagh dagger used for the murder. She shuddered.

"It's possible." Meinwen replaced her shoe and walked on. "But imagine, if you will, a young man, not very well off, who finds out a secret. He sees a way to make money from the knowledge. He doesn't need the money but desires it nonetheless, for the acquisition of it is his weakness. He is not an evil man, but when the secret well runs dry and threatens to expose him, he kills out of desperation."

Simon shook his head. "It's an interesting tale but if you're relating this to life you're off the mark. Grace Peters committed suicide."

"Did she?" Meinwen shrugged. "I have no proof, of course, but is it not possible that when she took her usual sleeping tablets this blackmailer gave her heroin and staged the hanging? Who is then to say she did not do it herself, either by accident or design?"

Jennifer gave her arm a squeeze. "It does seem a little far-fetched, dear, though I could use it as a plot for my next book." She grinned. "He could be blackmailing her for sex."

"Jennifer, please. We're trying to be serious." Simon pulled and they walked on.

"I am serious." Jennifer punched him on the bicep. "Older women are sexy."

"Let me continue." Meinwen fell into step with them. "This blackmailer thinks that's the end of it, but then discovers that his money pot told someone she was being blackmailed and may even have mentioned his name. What can he do about it? In a fit of desperation he takes a knife from the open case, plunges it into the back of the confidant and steals the letter."

Simon laughed. "It all sounds very plausible when you say it like that, my dear, but I still think--" He was interrupted by the beeping of his cell phone. "Yes? That's right." His face went through a series of expressions as Jennifer and Meinwen watched. He finished with "I'll be right there. Thank you."

"What was that about?"

"That was the police," Simon said. "They've picked up the stranger who asked for directions and they want me to identify him."

Chapter 26

Jennifer balled her hands into fists. "An identity parade? How exciting!"

Simon put a hand on her arm. "You'd better go back to the house, Jennifer." He tried to steer her in that direction but she shook it off.

"Not on your life. I was driving that night, remember? I've got as much right to be involved as you have."

"She's right, Simon. We'll all go." Meinwen began walking to the police station, looking back after a few yards. "Come on, slowcoaches."

Simon grimaced. "Why does she have to come with us? She wasn't there at all."

"She does seem to have some insights into the case." Jennifer skipped a step or two. "Come on, Simon. Don't be such a naggle-puss."

When they'd arrived at the station and introduced themselves to the desk sergeant, Inspector White came out, gave them visitors' badges and ushered them through to the interview rooms.

Jennifer took in the shabby walls and nicotine-coloured ceilings. "It's a bit dingy, isn't it? It looks much more salubrious on CSI."

"It's the cutbacks, miss." White showed them into a room where a constable sat with a small CCTV monitor. "It's all right for them to go spending millions on the new offices at Scotland Yard, but five grand for refurbishing this place was rejected because it was 'unnecessary.' You try telling that to the lads who work here." He gestured toward the screen. "That's the lad we picked up. Do you recognize him?"

Simon shook his head. "I'm afraid not. It was dark in the street. It could be him but I couldn't swear to it. He's not even wearing a hoodie any more."

White sighed.

* * * *

"Who is he?" Meinwen peered closer at the screen. "Do we know anything about him?"

White picked up a file. "His name is Jack Rogers, a student at Birmingham University who lives with his father there. He admits to being in Laverstone on the night of the murder but won't tell us why. We can't hold him for long without any evidence of wrongdoing."

On the screen a constable came in to give the man a cup of tea. "Can we hear what he's saying?" Simon asked.

White nodded and flicked a switch.

"Will somebody tell me what I'm here for?" Jack Rogers's voice was thickly accented. "They said I was a suspect in a murder case and I'm scared shitless. I haven't killed anybody. I don't even know who's been killed."

The constable paused at the door. "I'm sorry, sir. I can't discuss anything about the case with you. I'm sure someone will be in shortly."

"Shortly? I've been here two hours and that's not counting the ride down from Brum. I have rights, you know."

The constable said nothing as he left the room, the click of the lock echoed by the expression on Rogers's face.

Simon pointed at the screen. "That's him. I'd recognize that voice anywhere."

"Yes. That's him all right." Jennifer clutched at the inspector's arm. "Will you arrest him?"

"We've nothing to charge him with." White extracted himself from her grip. "There's no law against asking for directions."

Meinwen smiled at him. "Inspector? I'd like to ask him a few questions."

White shrugged. "It can't do any harm I suppose. Father? If you and your sister will remain here? The constable will stay with you." He nodded to the policeman at the desk.

He led Meinwen along the corridor into the interview room. Rogers looked up as they entered. White checked his watch.

"Interview with Jack Rogers. Fifteenth of April, Twelve-twenty AM. Present are Inspector White and Meinwen Jones, civilian assistant." He sat. "Mr Rogers, you are a suspect in the murder of Robert Markhew at The Larches last Tuesday night. We have a witness who has testified you asked for directions to the house at approximately nine-fifteen PM, shortly before the murder."

Jack shook his head. "I'm not saying anything. I didn't murder no one."

Meinwen leaned forward. "But you did go to the house. You went to see your mother, didn't you?"

Jack sneered and folded his arms. "My mother? My mother left me when I was two years old. I don't have a mother."

Meinwen nodded. "You may not have a relationship with her, but you know exactly who she is. Should I ask the inspector to compare your DNA with the residents of The Larches?"

Jack shook his head again, his eyes lowered to the table. "No." He unfolded his arms and looked at her. "There's no need. All right. I was at

The Larches, but only as far as the drive. I didn't go into the house."

"Is that where you met her?" Meinwen stared in his eyes.

"Yes, but it was only for a minute. I was gone ten minutes later. She can testify to that."

"Just who is your mother?" White opened his notebook.

"Susan Pargeter. She won't want it known she abandoned me, though. No one wants it bandied about they're a bad mother."

"What was the meeting for?"

Jack shrugged. "Guilt money. I'm a student, see. I need books and supplies and a laptop. Dad can't afford it so I traced her and asked her."

"Did she give it you?"

Jack nodded. "Five grand. She told me it was all she had."

"When did you leave Laverstone?"

"I caught the eleven twenty-three back to Birmingham."

Meinwen raised her eyebrows. "Two hours later? Why didn't you get an earlier train?"

"I stopped to celebrate, didn't I? Some pub between the house and the station." Jack smiled, and his eyes sparkled for the first time. Beneath the frightened, sullen exterior he was quite a handsome young man.

"Can anyone verify that?"

Jack shrugged. "Maybe. The landlord or an old bloke called Tom. We walked to the station together. He was catching the same train."

Meinwen touched his arm. "Tom? Did he have a last name?"

Jack shook his head. "Not that I remember."

Meinwen frowned.

* * * *

Jean accepted the tea from Amanda and stood at the window. Outside, Peter was pruning the roses and mulching them with shredded bark. "When I came out of church yesterday you were talking to that Welsh woman. What were you talking about?"

Amanda looked down. "She found out who I was, ma'am. Who I used to be. I had to reveal the real reason why I was trying to speak to Robert that night."

"To ask him for the money for your cosmetic surgery?"

"That's right. Not just cosmetic, though. I'll go mad without it."

"If I inherit the whole estate, you may go ahead and have the surgery done privately." She took a sip of the tea and glanced up at Amanda's beaming smile.

"Thank you, ma'am. That will save me years of waiting for NHS treatment."

Jean nodded. "I know. I looked up the figures for people waiting for the operation. The suicide rate is twice the national average. I'd rather keep you alive." She reached across and slapped her on the bottom. "I'm sure we can think of ways for you to pay off the debt to me."

* * * *

Meinwen was thoughtful as they left the police station and they walked part of the way back in silence. "Mind if we pop in to the White Art on our way home? I want to verify his story." She jerked her head to indicate Jack Rogers in the interview room.

Simon pulled on a pair of leather gloves. "Fair enough. A snifter of brandy wouldn't go amiss either."

Jennifer perked up. "I could probably manage a gin. Just the one, though, or the roast will spoil."

"And we couldn't have that." Simon patted her arm. "It would be such a waste when there are so many starving in Africa."

Jennifer's laughter faded in the face of Meinwen's frown. "Something our mother used to say all the time."

Meinwen nodded. "I see. I don't think mine ever did, not that she had two pennies to rub together. She couldn't abide waste, though. Whatever was left would go back into the pot for the next day."

The pub was busy and they had to fight their way through to the bar. "That was a good sermon today, Father," said one man as they passed.

"Aye. It was short," said another, causing the group to laugh. Meinwen looked at the priest's fixed smile and kept her own to herself.

"It's not like you to come in on a Sunday, Father." Mike grinned behind the bar. "What can I get you?"

"A brandy, a gin and tonic and a…" He looked at Meinwen.

"I'll have a pint of the Heavy please, Mike." Meinwen grinned at the barman, almost lost in the press of customers.

Simon fumbled in his pocket for the money but Meinwen slapped a ten-pound note on the table. "I'll get these. Have one yourself."

Mike poured the drinks and gave her the change. "Anything else?"

"Yes." Meinwen leaned forward and lowered her voice. "Do you remember a young man in here last Tuesday night, about half-past nine? He would have been flashing money about a bit."

"Aye." Mike replied. "It's always a bit quiet on a week night. Vodka shots he was drinking. He was here until eleven then dashed off to catch a train."

"Thanks." Meinwen worked her way past the other customers to Simon and Jennifer. "Rogers was telling the truth. He was here until eleven."

Simon took a sip of brandy. "I didn't know Susan Pargeter had a son. Fancy abandoning a child."

"Shush." Jennifer pulled at his arm. "You don't know the circumstances. You don't have room to talk, anyway."

"Oh?" Meinwen raised her eyebrows.

"He wasn't always a priest. He sowed his own wild oats in college."

Simon lowered his voice. "I had a son once. I wanted to marry his mother when I found out, but her family wouldn't hear of it. She dropped out of college and I never saw her again."

"How long ago was this?" Meinwen sipped her drink.

"A long time ago." Simon shrugged. "He'd be grown up now. I never even saw him as a baby."

"You must have loved her," said Meinwen. "I can imagine how heartbreaking it would have been to be denied fatherhood." She bit her lip. "In a literal sense, I mean."

"It was." Simon gazed through her for a moment. "Did you believe Rogers when he said Susan gave him money for college?"

"Not in the least." Meinwen drained her glass and put it down. "I think he may well be our blackmailer."

* * * *

Mary Markhew spent the afternoon in her bedroom with a DVD and a book. At least, that was what she told her mother at lunch. Jean might have approved of the historical romance had she bothered to look at the post arriving from Mary's online rental, but she would have confiscated Pirates of the Rutty Ark on sight. It was fortunate Mary hadn't shown it to her.

She slipped it in the player and lay on the bed, her fingers slipping under the elastic of her knickers. Minutes later, and without reference to the film, she began moaning with pleasure, her eyes half-lidded.

It wasn't Richard she was thinking of, but Peter.

* * * *

Jennifer paused as Meinwen turned up the hill instead of down it as the trio walked home. "Where are you going? The Herbage is this way."

Meinwen turned and walked backward to face him. "I have an errand to do. Nothing your profession would approve of."

"Ah." Simon gave her an upward nod. "Perhaps we'll see you later then. Will you be at Robert's funeral tomorrow?"

Meinwen raised her arms with a shrug. "I don't know. I'd like to, but being so involved with the case I don't think that Jean Markhew would appreciate my presence."

"Funerals are for those left behind." Jennifer leaned against the telephone box on the corner. "It gives them release."

"Then I will leave that dubious pleasure to her. See you."

"Bye." Simon shook his head as he watched her stump up the hill. "She's a strange woman."

"What did you expect?" Jennifer put her arm in his. "She has a different set of values to you. You can't always expect two such distinct belief systems to interlock."

"I suppose not. What's for lunch, anyway?"

"With any luck--" Jennifer picked up the pace. "--a lovely piece of beef if it hasn't burned to a crisp after all this time."

* * * *

Meinwen laboured up The Bank. "You have to be fit to live here," she said to no one in particular. The short row of terraced cottages at the top of the steep hill were just coming alive with colour, the grey stone of the walls gathering the warmth of the sun and sending it back in bursts of yellow from the late winter jasmines and the early broom and forsythias.

Of the four cottages, one had a plastic swing set in the garden, one had washing out, one showed no signs of life, and the last was pristinely kept. She chose the last one to knock at. It was opened by an elderly lady.

"Yes?" She looked Meinwen up and down. "I don't buy anything at the door and I've got no money or valuables in the house."

"I'm not selling anything, not even religion." Meinwen smiled at her and visibly relaxed. "I'm just looking for Old Tom."

"You won't find him. He's gone up to his brother's for a fortnight."

"Really? That's a shame." Meinwen took out her wallet and flashed a picture of her Aberdovey Hill Ramblers club membership card. It was in Welsh, but had a nice picture of her. "I'm from the premium bonds. He's come into a bit of money."

"Has he?" The woman smiled. "That'll be nice for him, he deserves a bit of a break. He looks after my garden for me, see?"

"It's beautiful." She turned and gave it an admiring look. "I like the way you've got herbs interspersed with the bulbs. That's the first rue I've seen this year."

The lady's smile was almost warm enough to bask in. "You know your herbs. Would you like to come in? I think I've got his brother's address in my book."

"Thank you. That would be kind." Meinwen followed, glad she had no ill intent toward the lady. The front door led directly into a sitting room where a wood-framed armchair was festooned with wool and pieces of knitting. A radio played softly in the background and the woman switched it off. "I can't afford a telly. Not even with the reduced license." She went into the kitchen. "It'll be in the drawer. Would you like a cup of tea?"

"No, thank you."

"I'm Edie, by the way." The woman pulled open a drawer and took out a thick book full of pieces of paper. "Edith, really, but everyone calls me Edie." She sat at the little table next to the glass-paned back door and started flicking through the loose papers. She seemed out of breath.

Meinwen sat in the other chair. "Have you got nettles in the garden?"

Edie looked up. "There're some behind the shed, I think." She gestured to the door. "Why?"

"May I pick some?"

"They're weeds. You can have as many as you like, but not so many as the caterpillars starve."

Meinwen went into the tiny back garden and found a patch of nettles with their first shoots crowding the gap between the shed and the garden wall. She picked a handful, glad that their sting hadn't yet developed. She returned to the kitchen where Edie was still sorting through her book.

"Do you have a pan?"

Edie indicated the cupboard next to the electric cooker. "What are you going to make?"

"An herbal remedy. You've got a touch of anaemia, and a bit of nettle tea will do you good."

Edie frowned. "If you say so." She began writing an address onto the back of an envelope in neat copperplate handwriting.

Meinwen stood at the hob until the infusion had simmered for five minutes then strained it into a cup. "You can add a bit of honey if it's too bitter."

"Thank you." Edie smiled. "Can I give you something for it?"
Meinwen shook her head. "Just the address of Tom's brother."

* * * *

The sun had set by the time Meinwen got back to The Herbage and drank a pot of Earl Grey in front on her computer. An hour of navigating the electoral registers furnished her with several pages of notes and a good idea of Jack Rogers's history.

He lived with his father, John Rogers, in a house in Lickey, about ten miles south of Birmingham, since his birth in 'eighty-five. The house had been bought by John and Susan Rogers in 'eighty-one and they had lived there until she left six years later.

Further investigation had revealed where Susan had moved to. In 'eighty-seven she had moved in with her mother, Grace Pargeter, who had, since her daughter had left home, moved to Laverstone, remarried and changed her name.

Meinwen felt pieces of the jigsaw clicking into place. Grace Pargeter had become Grace Peters until her supposed suicide the previous week.

Chapter 27

White entered the church with slow, measured footsteps, noting the simple white flowers for the funeral. Despite his even tread, his boots rang against the stone until he paused at the rood screen separating the choristers from the nave. He inspected the carvings, marvelling at the skill of the artisans.

He straightened when the priest appeared from just below the altar. "I was just admiring the woodwork. Fifteenth century, isn't it?"

"That's right." Simon raised an eyebrow. "I didn't know you had an interest in architecture, Inspector."

"I'm sure there are a lot of things you don't know about me, Father Brande." White gave a perfunctory smile. "I was passing the church and saw the door open. I dropped in to tell you we let Mr. Rogers go home last night. His alibi checked out. He was in the White Art at nine-thirty which rules him out for the murder."

"Yes." Simon buffed the altar cross with the sleeve of his cassock. "We asked Mike about that too, actually. I was sure it was going to be him. We're back to square one in the hunt for Richard, aren't we?"

"I'm afraid so." White hesitated. "Will you tell Ms. Jones or shall I?"

"She guessed he'd be cleared." Simon stepped backward. "But since I've got two funerals this afternoon I'd be grateful if you would. I've enough on my plate as it is."

White nodded. "I don't mind. There's not a lot more I can do until Mr. Godwin turns up. I just hope she doesn't give me any of that blasted foreign tea." He nodded. "Good day to you, Father."

* * * *

Mary Markhew slammed her bedside drawer shut and began to dress. Her bedroom looked out onto the rear garden and the irregular hum drew her to the window. Outside, Peter rode a large lawnmower over the fresh spring grass, the first cut of the year sending the scent of wet grass into the house.

Since today was her uncle's funeral it was a necessity she wore black. She chose her full-length velvet skirt and mock-Tudor top, the long sleeves complementing the handkerchief pattern of the hemline. Calf-length boots hid her striped tights from view and she spent half an hour applying make-up to give herself the effect of Cleopatra in mourning.

She looked out of the window again. Peter was just putting the mower away.

* * * *

"Inspector." Meinwen brandished a bowl of cereal. "Come in. I overslept, I'm afraid. I was supposed to open the shop this morning but I got a bit involved online and ended up not going to bed until three. What can I do for you?"

"I dropped in to tell you that I released Rogers. Since his alibi checked out we had no reason to hold him."

"I wouldn't be so sure if I were you." Meinwen waved her spoon at him. "I think we've got the time of the murder wrong. If I'm right, the murder was committed much earlier, which puts him right on the scene."

White sighed, closing his eyes for a second or two. "What make you think we have the timing wrong? Eric Chambers, the coroner, said the murder had occurred within three hours, ergo, between nine PM. and midnight."

Meinwen swallowed another mouthful of oats. "Assuming the room had remained at the same temperature for those three hours. But what if the temperature had dropped significantly after the first hour? That would have given the body a higher temperature prior to that."

White took out his notebook. "I can't fault your reasoning, but how do you arrive at the theory? There's no evidence to suggest he was killed any earlier. We have witnesses who heard him after nine-thirty and Miss Markhew said goodnight to him at nine forty-five."

"I think Mary was lying. Do you want a cup of tea?" She headed to the kitchen, leaving White no choice but to follow her.

"Where do you get that from? And yes, I'll have a tea if you've got some English tea bags."

"Tea comes from the Far East. None of it is English, unless I can tempt you with dried elderberry and nettle."

"No, thanks." White failed to hide his grimace. "I'll have the supermarket variety if you don't mind."

Meinwen laughed and dropped two tea bags into mugs. "What if Mary was lying when she claimed she'd said goodnight to her uncle? There's still that missing hundred pounds unaccounted for and we know that although Markhew only gave her twenty pounds a week she has a bigger wardrobe than most working girls."

"All the working girls I've met had very little in their wardrobes," said White, his face perfectly straight.

Meinwen glared. "You know what I mean."

"So you think that Mary took the money and murdered her uncle?"

White sat on a pine chair. "I find that a little hard to believe and I certainly don't see any evidence to support it."

"No." Meinwen brought the tea over and sat. "I don't think she killed her uncle but I do think that she took the money then pretended to come out of the study. That's why she wouldn't let Amanda go in. She assumed her uncle would ask Amanda where she was, since she hadn't said goodnight, thus proving she hadn't been in the study at all."

White sipped his tea and made a face. "What is this?"

"Tea, like you asked." Meinwen winked. "The soy milk takes a bit of getting used to."

"Soy?" He looked into his drink. "Is there any sugar?"

"No. I've honey or molasses if you want it sweetened."

"No sugar?"

"Just honey. Take it or leave it."

"I'll leave it, thanks," White put the mug down.

* * * *

Mary found Peter in the garage cleaning off the lawnmower. The grass had been a little too damp and had caked the blades in wet cuttings. He was rubbing it down with an oily rag.

"Peter?" Mary sauntered into the half darkness.

"Mary? Do you need something?" Peter stood, picking up a clean cloth to wipe his hands. "What is it?"

Mary stepped closer, running a hand over his chest. She'd watched her mother do that with her father, a long time ago. She leaned in close and whispered in his ear. "I want you to fuck me, right now, right here in this shed."

Peter dropped his rag.

* * * *

Meinwen and the inspector followed Amanda through the house and out the kitchen door. "I'm fairly sure she's in the garden. I saw her go toward the sheds about half an hour ago." The maid pointed the way.

"Thank you." White walked along the path and around the side of the house. They could hear noise coming from the garage, like someone kicking a metal plate over and over. They headed toward it.

White saw the tangled limbs and coughed loudly, turning away. Meinwen was not so prudish. "Don't mind us. You carry on. It good to see the influence of the rampant god at springtime. Copulation is a perfectly natural response to the flood of growth throughout the land."

Mary shrieked and disentangled herself, stepping away from Peter and pulling down her skirt.

Meinwen smiled. "I'm glad the potion worked. Lovely morning for it."

White waited until they were both decent, studiously ignoring the way Peter was smoothing his hair with sticky hands. "Can we have a word, Miss Markhew?"

"Anything you say to me can be said in front of Peter. I trust him absolutely, and I have no secrets." Mary's tone was reminiscent of her mother's but without the power.

Meinwen smiled. "I think you do, Mary. I think that on the night of your uncle's murder you stole a hundred pounds from his bedside table, and only pretended you'd said goodnight to him at nine forty-five to cover that up."

Mary's eyes flickered between the two of them. "You're right." She took Peter's arm. "I did take it. I've had to do a lot of that just to get by on the pitiful allowance he gave me. I'm fed up with lying about where I get my clothes and jewelry. I asked for a bigger allowance a hundred times but he'd never give it to me. Mother used to give me some. She remembers how expensive it is to be young."

"Did Richard know?"

"Probably." Mary shrugged. "He used to have to do things on the side as well. We're very similar."

"She's just protecting me." Peter threw off her touch. "Mary knows I took the money under orders from Mrs. Markhew."

"Don't be silly, Peter. Do run along now while I talk to these people."

"Run along?" Peter spat on the floor. "If that's the way you want it." He stalked out.

"Peter!" Mary took a few steps as if to follow him. "Don't be like that."

Meinwen watched him go. "Richard didn't really propose by webcam, did he?"

"No." Mary sat on the wing of the lawnmower. "It was in the back room of the White Art. We figured a marriage would please Uncle Robert and leave us free to pursue our own interests. We're just good mates really." She rearranged her skirts. "I know that he didn't kill Uncle Robert."

"So where is Richard Godwin?" White asked.

"I honestly don't know." Mary's voice rose in pitch, convincing Meinwen she was indeed telling the truth. "His phone's been switched off since Tuesday."

White sighed. "You've led us a merry chase, Miss Markhew. I've a good mind to arrest you for perverting the course of justice."

"Why? All I did was borrow a hundred quid."

White's voice dropped to an icy monotone. "Because of your lie, Miss Markhew, we were under the impression that your uncle was still alive at nine forty-five. Now he may have been dead before that. Everyone's alibis will have to be re-examined."

Mary shrugged. "Sorry. I was just trying to protect myself."

"At the cost of how many lives, Miss Markhew?" White turned and stalked back to the house, pulling out his phone.

Meinwen went the other way and caught up with Peter. "Don't be too hard on her."

Peter stopped, rubbing his eyes with his hands. "I don't know what to do about her. She begs me to...to love her and then treats me like a child."

Meinwen put a hand on his arm. "She'll grow into herself. She'll be her mother's daughter."

Peter gave a derisive bark of laughter. "Do you think so?"

"Yes." Meinwen nodded. "She just doesn't know what she wants yet. She doesn't love Richard, if that's any help."

"She doesn't?" Peter looked confused. "But I thought..."

"It was an engagement of convenience." Meinwen picked a sprig of early mint. "Made to please her uncle."

* * * *

The funeral went well, Jennifer thought, watching the clouds scud past the vestry window late that afternoon. It had been a good turnout for the old boy. His entire household had come, though several had commented upon Richard's absence. Mr. Waterman and his friend had stood respectfully at the back, leaving a handsome donation for the church upkeep fund as they left. Inspector White and his sergeant had stood even farther back, probably in the hope of apprehending Richard if he turned up. There were a few reporters but on the whole the funeral had passed beneath the journalism radar.

She'd watched the mourners at the graveside, knowing each was wondering who had reduced the charismatic Robert Markhew to the occupant of a plain pine box. They had filed away in silence, each mourning the man who had touched their lives so profoundly. A marker had already been commissioned in the local granite and a passage from the Bible would be engraved to ease him to redemption. Her brother had been shaking his head as he read the closing prayers. Much as she had liked the man, she didn't expect to meet him in Heaven.

Grace Peters's quiet memorial had been less well attended. Only Susan Pargeter and Inspector White had joined them for the five-hundred yard journey and witnessed the pot being placed in unconsecrated earth. An engraved slab would show the final resting place of a murderess. If no one else commissioned it, Jennifer intended to pay for it out of her own pocket. The woman had given her the plot of her next novel.

Chapter 28

Meinwen watched the sad little ceremony from a discreet distance as Grace Peters's ashes were interred. She took out her phone. "Directory enquiries? I'd like a number in Coventry, please. Harry Thomas. Thank you."

She waited to be connected. Who would have guessed that Old Tom was named for his surname?

"Two-three-nine-four. Hello?"

"Harry Thomas? My name is Meinwen Jones from Laverstone. May I ask if your brother is available?"

"Aye." The line went quiet. "Fred? A young lady on the phone for you." A moment later the line crackled again. "Hello?"

"Fred Thomas? This is Meinwen Jones, in Laverstone. It's very important that I ask you a couple of questions, if I may."

"Aye. Go on then." Meinwen heard a whistle of breath.

"Are you Old Tom, the gravedigger?"

"I am. What's this about?"

"Can I ask why you left so suddenly."

"It wasn't sudden, like. Not Really. Father Brande said to take a couple of weeks off."

"I see. And you caught the late train?"

"Aye."

"Thank you, Mr. Thomas." Meinwen disconnected and looked up to see that the small service had ended, then watched as Jennifer and Simon walked back to the church and Inspector White and Susan Pargeter headed toward the car park. She intercepted them as they left the cemetery, feeling suddenly awkward in front of the bereaved woman. "I'm sorry for your loss."

Susan started. "My loss? I liked the old dear and felt sorry for her, that's all."

Meinwen put a hand on her arm. "I know the truth and I know your secret. Can we talk?"

Susan glanced at the cars in the car park. Most of the residents of The Larches had left at the end of Robert's funeral. "I should get back to the house."

"It is important," Meinwen insisted. "We could go somewhere private."

The inspector raised an eyebrow. "I'm sure there'll be a spare room at the station. We could talk there."

Meinwen shook her head. "Thank you Inspector, but that would be a little intimidating, don't you think? My shop is only five minutes' walk away. We'd be comfortable there."

Susan pulled away. "I really have to get back. Another time, perhaps."

"Ms. Pargeter." White drew himself up to his full height. "Things will go badly if you don't talk to us now. We suspect the murder of Robert Markhew was committed earlier than we originally thought. That means that your son no longer has the alibi of being in the White Art public house."

Susan paled. "My son? You know about him?"

"The truth does not hide from the Goddess. Nor from the eyes of those who have the patience to see." Meinwen extended an arm. "Shall we?"

Susan nodded. "Let me just phone the house then and tell them I'll be a bit late back."

Meinwen nodded. She and the inspector withdrew a few feet to allow her to make the call in private. He tapped her on the arm. "Could you leave off the mumbo-jumbo? I prefer 'crime doesn't pay.'"

Meinwen patted his arm. "That's right. Usually it's the insurance companies that fork out."

* * * *

It was a good day for croquet, Jean thought as she measured the distance between her ball and Nicole's. Robert's favourite game--other than "hunt the sausage"--seemed a fitting tribute to the man she'd treated like a brother since her husband died. The balls flowed gracefully over the dense mat of freshly tended lawn and Amanda had served drinks in her funeral attire. She judged they had time for another game before the sun got too low to play, leaving her just enough time to thrash the staff before dinner.

* * * *

Meinwen led the way into the shop and sorted out another two chairs, placing them in a triangle to promote conversation. "Do sit. We just want a little chat with you."

Susan did as she was asked, glancing from Meinwen to White and back. "What about Jack? Is he in trouble?"

"He is if he doesn't have an alibi." White sat on one of the remaining chairs. "I can soon have him dragged back here unless he can prove he isn't the murderer."

"He isn't. Jack's a good lad who works hard at his studies. He was with me from seven until nine."

"What were you doing?" Meinwen sat back in her chair, her hand straying to her pentacle necklace. Holding it seemed to stave off her headache.

Susan rubbed her face with her hands. "He needed money. He'd had an argument with his father and wanted to move out and get his own place nearer the university. He lives about ten miles from it, you see. He told me he was coming and I dashed off to meet him from the train. That would be about seven. I took him for dinner at that Italian place on Cheap Street."

"I know the one." White wrote it down. "La Caverna. I can check that."

Susan nodded. "We talked for about an hour and a half. I can recommend the carbonara, by the way."

"Thanks. I'll give it a try." White looked up. "Beryl likes a good meal out."

"Well, when we finished eating I gave him the money I'd drawn out for him. He said it wasn't enough so I made a phone call to my solicitor and she lent me the money."

"At that time of night?" White frowned. "That doesn't sound likely."

Susan took a card from her wallet. "It's Isaacs and Du Pointe's on Market Street. Ms. du Point only works at night, though she has staff during the day."

"Why would a solicitor lend you money? I've never heard of solicitors lending money to their clients before."

Meinwen coughed. "I think I know the answer to that one. She lent it to you against your inheritance, didn't she?" She looked at the business card. It did indeed specify night hours.

Susan didn't even look surprised this time. "That's right. Mum didn't have much in the way of money, less than twelve thousand in fact, but she did own two houses outright." She smiled weakly at Meinwen. "I'm your new landlady, I'm afraid."

White gestured with his pen. "Wait a minute. Are you telling me you're Grace Peters's daughter?"

"That's exactly what she's saying." Meinwen picked up the solicitor's card and used it to emphasize her points. "She bought a house in Birmingham with her husband John in nineteen eighty-one and they had Jack in nineteen eighty-five." She looked at Susan for confirmation, who nodded. "Susan left in nineteen eighty-seven."

Susan nodded. "Rover made John redundant. It had been touch and go with the Longbridge plant for years, what with their ownership changing regularly, but they'd always kept him on until then. We used part of his redundancy to pay off the mortgage but he squandered the rest and turned to drinking. He got violent afterwards and when he broke my arm I knew I had to leave."

"Why did you leave your son behind?"

"He said he'd let me go if I left Jack." Susan looked into the middle distance. "I wanted to take him, but he threatened to hunt us down if I did." She shrugged. "He was always a good father and I wasn't afraid on Jack's behalf so I let him keep him." Her eyes caught Meinwen's. "It was the hardest thing I've ever done, but I was right to do it."

Meinwen chewed her lip. "So you moved in with your mam, changed your name back to Susan Pargeter and started a new life."

"That's right. Mum had remarried as well. Dad died during the Falklands War. Henry was a charmer. I wasn't surprised she fell in love with him. I stayed there for ten years until I met Robert and took on the role of nanny for Richard. Not that he needed it. Richard was an independent ten year old when I met him, almost resentful of the fact I had some of Robert's attention."

White tapped his notebook with his pencil. "Let's get back to last Tuesday for a minute. You left your son, Jack Rogers, and went to this solicitor--"

"Gillian du Pointe."

"Yes. Why was Jack looking for The Larches? Why didn't he just go with you or meet you back at the train station."

"I had to get back to work. Robert was in the habit of working at night and needed me to type up his files for him. Jack was in no hurry, so he said he'd meet me back there for the money before going home. I gave him the directions but he must have got lost. I met him back at the house at twenty past nine, we said our goodbyes and he left."

"Did you run after him?"

Susan nodded. "I did, actually. I wanted to ask him for his email address."

Meinwen nodded. "Then it was you Peter saw when he came back from the pub."

White smiled. "Thank you, Ms. Pargeter. Assuming the restaurant and Ms. du Pointe confirm your visits that will be both your alibis confirmed."

Susan nodded. "Thank you. You will keep this secret, won't you? I wouldn't like my past generally known."

"Of course." It was Meinwen's turn to smile. "You can be assured of my discretion."

"I appreciate that." Susan stood.

"Just one more thing."

Susan turned again. "Yes?"

"Why did you give your mother the heroin?"

* * * *

Jean Markhew whacked Nicole's croquet ball into the bushes and used the free shot to nudge hers into the finishing post. She grinned at the three other players. "My game, I think. I'll have to devise your forfeits."

She motioned to the maid. "Amanda? Collect up the set. You can leave the hoops out but the balls and mallets need to be put away."

"What about the yellow, ma'am?"

"The yellow? Oh, Nicole's." She stared at the secretary. "She can fetch that one herself."

* * * *

Even the inspector looked surprised. "What heroin?"

Susan slumped back into her chair. "How did you know?"

"Your mother had heroin in her system. She was being blackmailed and wouldn't have dared to ask Father Brande for it. Her only other regular visitor was her daughter. You were the only one she could ask."

Susan nodded. "Yes, I gave it to her and showed her how to use it. She wouldn't tell me who the blackmailer was, though, in case they came after me. She was at her wits' end and terrified of the truth coming out. She felt killing herself was the only way out. What could I do but help her?" Susan began to cry and Meinwen handed her a silk cloth. "I didn't help her do it or anything, just got her the packet of drugs."

Meinwen held out a hand to stifle White's questions. "Why did she kill her husband?"

Susan looked up, the tears stopping as anger flashed to the surface. "Henry abused her. When I left he began to resent the way she didn't keep the house as clean as I did, or the washing wasn't done on time, or she didn't cook as well as I had. He began by just being cruel to her. Turning off the television when she was watching something or refusing to take her out in the car. By the time she killed him she was black and blue almost constantly. He broke her leg and her arm. It was always an accident but I recognized the signs. She just couldn't take it any more."

"So she strangled him."

"More like she let him strangle himself. She made the knot in his rope self tightening."

White coughed. "Henry Peters died from auto-asphyxiation. He came and went, as it were."

Meinwen grimaced.

Susan clenched her teeth. "She was right to do it. I'd support anyone in the same situation."

Meinwen put her hand one the woman's knee. "Thank you for being honest with us."

White stood and helped her up. "Where did you get the heroin, Ms. Pargeter? From your son?"

Susan looked at him. "You'd never prove it. He doesn't use it and he doesn't deal in it. He just knew someone who knew someone."

"It doesn't matter." Meinwen shot a warning glance at White. "He won't be arrested, will he, Inspector?"

* * * *

Meinwen locked the shop. "This investigation has cost me a week's work. Is there any chance I can claim for loss of earnings?"

"Nope." White walked on in silence until Meinwen caught up. "I'll buy you a meal when we close the case. How about that?"

"Sounds like I'm not going to get a better offer." Meinwen laughed. "Fish and chips on the beach?"

"I can do fish and chips on the edge of the boating lake." White grinned. "I should prosecute for the drugs, you know."

"Does it really matter?" Meinwen asked. "Neither of them are users or dealers and Grace Peters is past caring. Concentrate on the blackmailer and the killer instead."

"I suppose." White walked on a little. "I wish I'd known."

"About what?"

"About Henry Peters. I'd have had his hide."

Meinwen shook her head. "The trouble with domestic abuse is that the abused don't think there's anyone to turn to for help."

"But there is. It's part of my job."

Meinwen nodded. "It's a funny thing but battered wives rarely want to get their husbands into trouble. They love them, see."

* * * *

The crack of a whip sounded like gunfire as it echoed from the walls of the white-painted house. Jean Markhew tested it again, first an overhand then a circular over-the-head crack, pulling the leather body of the single tail back to wrap like a strand of DNA around her body as it came to rest.

Nicole flinched. The whip hadn't touched her, not yet, but she knew this was going to hurt. The trunk of the beech tree felt rough against her naked arms and breasts, though Jean had allowed her to retain her black skirt and boots in an uncharacteristic gesture of public decency.

Not that there were any public present. The long garden was walled with hedges and trees, and no other houses overlooked the secluded lawn and specimen beech tree.

"Are you ready?" Jean's voice sounded too close for the four-foot whip. Nicole shook her head. "Yellow."

Jean tutted. "You can't safe-word before I've done anything. How would I trust you to safe-word when it hurts unbearably if you cry yellow before I've even started?"

"Sorry, Mistress." Nicole sniffed. "I hate whips. Always have."

"For now." Nicole could hear the smile in her voice. "Don't safe-word until you mean it. Shout, cry, scream all you like, but don't safe-word unless you have to."

Nicole nodded and Jean began with dog-tailing, a movement of the whip from side to side. No crack and hardly any sting, the frayed end of the cracker danced lightly across Nicole's back.

She closed her eyes. Perhaps whips weren't as scary as she'd thought.

* * * *

The email from Hertfordshire Constabulary stood out at the top of the list flagged as important. Meinwen smiled as she read it. Sergeant Peters was a good man. She clicked "print" and logged in to chat.

Scribe: Jennifer? Are you online?
Cacoethes: Yes? I'm writing, so I can't chat.
Scribe: Oh, okay. Just wanted to pass on the news.
Cacoethes: What news?
Scribe: LOL I thought you were busy.

Cacoethes: Not any more! Spill!
Scribe: I just spoke to Inspector White…
Cacoethes: Yes?
Scribe: He says that they've found Richard Godwin.
Cacoethes: Really? Where?
Scribe: Trying to board the Eurostar. They've arrested him.
Cacoethes: Oh God! Did he do it then?
Scribe: They think so. I'll let you know if I get more details.
Cacoethes: Do!
Scribe: Good night.
>>>*Scribe has logged off*
Cacoethes: Shygirl23? Are you there?

Chapter 29

Inspector White jumped when his phone rang and glanced at the clock on the mantelpiece. The television was showing a program for teenagers who should, since it was almost midnight, have been in bed long ago. He blinked himself into consciousness and pressed "answer."

"Ms. Jones? Do you know what time it is?"

"Half-eleven. Listen! I need you to announce you've caught Richard. It'll provoke the murderer into doing something rash."

"But we haven't caught him yet."

"It doesn't matter. I'm sure I can find him. Say you caught him boarding the Eurostar to Paris or something."

He frowned. "I'm not sure that's ethical… Well, all right. I'm willing to play along with it. I'll tell the duty staff."

He put the phone down and switched the television off. The cocoa Beryl had left him had gone cold long ago, leaving a thick skin on the top. White grimaced, spitting the mouthful back into the cup.

One phone call to the station then he was off to bed.

* * * *

Jennifer was waiting for him when Simon got up the next morning, pacing the length of the rectory hall. "They've caught Richard. You've got to do something about it, Simon. I know he's innocent."

Simon frowned. "How do you know he's been caught? Who told you?"

"Meinwen. It's all over the 'net."

Simon grunted. "Was it all over the 'net before she told you or afterwards?" Her face fell and he gave her a hug. "I'm sorry. I shouldn't have said that. If the police have found Richard then I'm sure they'll be able to clear him soon. If he really is innocent they won't be able to prove otherwise."

"I do hope you're right." Jennifer followed him into the kitchen. "When will we find out, do you think?"

"How should I know? You'd be better off asking Meinwen. It looks like she has the ear of the police, not me."

"I will, as soon as she's finished with that man."

Simon sighed. "What man?" He began filling a mug with coffee from the pot.

"I don't know who he was. He did seem vaguely familiar, but I could only see his back. That's the trouble with the study window being at the back of the house. I can't see anyone as they go up the drive to The Herbage, only when they get to the door."

"Perhaps he's one of her lovers. Or a devil she's induced into service. They could be having passionate, illicit sex right now on the dining room table."

"I doubt it. Firstly, she hasn't got a dining room and secondly--" The doorbell rang. "She's at the door."

Simon laughed and answered it. "You're up and about early. What can I do for you today?"

Meinwen bustled inside in her heavy black coat and fedora, two pheasant feathers wedged into its brim. "Is that coffee I can smell? May I have a cup? Hello, Jennifer." She went into the kitchen without waiting for an answer. "Ooh, it's fresh."

"A bit like her," Jennifer whispered to Simon.

Meinwen poured herself a mug of the coffee and bustled back out. "Mind if I take this with me? I'll bring the mug back later."

"Erm…" Jennifer raised a hand but Meinwen had already gone out of the door.

"Come on, Simon," she called back. "We've work to do."

"What?" Simon said. "I've got calls to make. My parishioners…"

"Do as you're told," said Jennifer, laughing at his discomfort as she fetched his coat. "You have to do as Meinwen says."

"What if she tells me to eat my greens?" Simon grinned as he shrugged on his overcoat.

"Ugh." Jennifer straightened his collar. "I wouldn't go that far."

Simon hurried out, grabbing his briefcase and half-jogging to catch up with the Welsh woman.

* * * *

Nicole woke up cold. The cover Jean had thrown over her the night before had slipped off onto the floor.

"Good morning." Amanda placed a cup of coffee within easy reach. "Mistress says you're excused of duties this morning. She's very pleased with you."

"Mistress? Jean, you mean?"

"Of course I mean Jean." Amanda smiled. "Take your time getting up. There's no hurry, but she'd like to see you in her room when you're ready."

Nicole nodded and shifted position. Her movements were accompanied by the rattle of a chain, and she looked with dismay at the shackles connecting her ankles to the bed. "Have you got the key?"

Amanda grinned. "No."

"Then how am I supposed to go to her room?"

Amanda smiled as she opened the curtains and went to leave. "That's for you to figure out," she said. "She didn't mention it to me."

Nicole watched her leave then sat up to drink her coffee, the chains rattling through the bars of the bed as she shifted position.

* * * *

Susan paused when she heard the Welsh woman calling her. She turned to see Meinwen striding along the pavement. "Are you coming to The Larches?"

"That's right." Meinwen nodded at the empty basket on Susan's arm. "Going shopping?"

"No. I've been up to the church to put some fresh flowers in."

They both watched the priest pound up to them and bend almost double, his hands on his knees, to catch his breath. "You run well for a vicar." Meinwen cocked her head to one side and half-smiled.

"I keep telling you. I'm a priest, not a vicar. Where are we going?" He straightened. "Hello, Susan."

"Just for a walk." Meinwen's stride belied her words as she fell into step with Susan.

"The Larches? Why are we going there again?"

"I need you to do something for me. Mrs. Markhew respects you when she won't give me the time of day. I need you to ask them all to come to my house this evening."

"That's not really true." Susan slowed her pace. "She just doesn't know you yet. You'll see, in time."

"Your house? Why?" Simon fell into step. "This would be a quicker walk if we went through the woods."

Meinwen shuddered. "I have some information that will shed light on the case and I need everyone to look at the murder with a fresh perspective."

"Oh." Simon fell silent for several minutes as they walked through streets still damp from the overnight rain. "Who was it at your house this morning? Jennifer saw a man knocking on your door."

"Ah. He brought me some very important information. That's why I want this meeting tonight."

"You're not going to tell me who it was, are you?"

Meinwen grinned. "And take all the fun out of Jennifer's guessing?"

"And mine." Susan looked at the woman. She was too full of secrets, that one. Full enough to burst.

They arrived at The Larches after a brisk twenty minutes, Simon red-faced and gasping like the world was about to end. He paused to regain his breath at the bottom of the drive. "Tell me why walking is better than driving again? My carbon footprint's about to become a carbon ankle."

"Because, A, walking is good for you, B, it saves burning fossil fuel unnecessarily and, C, I don't have a car."

"But I do."

"And, D, I don't trust your driving."

"I'm hurt. Very well. What time do you want them?"

"About nine?" Meinwen shrank back into the laurels bordering the gate. "I'll be right here."

Simon nodded, straightened up and took a deep breath. "Right. Wish me luck."

"Luck is an external influence denied by your God. But have some from mine."

"Thanks, I think." He took a last look at her and walked up the drive to the door.

"I'll leave you here, Father. Best we're not seen together. People might talk."

"As you wish, Susan. Good day." He pulled the antique doorbell as she strode to the back of the house, but once around the corner Susan paused to listen.

"Father Brande." Amanda's voice trilled. She sounded nervous. "The day just wouldn't feel the same without one of your visits. What can we do for you this time? Sing songs? Perform a dance?"

"I need to see Mrs. Markhew. It is rather urgent."

"Of course it is. I'll see if she's available. Would you like something to drink while you wait?"

"Tea would be nice. I missed my chance this morning with having to dash out."

"I'll see if there's anyone in the kitchen."

Susan scurried to the back door.

* * * *

Susan dried her hands on a tea towel as Amanda arrived in the kitchen. "Yes, love?"

"Would you make Father Brande a cup of tea, please? He's in the hall."

"Sure. Have you seen Catherine today? She's not in her room."

"I thought she was leaving?"

"She is, but her bags are still there."

Amanda shook her head. "If I see her I'll mention you want her. I have to go up to Mistress. Father Brande wants to see her."

"This early in the morning? She's not going to be pleased. I doubt she's even dressed."

* * * *

Meinwen hoisted herself onto the low wall opposite the drive of The Larches and took the coffee mug from her pocket. Not a single drop had spilled and it was still hot, despite the walk from the rectory.

She rested it on the wall and waited.

* * * *

Nicole used a metal nail file from her bedside drawer to unscrew the top rail from the foot of the bed. Taking out the screw at one side enabled her to lift it just far enough to slide the chain free. She hurried to the bathroom, enormously relieved.

* * * *

"Father Brande." Jean had dressed in black again. It was always good to be on the right side of the priest, even if she did consider him overly pompous.

"Jean." Simon stood and offered his hand. "It's good of you to see me."

"Yes, it is. What is it you want today?"

"Meinwen would like you to all come to The Herbage this evening. She has a matter of great importance to discuss with everyone about the murder."

"Oh?" Jean narrowed her eyes. "What might that be?"

"I'm afraid she wouldn't tell me."

"So you are her lapdog now, running errands for her. Very well. Tell her we will come."

"Thank you." Simon hesitated. "It has to be everybody, though."

"Of course. Except Richard, naturally. Is it true that the police have captured him? I know Mary couldn't believe it. I had to ask Nicole to verify it with the inspector."

"I'm sorry. I'm sure he's innocent."

"I expect he is. I don't know why he was boarding the Eurostar, though."

"Nor I." Simon folded his hands in a gesture of prayer. "I'm sure the police will clear him."

"Let us hope so." Jean ran her finger across the Pieta. "I must say that I wasn't keen on Mary and Richard marrying if he was a murderer but assuming he's innocent I look forward to the match."

"Richard will be very well off. At least Mary won't have to steal any more to buy clothes."

"My daughter didn't steal anything. It was just a small matter of her not wishing to disturb Robert when he was working, otherwise she would have just asked him for money he'd have been happy to give."

"I'm sure that's the case. No one thinks less of her, Jean. She's a lovely girl."

"Exactly." Jean shook his hand and motioned for Amanda to see him out. "Good day to you."

* * * *

Jean smiled at the half-naked woman. "That's a very sweet picture. Well done for having the initiative. What did you do? Take your bed apart?"

Nicole smiled back. "Yes, ma'am. That's exactly what I did."

Jean looked at her carefully. From the waist up she was every inch the business woman in her smart blouse, perfect make-up and hair tied neatly into butterfly clips. From the waist down, however, she was a naked slut.

"That image works for me," Jean said. "I might have you at your desk like that taking conference calls. It would amuse me."

"If you wish, ma'am." Nicole's cheeks weren't the only place heated with embarrassment at the scenario. "May I ask something, though?"

"Of course." Jean waited.

"How was I supposed to get out of bed to meet you in your room?"

Jean raised an eyebrow. "I left you your phone, didn't I? You could have asked me for release."

* * * *

"How did it go?" Meinwen strode back toward the rectory, leaving Simon to catch up with her again.

"They'll be there. She called me your lapdog for doing your dirty work, so thanks a bunch for the loss of respect."

"My dirty work?" Meinwen smiled. "Does that make you a dirty vicar?"

"That's C of E," said Simon. "Anyway, in the popular vernacular, I believe it makes me your bitch."

Meinwen stopped and looked up at him, her eyebrows raised. "Language, Father."

He grinned and carried on. "You should have seen Jean Markhew, all dressed in black again. I can't help wondering if it's for the sake of decorum or if it's her preferred colour. She either owns a lot of black clothes or else she goes to a lot of funerals."

"A bit of both, probably. My mam wore black more often than not."

"Yes, but…" Simon faltered. "Aren't you going to tell me what this surprise is?"

"Nope." Meinwen smiled. "If I told you, you'd tell Jennifer and then the whole world would know."

"I can keep a secret." Simon turned into his own drive, Meinwen following.

"Like the one about the ring, for example?"

Simon coughed. "That just slipped out."

"Exactly." Meinwen smiled and took the mug from her pocket as Simon opened the door and ushered her inside.

Jennifer sat on the sofa cradling a crying woman. She looked up as they bustled in. "It's Catherine, although I've no idea why she's crying. She says she'll only talk to you, Simon."

Meinwen put the cup on the table and crouched next to the girl. "Catherine? Everything will be all right. You can talk to us. We know your secret, Mrs. Godwin."

Chapter 30

With a glance at Jennifer for permission, Meinwen slid onto the sofa and put her arms around Catherine. "It's all right. There's nothing to be afraid of here."

Catherine shook her head, her long dark hair unkempt and tangled. Her sobs began to diminish as Meinwen rocked her like a child.

Simon looked across at Jennifer with raised eyebrows "Mrs. Godwin?" he mouthed.

His sister held up her hands in a silent "don't ask me" gesture. Meinwen caught the exchange. "I expect we could all do with a nice cup of tea. I think Catherine would like a little sugar to sweeten hers, as well."

"That's a good idea." Jennifer smiled acidly at her brother. "Why don't you go and make it, Simon?"

"Me?" Simon looked affronted. "All right, I'm going." He headed into the kitchen and began banging cups about.

Meinwen raised her eyebrows at Jennifer and gestured to the box of tissues. Jennifer handed them over, jerking her head in the direction of the kitchen and mouthing "men!"

Meinwen lifted Catherine's head up. "There, there. Tears are good but hope is better." She wiped away the tears around Catherine's eyes and gave her the tissue. Catherine attempted a smile and completed the task, finishing by blowing her nose.

"There now," said Meinwen, when the girl had composed herself. "What are all the tears in aid of?"

"They've caught Richard." Catherine sniffed, her eyes filling again. "They think he murdered his stepfather and they're going to send him to prison."

Meinwen wiped away another tear that ran down the girl's cheek. What was it about tears that she found so erotic? "Sometimes rumours are just rumours."

"But Amanda phoned the police station and confirmed it." She looked for the tissues again.

Meinwen handed her the box. "Have a little faith in the boys in blue. They won't put Richard away if he's innocent, will they? This is real life, not a television show. They're much cleverer than that. It's a long time since they put people in prison because they looked suspicious."

"Really?" Catherine dabbed at her eyes. "He won't go to prison and be ravished in the showers?"

"Not if he's innocent, no." Meinwen smiled.

"Unless he wants to be," Jennifer added.

Meinwen glared at her. "Look, here's Simon with the tea. Pull yourself together a bit and then you can tell us the whole story."

"I'll try." Catherine shuffled backward on the floor and gained the relative safety and aloofness of the armchair, hoisting herself into it but leaning forward defensively, her mug of sweet tea held in both hands and her head down as if she were inhaling eucalyptus for a cold.

"I came down here for Robert," she said, rubbing her pendant, a Celtic knot in a circular pattern, between thumb and forefinger. "I met him online in a chat room and he seemed to be everything I was looking for. He was my chance to get away from my family for a bit." She glanced at Simon, who had seated himself in the other armchair but unlike Catherine was filling the chair and the space around it with the air of a lord of the manor.

"I come from a big family, see," Catherine said. "Catholic. Mum never believed in birth control and I had four sisters and three brothers. Four, if you count Mikey, but he died at birth. We never had a spare penny. Dad was a fork-lift driver--good money if you haven't many mouths to feed. Mum did what she could but there were too many of us for her to work full-time, so she did part-time at the school crossing. Anyway, I went to college when I was sixteen. Just the local tech, nothing fancy, and that's where I learned about computers."

Meinwen nodded. "I can relate to that. Go on."

"I got a part time job in the chippy and saved up enough to buy a laptop. Just a basic one along with a broadband package. It got me out of myself, you see. Showed me other worlds I was missing. That's when I found the chat rooms."

"I can guess what you're missing out," Simon said. "There's really no need. I may be a priest but I have heard of sex." He grinned. "After all, my sister is quite the author of erotica."

"Are you?" Catherine's eyes widened. "I didn't know. What have you written?"

Jennifer shrugged, suddenly modest. "Simon's exaggerating. I've published one or two. Have you read She Died for Passion or The Clergyman's Confession?"

Catherine shook her head. "Sorry. I'll look out for them, though. I was more into Mills and Boon and Black Lace, I'm afraid." She hitched up her jeans to scratch her ankle, displaying a tattooed anklet chain in a Celtic weave.

Jennifer shrugged. "Perhaps I ought to spice up my books with bondage."

"What happened in the chat rooms?" Meinwen tried to steer the conversation back to Catherine's story.

"I met Robert a few weeks later," Catherine said. "I'd met all sorts by then. Men pretending to be girls and girls pretending to be men. I had to trawl through all the troglodytes in the country first. It was like a test. Those who didn't just want a quick shag wanted somebody to whip them, and a few of them sounded more like serial killers in the making. Robert was a breath of fresh air in a stuffy chip shop. I could see myself with him, you see. The more blogs and websites I found that told me about women who loved older men, the more I knew that I was one of them. We started talking about a relationship."

"Was he easy to talk to?"

"Not at first. He was different, though. He made me feel safe from the start, didn't try to make me do anything I didn't want to do, and pointed me to a few places where I could find out about him, prove to myself that he was a real person."

"Go on." Meinwen picked up her forgotten tea. It was already only lukewarm. She began to drink it anyway. Robert had never taken her that seriously.

"I wanted to meet him." Catherine smiled. "He was so careful. He made me set up a safe call first before he'd even tell me where he lived."

"A safe call?" Simon leaned forward in his chair.

"It's where you arrange for a friend to phone you to make sure you're all right," Meinwen explained. "The friend knows who you're meeting and where. If you're in trouble you say a pre-arranged codeword, such as 'I've got my lucky socks on' and the friend phones the police without the person you're meeting knowing that something is wrong."

Simon nodded. "That sounds very sensible. So did you wear your lucky socks when you met Robert?"

"I didn't have to," said Catherine. "He was a perfect gentleman. We met in the Corner Rooms Tea House on Lovat Street."

"It went well then?"

"It certainly did. I handed in my notice at the chippy and was back with my bag within a fortnight. He took me in on a month's trial and gave me a room."

"What happened then?" Meinwen thought about how close she had come to being in exactly the same situation.

"I had the duties of a maid to begin with, and cooking when Susan was off-duty. He gave me a uniform and everything. It was like being in an old film. We always had to wear stockings, too." She smiled for the first time since she'd been there. "That's when I met Richard. He was everything his stepfather was and more. He was my age you see, or near enough. I ended up looking after him more than I looked after Robert."

"How did Richard feel about this?" Jennifer was hunched forward, leaning on every word. Meinwen could imagine her writing it up as a novel.

"He fell in love with me. Asked him to marry him."

"When?" Simon sat up again. "He never told me."

"Valentine's Day. Robert wouldn't have approved of his precious heir marrying a poor girl from south of the river, though. That's why we had to marry in secret. He had a lot of debts and if Robert had found out he'd married me he would have cut him out of the will."

"Debts?" Meinwen's tone was nonchalant. "What were they for?"

Catherine shrugged. "College, I think. Student loans and a whopping overdraft. We kept the marriage secret by using the White Art instead of the house. Mike gave Richard a good rate for the room and kept our secret for us."

"Then Mr. Markhew insisted that Richard marry Mary."

Catherine's face clouded. "Yes. I didn't know about it at first. Richard told me the old man was suspicious about us. That's why he seemed to cool off toward me. I sort of thought Mary found out, but didn't think she'd give a toss either way. Richard was giving her money to keep her quiet, he said. She didn't love him, nor he her. They were more like brother and sister than anything." Catherine relinquished her mug. Jennifer took it off her and gave it to Simon, who put it on the coffee table.

"Richard was hoping for the inheritance before he told anyone that you and he were married then?"

"That's right. We saw each other a bit less for appearances' sake, but the sex was even better when we did manage it. The trouble came when Robert announced that Richard and Mary were engaged. I think Mrs. Markhew was pushing for it. Suddenly I realized that it was actually going to happen, and what would become of me? I was already his wife but I was being pushed out. I didn't know what to do. It's not like I could afford a solicitor."

"You confronted Richard?"

"What else could I do? I was devastated. He promised me that it was all a sham, that Mary didn't really want to marry him. It was all for the inheritance, you see. Richard promised to split it with her. He told me to be patient."

"This was in the park, wasn't it?" asked Jennifer. "I was in the woods and heard you, but I didn't know who Richard was talking to."

"By the wall, yes. I didn't think we'd be overheard there." Catherine frowned. "Anyway, I didn't want to be patient. I wanted my husband, all official-like. So I marched up to Mr. Markhew and had it out with him, interrupted his writing, as well."

"He didn't take it well, did he?"

"I should say not. He offered to buy me off there and then. Told me I'd come to him on false pretences and gave me my notice. We had a huge row about it and I stormed off. I didn't want to see either of them no more."

"What did you do then?" Meinwen shifted position on the sofa, glancing at the fascinated expressions of Simon and Jennifer.

Catherine gave a half smile. "I went to the cinema and saw the new Disney film. By the time I came out I'd calmed down a bit. I looked at my phone and found six missed calls from having it off in the cinema. I rang Richard to meet me in the park again."

"And you fought."

Catherine nodded, her fingers straying once more to her necklace. "He was furious with me because Robert had shouted at him, threatened to cut him out of the will altogether if he didn't get the marriage annulled."

"That's when you threw your wedding ring at him?"

Catherine laughed. "Yes, I was a bit dramatic. I stamped on it too! Richard stormed off back to the house and I went to the chippy." She sighed. "I sneaked back to the house at about half-past six, expecting Richard to find me and apologize. I hid in my room after that to just keep out of everybody's way. I didn't wake up again until the police came at nearly midnight and Robert was dead."

She looked at Meinwen. "I didn't have anything to do with his death, I swear."

"Nobody thinks you did." Jennifer rose from the sofa to cuddle the girl. "No one would suspect you of killing Robert, even if you did have an argument with him."

"I hope not." Catherine dabbed her eyes with a fresh tissue. "Richard didn't do it either. He's got more sense than that. You can't inherit by murder." She looked at each of the three faces.

Meinwen coughed. "If he's innocent, he'll soon be cleared."

Simon leaned forward. "How did you know about the marriage, Meinwen? I hadn't even got an inkling."

"You forget what I am. A woman knows these things." Meinwen got off the sofa and stretched her legs. "Besides, I remembered Catherine wore Celtic jewellery and guessed the ring Mary found must be hers. I did a search and found out that there was no record of her being married, so she must have married in secret and quite recently." She shrugged. "Richard wouldn't have dared order rings online in case someone asked him about the package or, worse still, it got delivered to The Larches and Robert opened it. There are only three jewellers in town, and only one that sells Celtic wedding bands. The rest was just charm and questions." She looked at Jennifer. "Mind if I use your bathroom?"

Jennifer made another cup of tea. When Meinwen returned, feeling a little fresher than she had done, she squatted in front of Catherine. "Here's your ring, Mary found it and would have claimed it for herself. Be a bit more careful with it in future?"

"Thanks." Catherine slipped it back on. "I didn't realize how much I'd miss it."

Meinwen held her fingers lightly to admire the ring in its rightful place. "I have one more question."

"Yes?"

"What cellphone did Richard have?"

Catherine shrugged. "A Nokia. One with a camera. I've got the number if you want it. Why?"

Meinwen shook her head. "I think the police found it at the scene."

Chapter 31

Meinwen stood. "I can't hang about here all day. I should be doing an inventory."

"Would anyone like another cup of tea?" Jennifer placed a hand on Catherine's knee and the girl looked up.

"No, thank you." Catherine sighed. "I need to think about all this and work out what I'm going to do."

"You're welcome to stay here. You can rest in my room if you like, and I can make up a bed on the sofa for you."

"I couldn't presume..." Catherine was hopeful.

Jennifer smiled and held out a hand to help her up from the chair. "Think nothing of it. I'll show you where my room is."

"Thank you."

Meinwen watched them go. "Remember I need you at the meeting at my house at nine."

Catherine stopped. "Must I? I don't think I could face any of them."

"I insist." Meinwen winked. "Don't worry, though. I'll hex anyone who says anything to you."

Catherine laughed. "All right." She took out her phone. "I'll set an alarm for eight."

Simon waited until they heard footsteps in his sister's room. "Do you think she was telling the truth?"

Meinwen nodded. "Probably. I can't see her murdering Mr. Markhew. What good would it have done? Would her marriage last if she'd killed her father-in-law? Richard wouldn't stay with a murderess."

"No." Simon tapped his finger against his lips. "He's a very trusting young man."

"You're very fond of him, aren't you?"

"I am. The lad shows a lot of promise. I had hoped he might go into the clergy, but he studied psychology at university instead of divinities."

"Did he now?" Meinwen tied her hair back. "That's interesting. Was he involved in his uncle's work at all?"

"The kinky books?" Simon shook his head. "I don't think so. Is it important?"

"Everything is important, Father." Meinwen smiled and patted him on the shoulder. "I must be off. I have things to do before the meeting."

"Do you know who the murderer is?"

Meinwen paused in the act of opening the door. "Let's just say that I know who it isn't." She smiled. "See you later."

* * * *

Jean Markhew took the key from her pocket and slipped the silver chain from Nicole's ankle, folding the chain in two and dropping it into her jewellery box.

Nicole rubbed at the reddened skin where the chain had chafed. "Thank you, ma'am."

Jean nodded. "Until we know how the will is going to be divided I cannot and will not claim you for my own, even if you wish it."

Nicole bowed her head. "I understand. I'm sure that the police will sort it out soon."

"I hope so." Jean removed a gold chain from the box on her dresser. "If you're amenable, I'd like you to wear this in the meantime."

Nicole stood up straight. "I would be honoured, ma'am." She dropped to one knee, drawing up her hair so the tattoo of the twin R's was exposed.

Jean threaded the chain around her neck and clicked the heart-shaped padlock into place.

* * * *

Meinwen took the long way round into town but had to hurry to get out of sight in case Simon left the rectory to go to St. Pity's. She didn't want him seeing her talking to Tom, who was trimming the grass around the tombs with a pair of long-handled shears.

"Afternoon," he said. "Come to look at Old Mab again?"

"Actually, it's you I've come to see." She took his arm and led him to the side of a tomb, out of sight of the church. "I know your secret."

* * * *

Meinwen pulled the coffee table in front of her chair at the shop and spread a silk cloth over it, shuffling and spreading her tarot deck. She studied the results. So many major arcana cards were unusual in a ten-card Celtic cross spread and she mused upon the positions of The Hierophant, The Hermit and The Lovers.

She shuffled the cards again and did two quick three-card draws to confirm what the full reading had told her then put them away again. The hermit had come between the two lovers but was occluded by the priest.

Could Robert be thought of as a hermit? She suspected so. His lifestyle had certainly been an alternative one.

When she left the shop at five, she happened to glance across at the bookshop. Mr. Jasfoup stood in the window watching her. He raised his hand in greeting.

Meinwen shuddered.

* * * *

When Catherine arrived at The Herbage at eight-thirty, accompanied by Simon and Jennifer, Meinwen let them in and showed them through to a sitting room crowded with chairs and stools.

"It'll be a bit of a squeeze." Meinwen moved a rug. "And one or two might have to sit on the floor but at least we'll be cozy." She went into the kitchen. "Catherine? Could I ask you to make up a pot of coffee and set the cups out? I want to lay out a few snacks."

Catherine followed her into the kitchen, spotting the crockery and all but colliding with Simon, who stood in the doorway.

"Is there anything I can do to help?" He clasped his hands together. "I'm quite handy with a teapot, I'm told."

Meinwen smiled. "By all means. A pot of green tea would be very welcome."

"Green tea?" He drew air through his teeth. "Ah well. If you insist."

Catherine laughed at the look on the priest's face.

Meinwen shook her head. "I'll make the green. You sort out some for yourself. There's a box of Assam in the cupboard. I bought it specially." She carried a tray of snacks to the living room and touched Catherine's arm. "It's ten minutes before the other guests arrive. Mind if I check my email?"

Catherine had just finished making a pot of coffee when the knocking came and would have answered the door had Simon not beaten her to it.

"What's all this about, Father?" Jean led the retinue from The Larches and glared at Meinwen. "I am getting heartily sick of all this kafuffle over the death of my brother-in-law."

"It won't be much longer," said Meinwen. "I assure you, this will all be resolved very shortly. That's part of the reason I asked you all here tonight."

"I hope so." Jean glared at Catherine. "Where have you been all day?"

"She's been with me." Meinwen folded her arms. "Mrs. Godwin and I have had quite a chat."

"Mrs. Godwin?" Jean looked puzzled, her eyes seeking her daughter.

Meinwen coughed. "Not Mary, Mrs. Markhew. Catherine. She and Richard married in secret six weeks ago."

It gave Catherine some satisfaction to see the look of shock that passed over the older woman's face.

"Oh," she said. "Oh."

"Simon?" Meinwen took charge again. "Would you help Mrs. Markhew to a seat and perhaps fetch her a glass of water?"

Simon steadied one of Jean's arms while Amanda took the other. When she was safely in one of the armchairs, Jean stared at Catherine. "That's why you wanted to leave. You have your own master now."

Catherine smiled. "I'm sorry for the deception but Robert would never have stood for it. He wanted Richard to marry Mary."

"I know." Jean composed herself. It was fascinating to watch, thought Catherine. It was as if she were two different people. All the confusion and hurt was drawn inside and enclosed in a hard, dominant exterior. Now she was as cold and as calculating as ever, despite the huge shock she'd just had--not only to her hopes for her daughter, but for her financial security.

"Where is…your husband?" Jean took a deep breath. "Was he really arrested?"

Catherine lowered her eyes. "He's been here all along. In Laverstone, I mean. Someone was trying to frame him."

"Don't worry about Richard's whereabouts just yet." Meinwen drew the attention back to herself.

"Where is he?" Jean leaned forward. "He's wanted by the police. If you're sheltering him…"

Meinwen raised a hand. "All will be revealed in good time." She pulled a sheet of paper from her printer tray. "Now, are we all here?" She read out the names on the sheet. "Mrs. Jean Markhew and her daughter Mary." She nodded to them both. "Mrs. Godwin, Susan Pargeter and Nicole Fielding." She caught their eyes as she called out their names. "Amanda James and Peter Numan." She put the paper down and smiled. "And Father Brande, Jennifer and myself, of course. You are all suspects in the murder of Robert Markhew seven days ago."

"This is preposterous." Jean began to rise in her chair.

"Sit down, Mrs. Markhew." Meinwen copied the older woman's tone and she did as she was told.

"Robert Markhew had dinner with Jean, Mary, Father Brande and his sister, Jennifer. They were served by Amanda." Meinwen lowered the paper and grinned. "I feel like Poirot doing this. Will the real murderer please stand?"

Jean frowned. "Do get on with it. Nobody would answer such a stupid request."

Meinwen dipped her head. "After dinner Robert and Simon discussed the death of Grace Peters in the study culminating in Robert coming out and asking for the morning's post when Amanda gave him a letter. He returned to the study but asked Simon to leave." She paused. "Why did he not receive it in the morning with the rest of the post?"

Susan coughed. "Because I hand-delivered it in the middle of the day."

Meinwen nodded. "Exactly. I should very much like to see that letter. Did you read it, Miss Pargeter?"

Susan shook her head. "No. Mother…Mrs. Peters had already sealed it, and it would have been a breach of my position to open it."

"A pity." Meinwen smiled. "Still, I commend your ethics." She twisted her computer chair around and sat. "The next we know of Robert Markhew was his argument, overheard by Peter Numan, with an unknown someone at nine-thirty."

"That was obviously Richard," said Jean. "He must have been there."

"Must he?" Meinwen held up a hand. "Bear with me for a little longer. No one else saw Mr. Markhew after that time."

"But Mary…" Jean began.

Meinwen held up her hand again. "For reasons of her own, which I believe are truthful, Mary did not say goodnight to him. The next sighting we have of Robert Markhew was at eleven-thirty when the study door was broken down and his body was discovered."

She paused and reached out for a cracker biscuit, breaking it into two pieces. "May I have a cup of the coffee?"

Amanda, who was sitting on the floor, waited for a nod from Jean before pouring it.

Meinwen took a sip and ate half the cracker. She waved a hand at the refreshments. "Do help yourselves."

Amanda poured a cup for Jean and Peter reached for the biscuits.

Meinwen began to count off the people on her fingers. "Jean, Mary and Amanda were all together until nine-ten. None of them have an alibi afterwards." She ignored Jean's protest. "Peter Numan was at the White

Art until nine-twenty, after which he shares an alibi with Nicole Fielding. Susan Pargeter has a verified alibi until nine twenty-five and none thereafter. Catherine Godwin has no alibi at all, and neither does her husband, Richard."

"There." Jean nodded sharply. "Need we look any further for the killer?"

Meinwen raised her eyebrow. "I think we do. The crux of the matter is the argument that Peter overheard when Robert was arguing at nine-thirty. But what if there was no one in the room with him at that time?"

"That's ridiculous." Peter gestured with a biscuit. "I know what I heard."

"I have no doubt you heard Robert arguing. What I am questioning is whether it was live."

There were several creased foreheads. Simon laughed. "What a ridiculous thing to say, Meinwen. What are you talking about?"

Nicole spoke up. "His laptop. He recorded his books all the time onto his laptop and I transcribed them afterwards. Think of it as a Dictaphone. He had speech recognition software installed and one of my jobs was to make sure the recordings and the documents matched."

Meinwen nodded. "I know. One of those recordings was of an argument between Catherine and Robert. I think it was set to play at nine-thirty, long after Robert was dead."

"Is that even possible?" Jean looked at Nicole. "I don't know enough about them."

"It's perfectly possible, Mother," Mary replied. "We covered it in IT at college."

"So the murder was committed even earlier than we thought?" Jennifer asked. "How early? Do we know?"

"That doesn't change the fact that Richard could still have done it," said Jean. "It's suspicious, the way he disappeared."

"He didn't go far away," said Meinwen. "Not very far away at all."

"Where then?" asked Jean.

Catherine looked up, realizing her husband had been upstairs all along.

Meinwen smiled. "Let's ask him, shall we?" She raised her voice. "Richard? Would you come downstairs, please?"

Chapter 32

Everyone's faces turned to the open stairwell as a young man came down.

"Richard!" Catherine rose from her chair and ran to him. He embraced her hard until she had to gasp for him to release her. He was reluctant and maintained a lighter contact, his fingertips gliding across her waist and shoulders.

"I'm sorry, Catherine." He buried his face in her hair for a moment. "It was best to be in hiding."

"I was so sure the police had caught you." She pulled his face down for a kiss. "I thought I'd lost you forever."

Meinwen was so pleased to see how much the young couple was in love. "My fault, I'm afraid. That was a ruse I made up. The inspector went along with it hoping to shake the murderer out of his complacency."

Jennifer pouted. "But I believed you. I told all my friends."

"I know. We were counting on you doing exactly that." Meinwen shrugged. "Sorry."

"Where have you been, Richard?" asked Jean. "The police have been looking for you all over the country."

"I know Aunty Jean, I'm sorry." Richard allowed himself to be led into the room where he perched on the edge of the armchair next to his wife. "I've been right here in Laverstone, all along. It was for the best."

"Did you kill your stepfather?" Nicole asked. "We've all been under suspicion for it."

Richard shook his head. "I didn't kill him. As much as Robert and I argued, I've never wanted him dead. I wish Catherine hadn't told him about us, though."

Mary punched him on the arm. "You might have told me. I was making plans for our wedding."

Richard laughed. "Sorry Mary. I know I'm not your type anyway. A marriage with me would have been a sham. A lucrative one for you, perhaps, but you should marry for love, not money."

Mary shook her head. "That's something the rich say."

Jean sat up straight in her armchair and asked again. "So tell us where you were all this time?"

Meinwen looked at the priest. "I think that Simon should answer that. I said every one of you had a secret. He was the only one not to give his up. I had to find out about it myself."

They all looked at Simon, who blushed beneath their gaze. "All right," he said, holding up his hands. "When I left The Larches after the murder I went down to the White Art where Richard was staying. It was all locked up, of course, but Mike let me in through the resident's door."

"That's right," said Richard. "I knew nothing about it until Father Brande told me. I was stunned."

Simon nodded. "It was obvious Richard would be the major suspect in the case and that even if he was innocent he'd have to testify against another member of his family. Probably Catherine, since she was about to be a major suspect as well."

"That was awful," said Richard, squeezing his wife's hand. "When you told me you'd had a fight with Robert and told him about our secret wedding, I knew he'd want to change his will. You knew how much I was banking on my inheritance, so I thought…"

"You thought that I had killed him?" Catherine's face fell. "How could you possibly think you'd married someone capable of murder?"

"Sorry." Richard shrugged.

"It was reasonable," said Simon. "You do have a quick temper."

"What could I do but flee?" asked Richard. "I didn't know where to go, though. That's where Simon helped me." He smiled at his extended family. "Simon's always helped me. Ever since my mother died he's been more of a father than Robert ever was. He offered me a place to hide."

"Yes." Simon smiled. "It was fortuitous, really. Old Tom had gone to see his brother for a few days. There was an opening at the church. Since Old Tom didn't really mix with the parishioners, I didn't think anyone would notice if Tom was a different man."

Richard shrugged. "It's quite interesting really. I never really realized there was so much to that job. It was quite peaceful to work in the church and graveyard. It was me who dug Robert's grave. I gave him a eulogy in my own way."

"That's all very well, Richard, but where does that leave us?" asked Jean. "Do you have a-- What's it called…an alibi for the time when Robert was murdered?"

Richard shrugged and gripped Catherine's hand even harder. "I was in my room at the Art. All I did all night was compose half a dozen letters to Robert and Catherine and read a book."

"You should have come forward," said Nicole. "The police would have sorted it out."

"I didn't dare," Richard replied. "I was sure that they would arrest me as soon as look at me."

"How did you find him?" asked Simon. "I thought he had the perfect hiding place, right out in plain sight."

"Mary found Catherine's ring and gave it to me," said Meinwen. "It's quite a distinctive one, I must say, and matches the necklace I saw her wearing when we interviewed her at The Larches. When I was in the churchyard looking at the old stone I saw two people making love on one of the tombstones."

"You didn't!" Simon was shocked. "Richard? You didn't, did you?"

Richard had the temerity to look sheepish. "I told you I'd never cheat on the woman I love. And I haven't. When I saw Catherine come to the church to pray I couldn't help revealing myself to her. I missed her terribly."

Catherine squeezed his hand and smiled up at him. He smiled back, raising her hand to kiss.

"I'm disappointed in you, Catherine," Meinwen said. "You lied about knowing where he was. At the very least you hampered the investigation. Unless you're very lucky you could be charged with obstructing a murder investigation. You distinctly told me you hadn't been in contact with him, let alone that you were shagging him at lunchtimes."

"Sorry." Catherine sniffed.

"Sorry won't cut it. You'll have to tell Inspector White and hope that he looks kindly on the folly of a newly-wed couple." She withdrew a sheet of paper from her printer tray. "The police are aware of your liaison already. I sent them DNA samples to find out the identity of 'Old Tom.' They came back as Catherine Latt and Richard Godwin. That's when I realized the wedding band Mary found and the one on Tom's finger were identical and therefore you were married."

"What about your cellphone?" asked Mary. "I tried to call you a hundred times."

Richard smiled and reached into his pocket. "I lost it on the night of the murder. I had to buy a new one." He laughed. "This new phone is great. I can read books on it, take photos and play games. Look, I've got some great shots of the church for your website, Simon. I'll show them to you later. One or two are from inside Robert's empty grave."

"What happened to your old one?" Meinwen asked. "Do you have any idea how it turned up outside your stepfather's study window?"

"I don't know," Richard said. "It must have been stolen in the pub. Mike said he'd keep a look out for it but it never turned up. I don't know how it got outside his window."

"The murderer was framing you," said Nicole. "It wasn't me. I was...occupied elsewhere."

Richard laughed and looked at Peter. "I can guess where, although

Peter was in the pub that night. I saw him."

"I was, yes." Peter grinned. "I was playing darts."

"I was reading, actually," said Nicole. "Admittedly, it was in Peter's room, but still…"

"That was a good idea of yours, Simon, to hide him as the curate," said Meinwen.

"Thanks." Simon grinned. "It would have worked, too, if he'd been able to keep his hands off a wife I didn't know he had."

"Sorry," Richard shook his head, pulling his lips back from his teeth. "I would have told you but I couldn't afford for Robert to find out."

"You could have told me in confession," Simon said. "I would have kept the secret."

"I didn't have anything to confess. There's no sin in being in love."

"You didn't help Richard at all," said Meinwen, looking Simon in the eye. "What you did actually made the case against him much worse."

"I see that now." Simon looked uncomfortable. "Sorry, Richard."

"You did what you thought was best, Father," said Richard. "Don't worry about it. If I'd been thinking clearly I would have gone and turned myself in straight away and let the police sort it out."

Nicole stared at them both for a moment. "So what's your story, Richard?"

He shrugged again. Even Meinwen was getting irritated with the gesture, more reminiscent of a teenager than of a married man. "You know Catherine and I had a row after she told Robert we'd got married?"

Most of the room nodded.

"Well, after she stamped on the ring and stormed off I went back to the house. There didn't seem to be any point in going to inside to talk to Robert, not until he'd calmed down about it, anyway, so I left the ring on the fountain for Catherine. She always went there in the morning with a cup of tea, so I assumed she'd find it and take it back. After that I went back to the Art and bummed about in my room all night."

"What about food?" asked Meinwen. "Surely someone saw you eat, or delivered your food."

"I was too upset to eat," he said. "I didn't see anyone apart from Father Brande that night."

"That's not good," said Nicole. "You don't have an alibi at all."

"Did you kill him?" asked Jean.

"Certainly not," said Richard. "I resent that."

Jean smiled with an expression more like a cobra about to strike. "I had to ask. Without an alibi, how could we know?"

"That's going to haunt me," said Richard. "If I'd known he was going to be killed I would have gone down into the bar where people could see me."

"If you'd known he was going to be killed, you could have warned him." Amanda stretched legs cramped from being caught between Jean's chair and the coffee table. "Then none of us would be here."

"Ifs and buts," said Meinwen. "They don't serve any purpose. The only way to clear Richard's name is if the real murderer confesses." She looked at each person in the room, not really expecting any of them to pipe up. "You know who you are and I don't want the confession tonight. Let's look again at the suspects."

She picked up the sheet of paper. "If Robert was murdered between say, nine o'clock and eleven-fifteen, when Simon got the call, we have a smaller suspect list. Richard, of course, and Catherine who was in her room. Jean and Mary had alibis for part of that time while they said their goodbyes to Simon and his sister, but after that they went to separate rooms alone. Nicole claims that she was in Peter's cottage until he returned at nine-thirty."

She paused. "I am satisfied with Amanda's lack of motive and Nicole and Peter's alibis are each other. A little suspect, perhaps, but again, they had little motive."

Nicole and Amanda let out sighs of relief, the others looked around the room, obviously wondering which of the others was the murderer.

"Susan's alibi is rock solid." Meinwen put the sheet down. "I didn't invite the police to this meeting on purpose though I will be informing Inspector White of my findings in the morning. I took a leaf out of Robert's book and had my computer record the whole discussion, should I need to hand it over to them. For now, it's been sent to a secure server."

There was an outbreak of muttering. Jean scowled. "You shouldn't have recorded us without permission. I find that highly underhanded."

Meinwen closed her eyes and gathered patience in as if it were a fog surrounding her. "It will not be seen unless it needs to be. I suggest that you all go back to The Larches and be prepared for the revelation I make in the morning, unless the culprit makes his confession to save me the trouble. I must point out that it would go better for them if they did." She ate the other half of the biscuit she'd started at the beginning of the discussion. "The meeting is over."

They began to stand, rubbing life into joints that had stiffened over the past hour. "Will that be the end of it then?" asked Jean as Amanda helped her on with her coat, "In the morning, I mean."

"I sincerely hope so, Mrs. Markhew," Meinwen replied.

"Why wait until morning?" Jean asked. "Aren't you afraid that the killer will try to stop you?"

"A little," said Meinwen, "but I have to be sure and tomorrow morning I'll know for certain."

"Would you like me to stay with you?" asked Peter after a glance at Jean. "You know I didn't do it and I used to be quite handy on the rugby field."

Meinwen smiled. "Thank you, but that's really not necessary." She leaned in close and whispered. "Besides, Mary is single again, remember?"

Peter smiled. "Good point. Er… You haven't got some of that love potion you mentioned handy, have you?"

Chapter 33

Meinwen stood at the door to say goodbye to the residents of The Larches. Inside, Jennifer began to tidy and Simon helped with coats. Susan had chauffeured Jean while the rest had come in Nicole's car, a fortunate circumstance since they were taking back two extra people.

She smiled to see Richard walking arm in arm with Catherine and getting into the back of Robert's Jaguar. Mary squeezed into the back of the Vauxhall, sandwiched between Peter and Amanda, with Nicole driving. How would Peter choose between Mary and Nicole? Nicole had deemed it a relationship of mutual convenience, but Meinwen was certain there was more to it than that.

"Will they survive the events of the last week or shatter like crystal?" Jennifer stood behind her with a glass of apple wine.

"It's all politics." Meinwen watched the two cars head off up the road. "They'll adjust in time." She turned to go inside.

Simon paused from piling empty bowls and cups on a tray. "How do you mean? Will they still all live with Richard once he becomes master of the house, do you think? That's assuming he's cleared of the murder charge, of course."

"I think they'll polarize between Jean and Richard." Meinwen carried a pair of Royal Doulton cups through to the kitchen. "My guess is that there'll be two camps and divided loyalties until Richard is mature enough to take over the master's position."

"At least he's married." Simon wiped his hands on a tea towel. "He won't be running a harem like Robert. To think that I knew him for ten years and never realized what was going on in that house. It's disgusting."

"Why?" Meinwen began filling up the washing bowl with hot water. "You just said you never knew. What harm were they doing to anyone? The only unhappiness was caused by Robert insisting Richard marry Mary."

"That's when all the trouble started." Simon started putting on his coat, although it was a clear night and hardly seemed worth it for the twenty-yard walk up the drive to the rectory.

"The trouble started with the blackmail." Meinwen looked up at the gibbous moon.

Jennifer, already wearing her fur-trimmed cape, lightly touched her arm. "I'm heading back. It's been an eventful day and I could do with a cocoa and bed."

Meinwen pulled her into a hug. "Goodnight then. Thanks for all your help tonight."

"I wouldn't have missed it for the world." Jennifer relaxed under the hug. "Thanks for not telling the police about Richard."

"Dim problem, *cariad*." Meinwen reached out and took her hands. "Just don't tell Inspector White or he'll have my guts for garters."

Jennifer smiled and nodded. "I promise. On my mother's grave."

Meinwen leaned forward and gave her a peck on the cheek. "Thanks. I'll see you tomorrow."

"Okay. Coming, Simon?"

The priest nodded. "I'll be along in a minute."

Meinwen saw her out then turned back to Simon "Would you like a tea or coffee before you go? Or a hot chocolate if you like. I'm going to have one."

Simon looked through the kitchen window at his own house where several lights came on. "All right. Any chance of an Irish coffee?"

"Only if you have the whiskey. I've no alcohol in the house at all other than a bottle or two of home-made wine, and that's only for sabbats and esbats."

"You observe the Sabbath, do you?" said Simon. "Which day?"

Meinwen smiled. "Every three months. Midsummer, midwinter and the spring and autumn equinoxes. The esbats are the four festivals that fall between them."

"Oh, I see. Dancing naked around stone circles and the like."

Meinwen laughed. "Sometimes. It's not a requirement, though, and in the middle of winter I don't take my clothes off for anybody." She winked. "Not outside, anyway."

Simon grinned. "I shouldn't be listening to this heathen talk."

"I'm sure you have equally odd rituals, when there are no parishioners to see. "Now how about that coffee?"

"Please." Simon sat on a pine chair while she boiled a kettle and washed up.

* * * *

"Come to bed, Richard."

Catherine tugged at her husband's arm. "I've never been able to sleep with you here before and certainly not as lady of the house."

Richard smiled. "Soon, love." He stroked her cheek with his finger. "I want to show you something first."

He led her upstairs to his stepfather's bedroom. "Have you ever been in here before?"

She nodded. "Once or twice last year. After we fell in love I was careful to avoid Robert's attention and he never asked for me to join him in here."

"Good." Richard led her inside and kissed her on the neck, drawing a moan from her lips as she surrendered to his touch. He slipped the buttons of her blouse and dropped it to the floor, then released her breasts and let them stand free, pert from the desire flowing through her. Her skirt soon joined the blouse. "Soon all this will be mine…"

Catherine nodded and her eyes closed, floating on his touch. His tongue across her nipples took her to the edge of bliss.

"…but you already belong to me."

* * * *

Simon stirred chocolate powder into the froth on his coffee. "What did you mean when you said the only unhappiness at The Larches was when Robert arranged the marriage?"

"Exactly that," Meinwen said. "The dynamics of the household was arranged around a tribal system with Robert at the top as the lord and the others all had a predefined niche in the microcosm of the house. He was the chief and the rest, apart from Richard and perhaps Mary, were his subjects." She finished washing up and dried her hands, leaving the dishes to dry naturally. Picking up her hot chocolate, she returned to the living room and sat on her computer chair. Simon followed and settled into the armchair Jean had used.

Meinwen took a sip and yawned. "Robert's sudden death changed the dynamics of the family. In one night it became a houseful of subjects with no one in charge. They carried on as normal as best they could but it was like a spinning top with nobody to wind it up again. Eventually it would have just tipped over on its side and stopped."

"So Jean took over?"

"Apparently." Meinwen nodded and sipped her coffee. "She was the eldest and most experienced. It's hardly surprising they looked to her for direction. Had Richard been there they would probably have looked to him instead."

"So will he have his own harem?"

Meinwen nodded. "Probably. Either they'll sort themselves out into a single unit again or they'll splinter into smaller groups, like part of a tribe breaking away to start another."

"Oh God!" Simon put his head in his hands. "The rot will spread."

"Don't be silly." Meinwen snorted and put her cup down at the side of her keyboard, hitting a few keys as she turned back. "They're a stable, polyamorous community. They do no harm to anyone. Some of your Christian groups would do well to emulate them."

"Rubbish. One man, one woman. That's the natural way of things."

"Not according to the Mormons." Meinwen raised an eyebrow. "And what of love? Even your Jesus said to love one another. "

"In matrimony." Simon waved away the argument. "It'll all change when one of them is declared the murderer."

"If you say so." Meinwen smiled and picked up her coffee again. The computer bleeped but she ignored it.

Simon leaned forward, nursing his coffee. "Why did you give the killer until the morning to confess? Surely you're putting yourself in danger."

"Why? Why do you think? Why would I give a killer another twelve hours freedom?"

"To let him get away?" Simon shook his head. "You're one of them, aren't you? One of these poly-wotsit subjects. You know Richard is the killer and you want him to get away so you can join him afterwards."

Meinwen laughed. "Certainly not. Think again, but be reasonable this time."

Simon looked at her, his mouth open. "You don't know who the killer is! That's clever. You want him to think you know and confess so that you look good when you say you 'knew all along.'"

Meinwen rocked her office chair. "That's a good theory but you're quite wrong. I know exactly who the killer is. I've set it all out in an email to the police which will be sent off in the morning."

"You haven't sent it yet?"

She shook her head. "Not yet, no, though it will go automatically whether I'm here or not." She smiled. "Third and final guess."

"All right." Simon closed his eyes. "You're setting a trap for him to try to come after you. That would force his hand and prove without doubt who the killer is."

Meinwen leaned back and half-closed her eyes. "I've no need to do that. I have all the evidence I need to send the killer to prison."

Simon sat waved a hand dismissively. "All right. I give up. Who is the killer?"

Meinwen smiled. "Let me tell you how I worked through the clues. See if you can come to the same conclusion as I did."

Simon put his cup on the coffee table and sat up, brushing away the lock of hair that habitually fell over his eye. "Go on then. This is exciting."

Meinwen raised an eyebrow. "The first clue is the telephone call. Richard had no motive to make it. If he was the killer, he would have wanted to get as far away as possible before anyone found the body and if he wasn't the killer he wouldn't have made it anyway."

"That makes sense, I suppose. So you've eliminated Richard purely on the phone call I received?"

"Not quite, no, though it gave me the impetus to believe he didn't do it. Who else would make that call, and why would they say they were Amanda? At eleven-fifteen all the residents except Richard were at the house, so it couldn't have been one of them at the station. That means that it must have been an accomplice of the murderer."

"Why tell me of the murder, though? Why not just leave the body to be discovered later?"

Meinwen shook her head. "All in good time. The effect of the call was that the murder was discovered at night rather than in the morning. This could mean one of two things. Either the killer wanted the body found before it began to deteriorate, which indicates they cared for him, or else the killer wanted to be present when the body was found."

"But only Amanda, Nicole, Peter and I were present," said Simon, "unless someone else was watching that we didn't know about. Jennifer stayed in the hall."

"Someone watching?" Meinwen smiled. "Hold that thought."

"Okay." Simon grinned and rubbed his hands together. "Go on."

"My next clue was the chair. Do you remember Amanda said it had been moved?"

"That was the day I was giving Mass. You told me afterwards, though. It could easily have been moved by the police when they investigated the scene."

"I thought so too. So I checked with Inspector White, or rather his sergeant, since it seems that the police have an internal server for all this information and the inspector doesn't like computers. The police make it a policy not to disturb anything at a crime scene, and he sent me a picture of the room taken that night. The chair is exactly where we found it."

"Perhaps Robert moved it then, or one of the people he argued with. Catherine, say, or the killer."

"Amanda didn't think so. She was surprised it was out of place. There were deep tread patterns in the carpet that suggested it was always on the same spot. She wouldn't have noticed the discrepancy otherwise. That's one of the reasons I eliminated her. She wouldn't have brought our attention to a detail like that if she was the killer. Combined with the fact she had no reason to make the phone call and she's no longer a suspect."

"What if she wanted the body found because she cared for him?"

Meinwen shook her head. "Her loyalties are firmly with Jean. That much is clear from watching her. She may have liked Robert or even loved him, but she didn't kill him."

Simon sat back again, rubbing his eyes. "What was the significance of the chair, then?"

"In its new position it hid Robert's laptop from the doorway. The killer had to be there to switch off the dictation program, leaving us to think the murder was committed later than it was. Whoever made the phone call wanted to be at the scene when the body was found so they could shut down the software which also means that they were conversant with using a computer."

"Clever. That eliminates Richard, doesn't it? It could still be Amanda though. Who doesn't know how to use a computer these days?"

"No." Meinwen drained her cup and twisted to put it down on the coffee table. "Amanda would be at the scene whenever the body was found because she'd be the one answering the door." She laughed. "You've fixated on the poor girl, now. Have you got a grudge against her? Trust me, she didn't do it."

Simon sighed. "If you insist, but there's something not quite right about her."

"This from a man in a dress." Meinwen grinned.

Simon wagged his finger at her. "That was a cheap shot and an old one. No points."

She laughed and stretched her legs out. "Fair enough."

"Is there anything else or is that the extent of your deductions?"

"There's more." Meinwen began to massage her calves. "Given that we've established Richard wasn't the killer, why was his cellphone and footprints found outside the window?"

"They were left there to frame him?"

"Exactly. If we believe Richard's story, he lost his Nokia at the pub. Who had the opportunity to steal it from him? To my knowledge, only you and Peter were at the pub on the night of the murder."

"There's still this mysterious watcher you mentioned."

"Indeed." Meinwen pointed at him. "That's right. The watcher saw everything."

Simon leaned forward again, his voice catching in his throat. "So who is the watcher?"

Chapter 34

Meinwen smiled, though it never reached her eyes. "I am the watcher, though I watch in hindsight through all the clues you left me."

"The clues I left you?" Simon laughed. "You think I'm the murderer?"

"Of course. Do you deny it?" Meinwen reached into the printer tray and took out a sheaf of papers. She sorted through them and pulled one out.

"You may have forgotten, but I'm a priest."

"A priest is not immune to committing offences before God."

Simon leaned back and scratched his ear, his blue eyes twinkling. "And how would a simple heathen know that?"

"I've studied you over the past week," Meinwen said. "You are not who your parishioners think you are. You have secrets, just like the rest of them, but I found them out."

"I was hiding Richard, big deal." Simon leaned over to the coffee table where a bowl of salted peanuts lay untouched after the meeting. He sorted through them, looking for unbroken ones. "It may have been foolish but it was hardly a sin."

"That's not your only secret, though, is it?" Meinwen stood. "Would you like another coffee?"

Simon looked at the dregs in his cup. "I'd better not. It might keep me awake."

"I'm surprised you manage to sleep at all," Meinwen said on her way to the kitchen. "I know I wouldn't with such a tarnished spirit."

"The state of my soul is between me and God and none of your concern."

"True." Meinwen sat again, fresh coffee instead of carob steaming in her mug. "It's your mortal deeds that concern me. It was only the discrepancy in time that drew my attention away from you as the killer in the first place."

"Why would I have killed Robert? He was a good friend and Richard's stepfather. What reason would I have had to kill him?"

"Because the letter he received from Grace Peters named you as the blackmailer." Meinwen sipped her coffee. "Oh, I know it was you blackmailing her. Who better to know her darkest secrets than her priest and confessor? You threatened her with exposure to the police and she kept you quiet with a payment of a thousand pounds a month."

Simon laughed. "You're talking out of your hat. You have no proof of any of this."

"Circumstantial, perhaps, but I can prove the withdrawals from Grace Peters' account match the deposits into yours."

"Donations to the church. I have a private source of income."

"Stocks and shares? A legacy?" Meinwen shook her head. "I think not. Only two people visited Grace Peters on a regular basis--you and her daughter."

Simon's face creased as he stood. "I don't need to listen to any more of this rubbish. Needless to say, you are no longer welcome in my home."

"Nor will you be after tomorrow," said Meinwen. "What will Jennifer do when the church reclaims its property? Where will she go when she discovers that her dear brother is a murderer?"

"You leave her out of this." Simon leaned over Meinwen, his face contorted in fury. "It's bad enough that you bandy about accusations about me without you going after her as well. What harm has she done to you?"

"Nothing." Meinwen sat back to give herself a little space from the snarling priest. "I quite like her, actually. She even helped me with the case. I just feel sorry for her. She'll be gutted to find out that you were the murderer."

"I'm going to sue you for slander. I know a good solicitor."

"Gillian du Pointe?" Meinwen smiled. "I know her too. Lovely woman. She was very helpful when I made enquiries about the services she offered."

Simon shook his head. "I have other friends I was at college with. I shall look forward to seeing your business close and you sent packing back to Aberdovey."

"If so I shall send you a postcard," said Meinwen. "Of course, I'll have to address it to Wandsworth Prison."

Simon dropped back into the armchair. "All right. Let's pretend what you're saying is true. How do you explain the phone call? The police have verified that it really happened. I didn't just phone the home number from my cell."

"That was easy. Once I'd met Tom in the graveyard and suspected who he really was I asked around. The neighbour of the real Old Tom told me where he was. It was easy for me to get in touch with him. It was Old Tom who phoned you that night, exactly as you asked him to, to tell you that he was on his way to his brother's."

Meinwen flipped a lever so that her chair could tilt and leaned backward, a half-smile on her face. "There was all the evidence I needed. Tom hadn't a clue about the murder, so when you told Jennifer Robert

Markhew was dead, there was only one way you could have known. You'd killed him yourself."

Simon yawned. "I suppose you can pretend that all the other clues point to me as well."

"Of course." Meinwen put her coffee cup on the mouse mat. "You certainly have the skill with computers that the murderer needed. I've seen your profile on Jennifer's for one thing and you've got the one in the church as well. You're more than capable of setting up an audio file to play at a predetermined time. You knew Robert's methods of working and knew enough about his program to extract the file of his argument with Catherine."

Simon leaned forward, inspecting his nails. "So could half the people in your investigation. Why would it have been me?"

"As I explained to The Larches people, the only purpose of that telephone call was to enable the killer to be on the scene when the body was discovered. Amanda and Peter have alibis, leaving it a choice between you and Nicole. Nicole, although she had the computer skills, had no motive to kill her employer."

"So it conveniently falls upon me to have done the deed." Simon yawned again, making a great show of patting his mouth with his hands. "Really, my dear, there's not a shred of evidence here that would hold up in court."

"There's certainly enough to send you to trial, though." Meinwen sat up again now that he was at a safe enough distance away. "Robert Markhew was dead before you even left the house with your sister after dinner. When he came back into the study with the letter from Grace Peters you were desperate to know what it said. You had already removed the dagger from the glass case while he was talking to Amanda in the hallway and when he refused to read it in front of you, you killed him and took it."

Simon shook his head. "I must admit I knew pagans had an active imagination but I never expected it to be this fanciful. I had thought you rather a level-headed woman but this is preposterous. How can you possibly believe in all this guff?"

"Because it's true, Simon." Meinwen smiled, knowing he was fighting a losing battle. "You turned the heating up to reduce the rate of cooling of the body, unlocked the study window, set the computer to play one of his dictation files--it was a lucky chance that you picked the one with an argument on it, unless he'd labeled it--and bid him a cheerful good night as if he was sitting at his desk as normal. No one was any the wiser."

"How would I know that no one would go in to see him before I returned? That would bring your theory crashing down."

"It was a risk you took," said Meinwen. "You knew Robert didn't like to be disturbed at night, and the dictation files would discourage anyone from knocking or coming in unannounced. When you returned, you climbed in through the window, turned the heating down and locked the study door, then planted the phone you'd stolen from Richard, left a set of footprints with his shoes and rejoined Jennifer on the drive, ."

"You seem to have made up a lovely theory," Simon said. "You should become a fiction writer. I know that Jennifer could give you some pointers, perhaps even introduce you to an agent."

"Perhaps I will write it up." Meinwen scratched her neck as she thought about the prospect. "If I do, though, I'll publish it under 'true crime.'"

"I wish you the best of luck." Simon stood again. "Of course, if you do it will give me the perfect opportunity to sue you for libel instead of slander. It might even bring people flocking to the parish and I'll be able to afford a new church roof."

"That will be someone else's problem by then." Meinwen stood as well. "The new parish priest's."

Simon smiled. "I wish you well on your journey back to Wales. Give my regards to the mountains. You've got until morning to leave."

"I'll certainly see them before you, Simon. You won't be seeing any mountains for a long time where you're going." She paused. "I'm only warning you about all this for Jennifer's sake, you know."

"I told you to leave her out of this." Simon picked up his coat.

"It's too late for that. She has a murderer for a brother, and unless you do something about it she'll be dragged through the courts with you. What then of your beloved church? It will come into disrepute just by association. If you really believe in God would you risk that?"

"What would you have me do, if I was the guilty party? Just hypothetically, of course."

She smiled. "You could hang yourself like Henry Peters was thought to have done. You could take an overdose like Grace before you hanged her, or stab yourself like you did Robert."

"Suicide?" Simon laughed. "That's a mortal sin."

"Not as bad as the blackmail and murders you've already committed." Meinwen picked her coffee cup up, her fingers brushing across her computer keyboard. It bleeped once. "There is an alternative, though."

"What's that?"

She took the cups into the kitchen, Simon following on her heels. "I can offer you a way out that doesn't involve death, but you would never see your sister or parish again, and people would think you were dead."

"Go on. What is this hypothetical method of escape?"

"Come back in the morning and I'll tell you. Just make sure you bring me a full confession to exonerate Richard and I'll do the rest." Meinwen led the way to the front door and opened it. She looked across to see Jennifer sat in front of her computer in the rectory. "Say hello to your sister for me."

"You're getting very tedious, Miss Jones." Simon pulled on his overcoat against the night's chill. "Good night to you."

"Don't take this lightly, Simon. My findings will be with Inspector White in the morning."

"If I were the one making wild accusations I would be afraid for my own safety." Simon turned and strode down the path to the rectory. Meinwen watched him go, then closed the door and leaned against it, letting all the pent-up tension out of her body with a sigh.

She went back to the living room and tidied up, putting the extra chairs back in the kitchen. She made a cup of green tea to flush the coffee toxins from her body and returned to her computer desk. It was still only eleven-thirty--early to someone used to meditating under the moon. She switched on the computer screen and twitched the mouse to force the computer out of hibernation.

The hard drive was almost full and Meinwen set about burning several copies of a video file to DVD. She had managed to stay calm during her talk with Simon but was relieved she'd taken the precaution of recording the past two hours as a streaming video file. It made an interesting addition to the evidence she'd collected, but she was glad she'd judged his character well enough to be confident he wouldn't just attack her. With the house empty and the doors locked, she began to shake at the thought of what he might have done had she misjudged him.

She logged on to her chat program.

Scribe: Daffyd?
Dovey_Daffyd: Hey Manny. You okay?
Scribe: Sure. He's gone. Thanks for keeping an eye on the cam feed.
Dovey_Daffyd: No worries. Did it go to plan?
Scribe: I'll know in the morning.

She closed the chat program and opened a browser window, typing in "Laverstone" and "unrepealed local statutes." There was precious little online about the town other than a short entry outlining the basic history and some photos of the local landscapes on a photo-sharing site. There were also numerous mentions on social networking sites and a badly maintained site for the Laverstone Times. Nothing pertaining to her query, however.

She checked the time. Was eleven-thirty too late for a telephone call? Perhaps not. She pulled out the business card for Isaacs and Du Pointe, Solicitors. Overnight business hours were printed clearly and Ms. du Pointe had been friendly enough when she'd asked about the services she offered.

Meinwen used the house phone to dial since her telephone provider gave her free calls in the evenings. "Miss du Pointe? This is Meinwen Jones from The Herbage."

"Yes, I remember. How can I help? Not another murder I hope?"

"No. The same one, actually. What are the laws relating to the justice at the hands of the lord of the manor?"

"Interesting you should ask. It was one of the first things I researched when I took over as solicitor here. Is there something specific you needed to know?" She laughed. "Did you know, for example, that it is still legal to shoot a Welshman with a bow and arrow, but only within the city walls of Chester and only on a Sunday after midnight?"

"What is the position on murder? Does the lord have jurisdiction over killers?"

"Technically, the Civil War, Laverstone, act of sixteen fifty-eight gives the lord of the manor the right to try anyone accused of killing in the Laverstone parish boundary. You have to be careful, though, because it refers to the boundary in existence in sixteen fifty-eight, not the one today which is considerably larger. There's a map detailing it at the manor."

"Is The Larches inside the boundary?"

"Alas, no." There was a pause and Meinwen could hear the woman take a sip of something then swallow. It made her want another cup of tea.

"What about Grace Peters's house?"

The came the sound of shuffling papers. "Hilltop? Yes, that's well within. Why? Have you identified the killer?"

"Yes." Meinwen took a deep breath. "Simon Brande."

"How ironic. You have proof of course?"

"Not of Grace Peters's murder, no. Only of his blackmailing her."

"Blackmail?" Gillian du Pointe's laugh was like music. "Even better.

If there's one thing generations of lords of Laverstone have ever agreed with, it's money. "

"Then he can be tried by Mr. Waterman?"

"Indeed he can, though it has to be in the presence of a bishop."

"Excellent." Meinwen couldn't help smiling. "Can I arrange a trial then?"

"Without involving the police? That's a very grey area."

"Nevertheless."

"Very well. When?"

"Tomorrow night? Eight-thirty?"

"Short notice indeed. It has to be in the original demesne, mind."

"Does that include the top of the waterfall?"

Chapter 35

The April sun had cleared the horizon but it was still cold enough to freeze particular parts of a witch's anatomy. That's why, when Meinwen rose at sunrise and went out in the garden, she was dressed in her heaviest winter woollies.

She lit a fire in her circle and meditated, her bottom going numb against the cold stone as she fed sticks into the small blaze. After an hour, when the noise from the distant M25 had grown to a noticeable hum, she let the flames die and returned indoors to warm up.

To take her mind off the day ahead she began to write notes for a book about Laverstone. Although she'd only been here a week, she had gleaned enough knowledge about the area to at least make a start and it would, given the chance, provide her with both a small income and increased traffic to her shop.

Half an hour later, just as she finished her Earl Grey, a knock sounded at the door.

"I wasn't sure you'd be up yet." Simon wore his cassock and carried a small book of common prayer. "Jennifer's still asleep. She doesn't tend to wake until eight, so I thought that I'd get this over with."

"You've decided to confess then?" Meinwen led the way back into the kitchen and put the kettle on for more tea.

"Confess what?" Simon sat. "I've done nothing to confess."

Meinwen raised an eyebrow. "I thought lying was a sin? Bearing falsehood unto God and all that."

"Perhaps you'd know about falsehoods more that I, with your accusations and ravings." Simon accepted the tea. "Thank you."

Meinwen leaned against the sink. "So why did you come?"

He stirred his tea, a creature of habit despite Meinwen not providing any sugar. "I want you to leave. Go back to Aberdovey or wherever it is you come from. It will be easier if you go voluntarily, though I can make a few impassioned speeches about the corruption of moral standards in allowing witches to live in our lovely town." He wagged a finger at her. "Thou shalt not suffer a witch to live."

"'Poisoner' not 'witch.'"

"Semantics." Simon grimaced at the tea and pushed it away. "History recognizes the replacement. Who in Britain would condemn me for preaching from the English text?"

"Not many," Meinwen admitted, "unless they were aware that you were a murderer."

"Give it a rest, girl." Simon rubbed the tiredness from his eyes. Despite his assurances of the previous evening it was clear that he had not slept well.

"I will after today. I warned you I'd be sending my findings to Inspector White. After that I shall have nothing more to do with the affair."

"Those findings are inflammatory and misleading," said Simon. "I wouldn't be surprised if you were arrested for wasting police time."

"I doubt it." Meinwen allowed herself a smile. "At the very least I'll have given them a focus for their investigation."

Simon glared at her. "You have no proof of anything. Why would you destroy so many lives just for the sake of sticking to your wild theory?"

"It is my duty to do so," Meinwen said. "Are you really prepared to let the case go to court with all the suffering it would cause to the parish and Jennifer?"

"My sister will stick by me," he said. "She won't believe I'm a murderer."

"And a blackmailer," Meinwen reminded him. "There's certainly evidence you did that."

"Circumstantial at best." Simon glanced at his watch. "Grace Peters killed herself. I am not responsible for that. I don't even know where she got the pills from nor why she chose to hang herself afterwards."

"You tied the rope and pushed her off, unaware she'd already taken the heroin. You could have left her alone and she'd have been dead but you couldn't take the risk she'd expose you. If only you'd known about the letter, you could have intercepted it and not murdered at all."

"If I was the blackmailer I would have to say that she brought it upon herself. She was a self-confessed murderer. Robert told me."

"She was a battered wife before that. As her priest you must have known and yet you did nothing. Without any of your other sins this would condemn you in the hearts of your parishioners."

Simon's fingers traversed the gilt cross on the cover of his prayer book. "I did know about the abuse, yes. But she told me within the sanctity of the confessional. I couldn't tell anyone. I urged her to seek professional help but she was too ashamed."

"She confessed she'd murdered him, too. That didn't stop you acting upon it."

Simon smiled. "I prayed for her. She was absolved of the sin. She wasn't absolved of trying to commit suicide, though, and for that she will remain in Hell for eternity."

Meinwen shook her head. "It is a cruel place, your world, to be driven to such a desperate act and yet be condemned for it."

"Is yours any better? Blood is spilled upon your altars, witch."

Meinwen nodded. "I can't deny it though times have changed and the only blood spilled now is by those willing to make it. We live by rules which pre-date those of the church."

Simon stood, his chair scraping along the tiled floor. "I didn't come here to debate theology. Jennifer will soon be up and I must go. I give you a final warning. Leave today and I won't hound you out."

"And I give you a final warning, Father Brande. Give me your confession and the reputation of your church will be spared. Besides, what about Richard?"

"Richard?" Simon paused. "All the evidence against him is circumstantial. At best he'll get a suspended sentence for perverting the course of justice."

"What will my revelation do to him, though? He respects you. How will he feel when he realizes his father is a murderer?"

Simon scowled. "He'll survive. They all will."

"But to know that the blood of a murderer runs through his veins?"

Simon narrowed his eyes. "What are you talking about?"

"Richard is your son by blood as well as by faith, isn't he?"

"What makes you say that?"

"You told me about your time at university and the woman who broke your heart. That was Edith, wasn't it? Richard Godwin's mother. It must have given you a shock when she turned up as the wife of Robert Markhew. It was sweet of her to give him a family name that harked back to the man she loved. 'Godwin' from 'won from God.'"

"She was Meredith Brake when I knew her. She was the one woman I've loved in all my life." Simon looked down at the floor. "She never contacted me again. When she came to Laverstone she begged me not to reveal our past. I worked out that Richard was mine from his birth date. He doesn't know, of course."

"Then for his sake I ask you to confess. That's the one secret you kept from me that I'm prepared to keep hidden."

"What if I disappear? I promise that you will never see or hear from me again."

"And let you get away with murder?" Meinwen took a sheet of paper from the printer tray and placed it onto the table with a pen. "I cannot allow that. I gave you your alternatives last night."

Simon pulled the chair back again. "I cannot contemplate suicide. It is a grievous sin that cannot be forgiven."

"Your beliefs damn your soul. To a pagan, death by any means releases you to rejoin the Great Spirit."

"I will not regret my faith. What was your alternative resolution?"

"Write your confession and then we'll talk." She crossed the room and opened the door. "Sunset is at three minutes past eight this evening. You have until seven to settle your affairs and meet me at the bandstand in the park." Her whole demeanour hardened. "Do not disappoint me in this."

* * * *

Richard awoke to a knock on the door. "Who is it?"

His voice roused his sleeping wife, who opened her eyes. "This is the first time since our marriage that I've woken up with you beside me."

Richard smiled and looked toward the door.

"It's Amanda, sir, with your breakfast."

"Come in." Richard shuffled upward so that he was sitting with his back to the headboard and twitched the duvet over his wife's naked breasts.

Amanda pushed open the door. "Mistress sends this with her compliments, sir, and wondered if she could talk with you when you're ready?"

"Of course." He smoothed out the sheets so Amanda could put the tray on his lap. "This looks good. Toast, scrambled eggs, bacon." He grinned. "A step up from Mike's charcoal sandwiches at the White Art."

"Thank you, sir." Amanda smiled. "Would you like your tea poured?"

"No thanks, we can manage." Richard nudged his wife to sit up. "Tell my aunt that I'll see her in the conservatory at eleven, would you? I want to phone that woman first and find out who really killed my stepfather."

"As you wish, sir." Amanda left the room, closing the door behind her.

"I'll be glad when all this is over." Richard tore off a piece of bacon and put it between Catherine's teeth. She chewed slowly then sat up. He grabbed the tray to prevent it spilling.

"Then you'll be the master of the house and I shall be the mistress."

Richard laughed. "In name, perhaps, but behind closed doors you'll still be my little angel." He grinned at her pout.

"Do you still love me?"

"Of course." Richard leaned over and kissed her. "That's why I shall take on more submissives, so you don't have to do the cleaning any more."

Catherine reached for a piece of buttered toast. "Will you carry on the tradition of cooking for the staff?"

"Once a week," Richard promised, "but only if you can't. Otherwise it's a job for the mistress of the house."

Chapter 36

After meeting Simon at the bandstand, Meinwen led him through the woods and up the steep path to the falls where she had arranged to meet Harold Waterman, the mysterious lord of the manor, his partner and their lawyer. Her torch lit the path in a very small radius, forcing him to stumble over loose stones and roots. Unseen wings fluttered through the branches and small beasts scurried past.

"I thought you didn't like the woods?"

"I don't." Meinwen didn't glance around. "Most of the time I feel as if I'm being watched. Did you know there was a monolith at the top of the falls?"

"In the clearing, yes. What of it?"

"It's part of a stone circle enclosing the whole town."

"More of your mumbo jumbo?"

"If you like." She fell silent for a moment. "It makes the whole town harmonious with the ley lines."

"Pah." Simon spat as they reached the top of the steep path, the waterfall to their left. "Now what? If you think I'm doing anything stupid you're very much mistaken. I could just throw you over the edge right now. It'd be a terrible accident."

"I'd rather you didn't." Meinwen gestured with her torch. "There'd be witnesses."

Three figures stood a little way back from the leat, two with old-fashioned lanterns and one, a woman, with no source of light at all. The woman approached and Meinwen stepped forward to meet her.

She shuddered at the two men left in the background. Harold Waterman and his friend Mr. Jasfoup dressed in a bishop's cloak and mitre. It was good of them to agree with her idea and Mr. Jasfoup's disguise would have fooled his mother, if he had one. She wondered if he was really a bishop. It would explain why he made her flesh creep.

Gillian du Pointe walked up to them and dropped a bag on the ground. Meinwen looked into her eyes. They were almost colourless and reflected the vibrant pinks of the early evening sky.

Gillian looked directly at Simon and unfurled a parchment scroll adorned with the seal of Laverstone. "Simon Brande. You have been found guilty of the crime of blackmail within the demesne of Laverstone."

Simon snarled. "What's going on? Miss du Pointe? You've no authority here. I'm going home."

"You don't really have the opportunity for questions." Gillian kicked the bag toward him. "My authority comes from the lord of Laverstone manor and Bishop Mauvais of the Franciscan monastery in St. Albans. Take off your clothes and put these on."

Simon stared at her. "I shall do no such thing. Meinwen? What is this absurd arrangement you've made?"

"It's your other choice." Meinwen turned toward him. "One that will fit very well with your faith. You are to atone for your sins as a monk under a vow of silence." She nodded toward the two men. "The abbey will hide you from justice and keep the good name of your church out of disrepute."

Simon snorted. "I'm not becoming a bloody monk. You have no proof I did anything and saving Richard heartache isn't worth this."

Meinwen indicated the waterfall and the two-hundred-foot drop to the rocks below. "Then jump. No one will stop you. In the eyes of the parish you will be dead either way, thus saving the reputations of your sister, your son and your parishioners."

"I won't." Simon drew even farther from the edge. "I can say the confession was made under duress."

"Then face the consequences like a man." Meinwen said. "We'll go to Inspector White together. I have your confession. I'm sure that Jennifer and Richard will get over it in time. They might even visit you in prison."

Simon looked at the churning water and back at Meinwen. He sighed and began to unbutton his coat.

Chapter 37

Meinwen looked up into the imposing features of Inspector White, never at his best when woken before dawn to look for a body in the river.

He took a sip from a plastic traveller's coffee mug. "You should have told me sooner. You could have been killed, confronting him like that while you were alone in your house. There's nothing more dangerous than a cornered beast."

Meinwen nodded, her gaze cast to the ground. The inspector's boots could do with a clean, she thought. It was probably only mud from the woods but it still gave a less than favourable impression. "I realize that in hindsight, Inspector. I have the whole thing here." She handed him a padded envelope. "That contains all my notes on the case, plus Simon's confession and a DVD of the talk I had with him the night before last. There would be enough there to convict him if he hadn't…"

"There's little you could have done." White looked over the edge to where police divers were searching the river with floodlights. "If he hadn't done it like this he'd have found another way. It saves the taxpayers a costly trial, mind. I'm just surprised that it turned out to be him."

"You never expect a priest to be a murderer."

"Still…" White looked at the churning water. "To throw yourself into that…" He shook his head. "It's like Sherlock Holmes at the Reichenbach Falls."

Meinwen sighed. "And I was his Moriarty."

White nodded. "Just be glad that you called me first. If he hadn't jumped by the time you got here he might have tried to take you with him." He returned her phone and went to supervise the search, tucking the envelope into his voluminous overcoat pocket.

Meinwen looked at her received messages. The most recent had been from Simon at eleven-fifteen last night.

I have one last secret to reveal. Meet me at Lover's Leap.

She had been safely at home then, freshly showered and broadcasting on webcam while chatting to Jennifer, worried about her missing brother. She'd called White then the manor, giving Gillian and Harold good reason for having their footprints at the scene. Gillian had then wiped Simon's cell clean of fingerprints and thrown it into the waterfall.

"Penny for your thoughts, Ms. Jones?"

Meinwen looked up into the smiling face of Sergeant Peters.

"You looked miles away," he said. "I've brought you a cup of tea.

You must be freezing."

She smiled back. "Sorry. It's been one hell of a week. I was debating whether to stay here or go back to Wales."

"Oh, stay." Peters stopped a little way from the crime scene and took a sandwich from his overcoat pocket. "Nobody will blame you for any of this. They've got you to thank, after all. I wouldn't be surprised if you got a little compensation for your time. The crown will seize his bank accounts and refund the blackmail money out of the Criminal Compensation Fund. It'll go to Grace Peters's estate."

Meinwen smiled. "Susan Pargeter at The Larches will be happy."

Peters nodded, biting into his sandwich. "Aye, she's going to get a windfall. We'd have never cottoned on if he hadn't returned the twenty grand Sir Robert had set up as a fund transfer from his account." He offered her the sandwich packet. "Want one? Tandoori chicken and beetroot."

"No, thanks." Meinwen shook her head.

"Sorry. I forgot that you people are vegetarians."

Meinwen was about to correct him when there was a shout from one of the divers. "What's happening?"

The sergeant looked across, interpreting White's gestures. "They've found an arm. Poor bugger must have had it wrenched clean off on the rocks as he went down."

* * * *

Jean Markhew entered the conservatory to find Richard sitting in the single wicker chair. He smiled as the door opened. "Good morning, Jean. You wanted to see me?"

She replaced the frown that crossed her face with a smile. How dare he sit in her chair? "Yes, thank you, Richard. I appreciate it."

"My pleasure." Richard rang the small handbell. "Coffee for two," he said when Amanda entered. The maid curtsied and glanced toward Jean for confirmation before leaving. Richard waited for the door to close behind her. "Thank you for taking care of the house and staff. Had I thought more clearly I would never have left."

"I'm sure Simon meant well," Jean hesitated, sucking at her bottom lip. "About the staff. My role toward them has changed significantly during the time you were away."

"Oh?" Richard raised his eyebrows. "I am well aware of what your position was. Have you now decided to take his place?"

"Yes." Jean elected to be blunt. "They look to me to guide them now."

"I see." Richard inspected his fingernails, looking up at her with his head to one side. "The worm turns, then? Did you kill my stepfather?"

"I did not." Jean pursed her lips at the accusation. "I merely stepped in to fill the void left by his passing. I thought you were going to ring that woman and find out who the murderer was?"

"She wouldn't tell me yet. She suggested I wait until the police announce it." Richard looked toward the door as it opened. "Here's the coffee." He waited until Amanda had bent to place the tray on the ironwork table and put a hand over the maid's neck to stop her rising. Even through the fresh scabs the new mark was clear--the double R symbol enclosed by a J. "How many of them have you claimed?"

"Only this one, though Susan and Nicole have both sworn fealty to me. Peter was holding a torch for Mary and Catherine, of course, elected to leave. I couldn't understand that until yesterday."

Richard allowed Amanda to rise and stand behind her mistress. "Then I propose you keep a position of power. Second to me, of course and Catherine is exclusively mine. You will need to find a replacement for her. I can advertise in the usual places."

Jean nodded. "As you wish. Will you be keeping the others on?"

"If they want to stay. I'll allow them to leave without penalty if they choose to, or else sign annually renewable contracts."

"What about Mary?"

Richard shrugged. "What about her? Now that I am no longer obliged to marry her I have no interest. She can stay or go as she desires."

"She enjoys Peter's company."

"Then she can stay." Richard smiled and held out a coffee cup. "Would you like a little sugar with your bitter pill?"

* * * *

"So that's how I feel," said Peter, his gaze centred upon Mary's booted feet. "I love you, see. It near broke my heart when you got engaged to Mr. Richard."

"I know." Mary patted his leg and he looked up. "I've known that you were in love with me for ages but didn't want to rock the boat with Richard. When I get my inheritance I shall be able to do what I like, though."

"Would you consider marrying me?" Peter smiled, his muscles

rippling as he relaxed.

"No." Mary laughed at the sudden dejected expression. "I like you a lot, Peter, but I like Nicole too. She and I have been lovers for nearly a year now. I couldn't just give her up. I don't know how I'd have coped if she hadn't twisted the accounts in my favour."

"You wouldn't have to give her up." Peter grinned. "We could both be your partners. We could all be each other's partners."

Mary nodded. "It's worth a try. It worked for Uncle Robert, after all."

* * * *

Catherine sat on the floor between Richard's legs, her head cradled in his lap. He stroked her hair and talked to her. "You've had poorer and worse. From now on the marriage is going to be richer and better." He looked up and nodded. Jean shaved a small patch on the back of Catherine's neck and looked down at him.

"The usual." Richard smiled as the tattoo gun began to buzz. "Why waste a design when the initials are identical? Just leave out your J this time."

* * * *

At eight-thirty that night Gillian du Pointe knocked on the door of The Larches and waited. An early dinner with Harold had left her just enough time to make her first appointment of the night. The business of an evening solicitor was lucrative. People didn't always have time in their busy daytime schedules to see her, and for an extra sixty pounds an hour she was more than happy to make house calls.

It took Amanda a little over a minute to answer the door. Gillian didn't even raise an eyebrow at the oddly buttoned blouse. She held out her card. "I have an appointment with Mr. Godwin and Mrs. Markhew. I believe they're expecting me."

"Of course, Ms. du Pointe." Amanda opened the door wider.

Gillian hesitated, looking at her watch.

"Won't you come in?"

"Thank you." Gillian strode into the hall and paused, her gaze lingering on the Pieta.

Amanda closed the front door. "They're waiting for you in the sitting room."

Gillian entered, nodding to the assembled family. She glanced at each of them in turn while she opened her briefcase and took out the papers relating to Robert Markhew's will and the estate and holdings. Jean Markhew was flushed, the pulse in her carotid artery beating at an elevated rate, revealing that it was she Amanda had been with prior to her arrival.

She flicked open the folder. "Thank you for arranging this appointment. This won't take long now that the police have successfully identified the killer of the late Mr. Markhew." She opened the will and read out the standard clauses.

Jean leaned forward. "Just skip to who gets what."

Gillian raised an eyebrow. "Very well." She turned to the following page. "To my stepson, Richard Godwin, I bequeath the property known as The Larches, the grounds and the contents, excluding those belonging personally to any guest or resident thereof, plus the sum of four hundred and fifty thousand pounds, all stocks and portfolios in my name, and the full rights to edit, publish and otherwise dispose of my creative works."

Richard let out a huge sigh of relief and clutched Catherine's hand, grinning. Catherine leaned toward him for a kiss.

Gillian coughed to recover their attention. "To my sister-in-law, Jean Markhew, I bequeath the sum of fifty thousand pounds and the right to live in The Larches in perpetuity, as this has become her home. To her daughter Mary I leave the sum of two hundred and fifty thousand pounds to begin a new life."

Jean looked annoyed. This was hardly surprising since she had inherited so much less than her nephew. Mary, on the other hand, looked ecstatic, balling her hands into fists and shaking with glee.

Gillian went on "To my housekeeper Susan Pargeter I bequeath the sum of one hundred thousand pounds and to my devoted secretary Nicole Fielding and my companion Peter Numan I bequeath the sum of fifty thousand pounds each. The remainder of my estate I decree to be divided equally between Amanda James and Catherine Latt, after a tithe of ten percent for the church of Our Lady of Pity."

The solicitor smiled. "That concludes the last will and testament of Robert Markhew. As the new owner of the house and largest beneficiary I will address my bill to you, Mr. Godwin."

"What about the twenty thousand that went out of Robert's account?" asked Jean.

Gillian gave her a tight-lipped smile. "Oddly that transaction was initiated after Sir Robert's death, then cancelled and recalled shortly afterwards. You'll find it's all accounted for, though it left an odd trail in the recipient's bank account." She looked at her notes. "St. Pity's Fund for Deprived Boys. I expect they'll be a bit upset but you could always make them a donation."

Richard was still grinning. "Thank you, Ms. du Pointe. Amanda will see you out."

* * * *

Jean stood as soon as the solicitor had left the room. "I never did like that woman. How could Robert leave me less than his servants?"

Richard kissed her on the cheek. "At least you will always have a place to live, Aunt, though I'd appreciate it if you could move your things into Catherine's old room by the end of the week."

* * * *

"Meinwen?" Jennifer leaned over the wall toward the woman sitting in front of her fire pit.

Meinwen looked up. She looked tired and her eyes were blotchy, as if she'd been crying too. "Hello. I wasn't sure you'd want to see me after all that's happened."

"It wasn't your fault." Jennifer hesitated. "I saw your fire and brought out a couple of blankets. Do you mind if I sit with you a bit? I've gone off prayer as a cure-all."

"Not at all." Meinwen helped her to climb over the stone wall. "A friendly ear is something we all need at times."

"Thanks." Jennifer sat next to the fire and warmed her hands. "I've got the internet and the Women's Institute, but they all know me as 'Jenny Butcher, crime fiction author.' Only you know the real Jennifer Brande, really." She went silent for a moment and Meinwen let her be, feeding the fire with sticks and the remnants of an old chair "He's dead, you know. They found his arm and matched his fingerprints. Inspector White has just been 'round."

"I'm sorry." Meinwen stared into the flames. "What will you do now?"

"I don't know. The bishop phoned me. He says I can stay in the house until they appoint a new priest for the parish. After that…" She shrugged.

Meinwen patted her knee. "You're welcome to share my hearth."

Jennifer politely removed the witch's hand. "I'm not that sort of girl.

I prefer boys."

Meinwen laughed. "So do I." She put some extra sticks on the fire. "I hear that the internet is great for meeting people."

* * * *

Brother Simon knelt on the hard stone flags, his shoulder still swathed in bandages under the coarse linen of his robes. In lieu of clasped hands he clutched the rosary at his belt, gazing up at the sunlight streaming through the great rose window on the Abbey of St. Albans. At the altar, the abbot was saying Mass, but the words were lost in the voices of angels. He smiled, lips mumbling prayers despite the stitched stump of his missing tongue.

* * * *

Nurse Chapman marked the medication cart and moved on. They'd named the unknown patient in room twenty-three "Brother Robert" since that was the only name he could mumble when he was brought into A&E suffering from blood loss and hypothermia. He'd been lucky the water had been so cold else he'd have died long before. He thought the psychiatric wing was an abbey and who was to say it wasn't?

Epilogue

Jennifer hit "save" when she heard the knock on the door. Although the computer auto-saved her work, she didn't want to have to re-write the last half a dozen paragraphs. She'd have to edit them when the book was finished, of course, but for now she valued the free-flow of writing more.

She got up and answered the door. Even now, a month after the quiet, empty-coffin funeral, she still expected Simon to come waltzing in, dropping his bag and coat onto the pew. She thought it a measure of her faith that she still believed he was alive somewhere.

"Tom? What are you doing here?" The groundsman and curate raised his hat.

"I'm sorry, Miss Brande. I've got to deliver this letter to you. It's from the bishop. He said it had to be delivered by hand."

Jennifer took the letter, knowing that it was a notice of eviction. "It's all right, Tom. I knew it would come, sooner or later."

Tom nodded. "Well, I'm sorry all the same." He raised his cap again and turned back toward the church.

Jennifer closed the door and opened the embossed envelope. She had two weeks to vacate the rectory before the new parish priest, Father Harrison, moved in.

She dropped the letter on the table and returned to the computer. She was no longer in the mood to write about the incestuous relationships and kinky sex of a modern well-to-do family. She logged on to her chat program.

Within moments she was pinged.

Sir Real: Are you there?
Cacoethes: Yes. Not really up to chatting, though. I've had bad news.
Sir Real: Oh? Anything I can help with?
Cacoethes: *laughs* Not unless you know somewhere I can live. I've just been given two weeks' notice of eviction.
Sir Real: Oh dear. *hug* I could probably sort something out.
Cacoethes: Really?
Sir Real: Yes. You can move in here.
Cacoethes: Honestly? Thank you, Sir Real.
Sir Real: It's my pleasure, or will be. Call me Richard.

About Rachel Green

Rachel Green is a kinky, English lesbian who writes constantly with a cup of tea on her desk. Screaming Yellow is set in the fictional town of Laverstone, the scene of her paranormal humour stories involving Harold Waterman and his friend Jasfoup.

On the rare occasions she's not at her desk, Rachel is either out walking her dogs through the Derbyshire countryside (though not once has she run into the Bronte's) or painting in watercolours or oils. She is also an accomplished swordswoman with the rapier, the saber and the Japanese katana and practised the art of ju-jitsu until she broke both her legs.

She also writes poetry and twitters haiku daily. Follow her @leatherdykeuk

If you're very nice to her, she might show you her canes. No, not the kind for walking with.

Rachel's Website: www.leatherdyke.co.uk
Reader eMail: leatherdykeuk@gmail.com